WELL... IT'S YOUR COW

An Anecdotal Anthology

SAM KNIGHT FRANCES PAULI R.J.J. GOUDE
LEE FRENCH ELIZABETH R. ALIX
JOYCE REYNOLDS WARD WILLIAM GRAVES
OLIVIA BAXTER HUDSON SANAN KOLVA
FROG AND ESTHER JONES MADISON KELLER
DEBY FREDERICKS THOMAS GONDOLFI
G. R. THERON KAYE THORNBRUGH
VOSS FOSTER BETHANY LOY
MANNY FRISHBERG AND INTRODUCING
RYAN RIDDELL

Edited by
FROG JONES

ISBN-13: 978-1-7322477-1-0 (Paperback edition)

Edited by Frog Jones

Cover Art by Albert Holaso

Cover Design by Esther Jones

CONTENTS

INTRODUCTION

FROG JONES

You have to be careful, at a nerd convention, what it is you say.

At many conventions I attend, a bulletin gets published every day. Within this bulletin, one of the most interesting sections is almost always the "things overheard today" section. You see, weird stories come up when nerds start talking to each other, because our tales of what we've done don't have to come close to reality.

I mean, if you thought *fishing* causes people to tell tales, then you haven't seen what happens when *speculative fiction authors* start talking to each other.

I say that because, in order to introduce this anthology, I have to tell you a story. And, in a weird twist for me, this one isn't fiction.

It begins when a wild hair climbed into my nether regions and I hand-built a catapult. Specifically, I built a Roman onager, a torsion-driven field artillery piece. Which is the sort of thing one does when one is not entirely in one's right mind.

A friend of mine at the time had a cow pasture with exactly two steers occupying the field. The field angled downhill from his driveway and made for a near-perfect test range for Ultima Ratio

Regum (the name I stenciled on the side of my ancient artillery piece). And so it was, on a cool spring morning, a group of my friends gathered together in this driveway to hurl cantaloupe into a cow pasture.

Here's a thing I bet you didn't know: cattle, on the whole, do not get a lot of sugar in their regular diet. They eat mostly grains and grass. But it turns out, if you start chucking cantaloupe into their pasture, they will definitely eat it.

And then they will be on the biggest sugar buzz of their life.

After about a dozen or so pieces of what, at the time, I was beginning to think of as "cattle candy," these two steers were running around the pasture as though they were Golden Retrievers excited to see a person. They ran, and they frolicked, and they generally acted with more energy than I have *ever* seen a bovine display. And I grew up in a small town in Eastern Washington, so I am not unfamiliar with the species as a whole.

But that's what comes of feeding six or so cantaloupe per animal to creatures that do not usually consume fructose.

The thing is, one can only purchase so much cantaloupe at a time, and after a dozen shots we'd run out of ammo. That is, we'd run out of ammo until Dan brought out the coconut. Some basic physics, here. A coconut is far smaller and lighter than a cantaloupe. The force applied by the onager was going to be the same, and F=MV, which means as M decreases but F remains constant...V is going to see a bit of an uptick. Furthermore, I'm pretty sure if one were to accidentally noggin a cow with a cantaloupe, you might concuss the cow, but the melon breaks before the bone does. For proof, get on YouTube and search for "Watermelon Slingshot Fail" or, alternatively, "Right in the Kisser."

See how the melon shatters and blows, leaving the skull intact?

Ok, now imagine a coconut. Yeah.

Now, on the more reckless side of the equation, the odds that, in the entire cow pasture, this relatively small coconut manages to encounter one of the two steers is pretty low. Plus, we all kinda wanted to see how far we could get this smaller, more dangerous projectile to fly. And so it was, with a mild sense of trepidation, that I found myself cocking the throwing arm of my onager and loading a small piece of hard, brown death into the sling.

And then I paused. For just a moment, I looked over at my friend who owned these bovines, and I said the following words:

"So, do we think this is a good idea?"

It should be noted that *anytime you find yourself asking this question* the correct answer is NO. The very fact that you're asking means you know *damn well* what you're doing is a terrible idea. But you ask, as a way of placing the burden of your stupidity on someone other than yourself.

On the other hand, we all really wanted to see this thing let off the chain. So the owner of the bovines replied by saying... something. I'm not honestly sure; it is lost in the mists of time. Because, you see, one of our other friends had his cell phone out, and the microphone was closer to me. Thus we can hear my fateful question, the response is garbled, and then you hear my reply:

"Well, it's your cow."

Followed immediately by the quick *chunk* of me sending a lethal brown mistake downrange at a *really* heightened velocity.

Here's another fun fact about bovines: When you spend all afternoon flinging cattle candy into a pasture out of a weird machine, you train them. You train them that the thing coming out of the siege engine is not only delicious, but indeed the greatest treat they will ever receive in their life. You train them that they need to get to the thing faster than the *other* cow, because they want the lion's share of that sweet, sweet goodness. And all the while, they're getting faster and faster, because you're putting them on a plane of sugar high they didn't even conceive of until now.

Which means my original calculations vis-à-vis the head size of a steer in a pasture and the likeliness of the coconut intersecting with that small patch of real estate were deeply flawed, as in fact each bovine head did not represent *a point* at which a coconut intersection could kill one of them. No, rather each steer became *the centerpoint* of a radius dictated by said steer's reaction time and acceleration (such acceleration having been greatly increased by previous sugar-fueling).

And I did not realize this flaw until one of the steers lunged toward the hard, brown missile in midair, mouth open, bovine tongue flapping to the wind, trying to catch its sweet nectar.

Now, if this were one of my fiction stories, that cow would take damage at this point. But, sadly for the writer in me and happily for my checkbook, the steer missed by inches, the coconut whiffing past its outstretched maw and bouncing harmlessly into the pasture. No animals were actually harmed in the writing of this foreword.

But that moment, where that 1,000-pound animal craned out its neck and opened its jaws, is one of those moments that will always live in my mind.

So, at the beginning of this foreword I started talking about being careful of your words at a convention, then I told this story about a cow. Non sequitur? Not quite. I told you that story so I could tell you this one.

This is a story about Radcon 2017. Radcon is an awesome little con in Pasco, Washington. I've always loved geek cons in places that are not typically known for geeky things. The unbottling of nerdery that happens at the con becomes that much more epic as a result of societal pressure, and Radcon is no exception.

Now, at this particular Radcon, there's a launch party going on. Sanan Kolva (whose name you may notice amongst the stories of this very book) is launching her wonderful novel *Shrouded Sky,* and all her author-friends are getting down with a cake she's brought. See how these stories merge? I was on a bit of a sugar buzz.

Now, I don't know *how* the conversation worked its way around to my catapult, but it did. And from there, the coconut-cow story simply *had* to be told. And so, surrounded by speculative fiction authors, I told the same story I have told unto you.

You have to be careful about these things.

Because after the story came the video. It's still on Facebook, shared under my friend's account, and it has forever recorded my two fateful lines.

"So, do we think this is a good idea?"

"Well... it's your cow."

And Frances Pauli (whose name you may also notice amongst the authors of this very book) did speak, and say "Those words would be a great opening to any story."

And we were off. Because each author had their own take on those two lines, and what would happen if you used them in the opening. And I was on a sugar buzz. And, after all, it was my damned coconut-cow story anyways. And so I said, "Woo! Let's do an anthology."

Thus condemning myself to editing this book by reason of a catapult I built in my garage seven years ago.

What you will find contained within these pages is a complete mish-mash of tales. You will read horror, comedy, fantasy, tragedy, and romance. You will read cyberpunk, you will read of furries, and you will read of alien invasions and faeries and cows strapped to hang gliders being mistaken for wyvern. This is not, in short, an anthology bound together by any kind of a theme.

Instead, it's an anthology bound together by those two lines. See, every one of these stories begins with those same two lines of dialogue. In editing this anthology, I watched all of these magnificent authors start at *exactly* the same place, with *exactly* the same words, and immediately hare off into their own worlds. You're going to get a little sampler of everything in these pages, but more importantly you, too, are going to be able to watch the minds of these authors as they process the same lines in ways you have yet to imagine.

I started this anthology on a sugar-fueled, sleep-deprived impulse, the way one responds to a dare around a campfire at midnight. But the authors contained in these pages have brought such a wealth of storytelling to those fateful words of mine that they are really no longer words *of mine.*

They're ours.

So step up. Each story will give you something different, something new. Like loading a coconut into a catapult, we've really let these folks off the chain. You're going to be happy with the result. After all... It's their cow.

COWS ON THE WING

SAM KNIGHT

About the Author: As well as being Distribution Manager for WordFire Press, Sam Knight is Senior Editor for Villainous Press and has curated and edited four anthologies. He is the author of five children's books, four short story collections, two novels, and nearly three dozen short stories, including two media tie-ins co-authored with Kevin J. Anderson.

A stay-at-home father, Sam attempts to be a full-time writer, but there are only so many hours left in a day after kids. Once upon a time, he was known to quote books the way some people quote movies, but now he claims having a family has made him forgetful, as a survival adaptation. He can be found at SamKnight.com and contacted at Sam@samknight.com.

Cows on the Wing
Sam Knight

"So, do we think this is a good idea?"

"Well...it's your cow."

"Bloody right it is!" With that bit of effrontery, cemented by downing the last of the whisky in the bottle he'd shared with his twin brother, Nacky McDurn firmly planted his foot on the bovine's backside and shoved it off the cliff.

The unwilling cow disappeared into the darkness of the night sky with a trailing bellow.

Nicky McDurn, faithfully video recording his brother's antics, raced to the edge of the cliff, smartphone in hand.

"When a cow flies, she says." Nacky sniffed, stood up straight, and wiped his nose with the back of his hand. "That'll show her!"

"Nacky! Ferthelovagod! Look at this!" Nicky waved his brother forward. "It worked! It's frickin' flyin'!" Nicky took another step forward, eyes on the glowing screen of his phone, and promptly followed the cow out into the dark void, also trailing a bellow.

The light from the phone gone, Nacky took two steps forward in the sudden darkness, drunkenly swiping out a hand to catch someone who was no longer there. "Nicky?"

His voice sounded small and lonely in the night.

"Nicky?"

Forgotten, the empty whiskey bottle slipped from his numb fingers, hit a rock, and shattered.

The sound startled the confused Nacky who promptly did the same thing he had done since the moment before his birth: he followed his twin brother's example.

In the pool of light under the streetlamp, Constable Athey bent down and picked up the limp form of Hackett Dawley, tossing the drunken man over his shoulder. The jolt of the constable's shoulder hitting the scrawny man in the belly woke him and nearly caused a forceful ejection of expensive liquid down the constable's back.

Hackett squirmed, trying to get free, knocking the constable's custodian helmet askew.

"Settle down," Athey told him while righting his helmet. "I'm just takin' you home, ya drunken bastard."

The familiar voice calmed Hackett, who lifted his head to see where he was. Between lampposts, he found himself unable to pick out the street in the darkness, but the rising harvest moon caught his eye.

" 'S beauful!" Hackett tried to tell Constable Athey. "Friggin' beauful!"

"Yep." The constable continued onward, his back to the golden orb.

A dark shape passed in front of the lunar spectacle. "Ha!" Hackett began laughing, trying to raise his arm high enough to point at it. "Goddam cow jump 'ver da moo!"

"Yup. Carol will probably ask me to carry you up to the room." Constable Athey sighed heavily and adjusted Hackett's weight on his shoulder as he walked. "Again."

TAD DONNALLY FROZE. HIS ARM WAS UP TO HIS SHOULDER through the glass window he'd broken with the brick, and his fingers stopped trying to work open the interior latch. The siren was unlike any he'd ever heard before. Lower pitched than normal, the sound was coming at him from the sky.

Fear held him in place as he looked up, searching the night sky. This house wasn't supposed to have an alarm. He'd cased the place and tested it beforehand to make sure.

The sound above him stopped and then started up again, closer.

The friggin' coppers were using drones now?

The strange sound passed right over his head at the same time as he spotted a large dark triangular shape flying past in the sky. Liquid hit the pavement next to his feet with a smacking sound and Tad felt it splattering over him—then he was off at a full run.

Friggin' cops had marked him! He couldn't see the stuff in the dark, but he could smell it, and he was sure it would show up under ultraviolet.

As he rounded the corner to his girlfriend's flat, his wet shoes sent him sliding sideways like an old slapstick movie actor. Pain lanced through his elbow as he lost his balance and fell. Scrabbling back to his feet and cradling his arm, he raced on and was at his girlfriend's door in seconds, pounding on it nearly as loudly as his heart pounded in his ears.

"Biddy! Open up! 'S me! Tad!" He pounded again, looking to the sky for dark shapes gliding by. He couldn't hear the siren anymore, but he needed out of these clothes before anyone came looking. "Biddy! I've broken me arm! Open up!"

A light clicked on and a bedraggled young woman with red curly hair opened the door. The angry fist on her hip pulled up the hem of her oversized night shirt. "What the hell you want this time of night?" She grabbed at her nose. "Cod! You smell like piss!"

THE SCREEN GLOWED GREEN WITH THE NIGHT-VISION IMAGE, making Charles Washburn's pasty face even more ghoulish as he stared at it, unmoving. The image showed the silhouette of the ridge he'd seen the ABC, the Alien Big Cat, walk across last year. No one believed him, of course. It seemed no matter how many people saw ABCs, no one else ever believed. Why was it so ridiculous to accept a panther was loose in the country side?

He'd show them. Even if it took forever.

Which it was starting to.

Charles lifted his energy drink to his lips and took in a

mouthful. He'd had so many over the last few years they'd become flavorless. He sat the can down, picked his nightscope up, and did his routine scan of the rest of the countryside, just in case the beast was ranging through a different field. The full moon was a boon, greatly increasing both the resolution of his scope and the distance he could see.

But there was still nothing out there.

Sometimes Charles doubted himself, but if he hadn't given in when Aggie divorced him over this, he wasn't going to give in now. There was something strange out in the countryside, something that shouldn't be there, and he was going to prove it to the world.

The strange sound, coming from the sky above him, was not the something strange Charles was looking for, so it took a moment for the low pitched bellow to garner his attention. Looking up, he spotted the odd shape gliding slowly through the sky, blocking out stars as it passed over him.

"What the...?"

Charles brought the nightscope up, accidentally pointing it at the moon first and blinding the sensitive instrument. When the image settled, Charles quickly scanned the sky. He found the dark shadow lazily turning a wide circle, as if it were searching for something. It had a large, square shaped head, and squat legs and body, but it was the odd, perfectly triangular shaped wings that gave it away.

"Jesus Christ! A frickin' wyvern!"

LANA GERRITY PULLED HER TWEED JACKET TIGHT AND STEPPED out into the pre-dawn light, taking a deep breath of the fresh air. Fresh except for the barnyard smell, anyway, but she was used to that. It had taken her forty years to get used to it, but she had. And then her good-for-nothin' husband up and died on her.

That same thought went through her mind every morning as she went out to milk the cows and collect eggs from the hens.

She'd always hated animals. The whole of the countryside, truth be told. A city girl through and through, she'd made the mistake of falling for a poor, simple farmer and ended up spending her entire life living someplace she hadn't wanted to be.

And now he was gone, and she was still here, too damned poor to go anywhere else.

With a heavy sigh and one hand on her tired old back, Lana picked up the milk bucket and headed for the barn with a shuffling limp. The cows were already lined up, lowing to be milked.

"Bossy Bessies! I'm comin', I'm comin'," she muttered as she entered the barn. She stopped and looked around, waiting for her rheumy eyes to adjust to the dim light. The dust motes, floating through the sunbeams just appearing through the cracks of the barn walls, didn't help her vision any more than they helped her sinuses.

Waddling to the milking stool, she dropped the bucket and scooched it into place with her foot. It always amazed her how the cows came in and got into their proper places to get milked. But she wasn't going to complain about that! Anything that actually made things easier was a good thing.

With a groan she sat down and reached for the udder of the cow in front of her. She hesitated, hands on teats, and leaned her head back to look down the row of waiting cows. A frown added to the wrinkles on her forehead.

"Weren't there only five of you before?"

THE TWO METAL TEN-GALLON MILK CANS RATTLED AGAINST EACH other in the back of Lana Gerrity's electric cart as she drove into town. Her face was pinched in thought as she absentmindedly held her jacket closed with one hand and steered with the other, avoiding the same potholes that had vexed her for twenty years.

Twenty years.

That's how long she'd been driving the fresh morning milk into town. The other two milkings went into a small storage tank monitored by a pasteurization service, but the first one of the day went to Lambert's Creamery. It was only the freshest for them!

Lana approved of that.

Not only did it put money in her pocket, but Lambert's Creamery produced the finest products around. Fresh did make a difference.

Twenty years.

For some reason Lana couldn't remember having *six* cows. They were nasty, filthy things, so she had never treated them like pets or named them, and she wasn't too surprised she couldn't remember one of the beasts, but she was sure of one thing: she had never needed to use two ten-gallon milk cans before. One had always been enough.

And two was a pain in the ass.

She made up her mind. It was time to sell one of the cows.

"YEAH, THAT'S WHAT I TOLD 'IM! WHEN A COW FLIES!" GIANNA Keegan was doing her long nails while talking on the phone when Lana Gerrity came into the creamery's office, holding her jacket closed tight with one hand. "I know, right! Ha! That's what I said. Anyways, gotta run."

Gianna hung up the phone, careful not to mess up her fingernails, and then capped the bottle of blue polish. "Good morning, Mrs. Gerrity. How are you today?"

"Eh! I've finally gone berco!" Lana handed Gianna her bill of lading. "Need to start sellin' off the cows before I go arseways."

"Don't say that!" Gianna's tsked. "What would we be without you?" She gingerly took the bill by the corner, trying to protect her blue nail polish. Looking at it she said, "This is two and a half gallons more'n you've ever brought us before."

"Told you." Lana pointed to her own temple and circled her finger. "Berco."

"I've got to check with Mr. Lambert. I don't know if I can pay for this much."

"Ask him if he wants to buy a cow while you're at it."

"THERE YOU HAVE IT! DRAGONS RULE OUR SKIES ONCE AGAIN!" The radio announcer's voice sounded terribly excited, yet completely bored at the same time. "We've uploaded Charles Washburn's video to our website so you can see for yourself. Make sure you 'Like' us while you're there, and 'Follow' us for all the latest news!"

Constable Athey shook his head and turned the car radio off as he reached his aunt's driveway. A delivery truck was pulling out. He returned the friendly wave before he recognized Mr. Lambert driving the truck. Athey wondered if there had been problems with his aunt's morning delivery of milk and eggs to Mr. Lambert's creamery.

He pulled in and parked next to the little electric farm cart, eyeballing it for any signs of trouble.

"Radley!" Lana stepped out onto the porch and pulled her jacket tight around her. "How many times do I have to tell you? You don't have to check on me every single day!"

Athey took off the helmet he had just put on and smiled. "I promised Uncle—"

"It's been two years! You don't have to keep a promise to a dead man! I'm not going to!"

Her words and defiant attitude stopped Athey in his tracks. He'd never seen his aunt look so...alive.

"I'm selling the farm!" Lana announced proudly. "Isn't it wonderful?" She looked as though she wanted to twirl in place but thought better of it.

Athey's mouth worked up and down a few times, but no words came out.

"Mr. Lambert took pity on me." She chuckled. "He could tell

right off I've gone too batty to count cows, let alone take care of this place anymore, so he's pretending he wanted to expand his business, and he's going to purchase this whole damned farm!"

Lana turned slowly and took in the view around her as if for the first time. "This may be the best day of my life. I think I'm going to like being berco."

STILL IN A BIT OF A DAZE FROM THE NEWS, CONSTABLE ATHEY washed out his teacup and kissed his aunt goodbye before donning his helmet again. He was at the door to his car, helmet in hand, when the wind picked up and gave rise to a ruffling sound, catching his attention. A six-foot high tangle of brightly colored fabric and bent aluminum, blown by the wind like a technicolor tumbleweed, rolled across his aunt's pasture. It took a lazy hop and sailed over the fence with ease, landing and bouncing down the street like a child's runaway ball.

Sighing, Athey put on his helmet and gave chase. He still had three hours before he was on duty, but then, technically, he was always—

The sound of screeching tires made him wince. Scraping sounds, which he imagined to be caused by the ball rolling over the top of a car, made him wince even more.

He picked up his pace. Whoever was driving the car had likely seen the mess jump the fence and would try to blame his aunt for it. He was glad to be at his aunt's at this exact moment in time, so he could explain it wasn't hers before things got out of hand.

The sound of a slamming car door was followed by a cursing voice just as Constable Athey hurried into view of the accident. The cursing made him wince most of all. He recognized the voice all too well as that of Chief Inspector Harold Yancey: his boss.

Who, Athey now saw, had been driving a brand-new 'I'm having a midlife-crisis-red' sports car.

And the woman in the skimpy dress getting out of the

passenger side was neither Chief Inspector Yancey's wife nor his teenage daughter.

Athey stumbled as his feet and his brain argued over whether or not he could run back out of sight and hide, sorry to be at his aunt's at this exact moment in time when everything had gotten out of hand.

"AFTERNOON, ATHEY." CONSTABLE CAROL DAWLEY NODDED AS she greeted Constable Athey at the top of the driveway to Rabbie Harrington's farm.

Athey donned his helmet and nodded curtly back. "Dawley." He never allowed his eyes to linger on the female constable. He liked her a little too much.

"Are you all right?" Dawley asked. "You look a little ... peaked."

"It's been a strange afternoon, that's all." He changed the subject. "How was Hackett this morning? Little rough around the edges?" Carrying her drunken brother home a couple of nights a week was a good excuse to see her, but Athey had never been able to work up enough nerve to actually talk to her in any way other than professionally.

"More than a little," she said as they left the driveway and headed for the barn. "He was so far gone he swears he saw a flying cow last night." Dawley gave him a sad smile. "Thank you again for bringing him home."

They reached the barn and Dawley led him around to the small side door. "Mr. Harrington reported a hang glider was stolen from his barn sometime last night," she said opening the door.

"A hang glider, you say?" Athey hesitated in his step.

"Yeah. Can you believe it? Apparently, it was specially made to accommodate someone of his size. Can't imagine it's smaller than a plane. Anyway, I found some evidence I was told could also pertain to a call you took earlier."

"Which of the morning's calls are you referring to?" Athey

asked. Dawley couldn't possibly know about the incident with Chief Inspector Yancey, could she? There hadn't been a radio call, and Yancey hadn't decided whether or not to even let Athey even write up a report.

The humor in Dawley's eyes faded. She must've noted the pained look on his face. "The McDurns. I heard they went missing. Again."

"Oh! Right. That one." Athey felt inordinately relieved he wouldn't have to talk to Constable Dawley about improper sexual escapades. "Sorry. I'd nearly forgotten that one. Their mum is worried the dragon ate them last night. Said a cow's been eaten as well."

"Ah, the dragon. Ate the cow, did it?"

"That's what ol' Mrs. McDurn said." Athey shook his head. "Not a trace of hide nor hair left of it."

"I suppose there'd be insurance money in there somewhere." Dawley lead the way into the barn, pulling out her torch and shining the light around. "That poor old lady. Imagine still takin' care of those boys all these years, like they was five years old this whole time. I don't know how she's afforded it."

Her light fell upon an empty liquor bottle and small square object just inside the door.

"A wallet?" Athey asked.

"Mmm-hmm. Nacky McDurn's."

"Why doesn't that surprise me?"

"Because nothing the McDurn brothers do surprises any of us anymore," Dawley said.

"I still don't see why you needed me here."

"Because the McDurn brothers were reported missing to you this morning and this evidence links them to the theft of a hang glider." She cocked her head at him. "I need a second to back me up before I get authorization to order a search along the cliffs."

"You think they're dead?"

She raised the beam of light up six inches and showed him an empty liquor bottle. "Dead, drunk ... dead drunk, maybe? All those two would have to do is dare each other to get high while they were high..."

"You're right." Athey shook his head. "I wouldn't put that past them. Nothing the McDurn brothers do surprises me anymore."

"I'll put out a call to keep an eye out for the hang-glider as well," Dawley said. "If someone's spotted it, it may narrow down our search area."

"I may have a lead on that." Athey's face went sour. "Or I may not. Depends upon what the official report ends up saying. I'll have to get back to you on it."

Constable Dawley raised her eyebrows and matched his pained look.

"You don't want to know. Trust me."

"HAVEN'T SEEN THE MCDURNS. NOT SINCE I TOLD 'EM TO PISS off." Gianna Keegan examined the chip in her blue nail polish.

"When exactly was that?" Constable Athey asked, notepad ready should Gianna offer anything remotely useful. His expectations were low. No one else had seen the McDurn brothers either, and he knew Gianna well enough to know she'd have already gabbed to everyone if she even thought she knew anything. He considered her one of the local gossip girls and did his best to stay out of their melodramatic machinations since the time they set out to prove, once and for all, whether he was gay.

"Six-ish last night. Nicky kept goading Nacky to grab me bum, talkin' on 'bout how it might look rock hard, but had to be softer than angel feathers." Her eyes flicked from her nails to Athey's face for a microsecond.

He ignored it. She'd been the gossip girl most concerned with seeing if she could rouse his attentions.

"Where at?" Athey scribbled six o'clock in his notes.

"On me bum."

"No. I mean where did this happen?"

"Didn't happen. Nothin' the bastard done has ever been good for no one but 'imself. I told him he could have some of this when cows fly."

Athey ignored her encompassing hand gestures. "I mean where did you last see the McDurn brothers?"

"Down at the pub. Me and the girls was havin' a pint. Nicky and Nacky were havin' a barrel." Gianna rolled her eyes and gave out a loud exasperated breath. "Them boys can drink. Almost felt bad for poor Hackett when the twins gave up on me and started drinkin' with him. I knew right then his night was done."

"So Hackett Dawley might know where they went after the pub?"

"Might," Gianna said. "His eyes was so crossed, like as not, he didn't leave the pub last night."

Athey's radio crackled and Constable Dawley's voice called for his attention.

"This is Athey, go ahead," he said, excusing himself from Gianna with a polite hand wave.

"The chopper spotted two bodies halfway down the cliff at Bodger's Point."

"On my way."

"What?" Gianna's voice went up through the octave scale until she sounded like she was auditioning to voice an animated mouse. "Nicky and Nacky? They can't be dead! They's the only ones what even look at me!"

"How we going to get down there?" Constable Athey looked over the edge of the cliff. Someone's legs were visible on a ledge about a hundred and fifty feet down.

"I called the fire department," Constable Dawley answered. "They're going to send a rescue chopper out with a basket to collect the bodies for us."

People, following the exciting lure of the flashing lights, had started gathering in groups around both the top and bottom of the cliffs, pointing and milling about. Some of them moved within hearing range of the constables' conversation, so Athey motioned for Dawley to walk with him as they talked.

"Notice the footprints." She pointed into an area marked off with yellow tape to keep people out.

"I see the broken whiskey bottle."

"There's no sign of either of them running to jump off the cliff like they were using the glider. It looks like they both fell. My guess is they were getting ready to use the glider, the wind caught it, took it away from them, and they both fell off trying to catch it. We can't be sure though. A lot of it was obscured by cow tracks."

"Cow? There's no pasture up here." Athey turned and looked across the landscape to make sure his memory was serving correctly.

"Could be the one Mrs. McDurn reported missing. Their farm's only a mile or so off."

"You're probably right." Athey took off his helmet and wiped his brow.

"Hackett called me back," Dawley said. "He doesn't remember the McDurns leaving the pub last night. Not that it matters much now."

They went quiet as they walked around another group of approaching gawkers.

"Who are all of these people?" Dawley asked when they were out of earshot. "I've never seen half of them before."

"Wyvern hunters. The town's filling up with them. Bed and Breakfasts are all full."

"W—" Dawley looked around again. "What's a wyvern?"

GIANNA KEEGAN WAILED AS THE FIRST SHOVEL OF DIRT HIT THE twin coffins. Her blue fingernails matched her tight dress. Anyone who would listen to her had been told the story of how the brothers had been fighting for her attentions that night.

Old Mrs. McDurn had refused to listen. With a sour face, she turned and hurried away from her boys' graves as soon as the funeral ended. It was all Constable Athey could do to catch up.

"My condolences, Mrs. McDurn." He huffed as he reached her.

"Good riddance," she muttered.

Athey ignored the comment and held out an evidence bag. "We only found one of their phones, but I thought you might like to have it back. I'm sorry ... it's broken."

The old woman waved her hand in refusal. "They only had the one phone. Refused to work hard enough to earn a second." She stopped and looked Athey in the eye. "Just like their worthless father, they was. But I learned my lesson from him, I did!" Her eyes twinkled and she smirked. "I made damned sure their life insurance was paid up."

Athey stayed where he was, stunned, as the woman strutted away.

"Heya," Constable Dawley said as she walked up. "I heard your aunt is moving."

"Moved," he said, turning away from the old woman and putting the phone into his pocket. "Packed her suitcase and left yesterday. Said she didn't need the rest of it."

"Really?"

"I've never seen her so happy."

"Huh." Dawley stood next to Athey as they watched Charles Washburn, looking paler than ever in the daylight, hesitantly approach a sobbing Gianna Keegan and offer his condolences.

"Heard he's made some money, giving television interviews about the wyvern he says he saw," Dawley said, pointing her nose toward Charles.

"So's every business in town." Athey nodded. "Biggest thing to happen round here in my lifetime."

Charles' supportive embrace lasted a moment longer than it should have when he seemed to try to pull away but couldn't. And then it lasted another moment longer than it should have as he settled into the embrace. And then Gianna was kissing him. Charles' evident surprise was only matched by Gianna's eagerness.

"Wow." Dawley raised her eyebrows.

Athey turned away. He'd been on the unwilling end of that embrace once and felt a little guilty about not throwing a life preserver to a drowning man. But not guilty enough to take action. Charles Washburn had been a miserable lout since his divorce. Maybe this would work out for the best.

"You suppose the insurance company will really accept a dragon ate that cow?" Dawley asked.

"Not any more tha—"

"Oh, sorry!" Biddy Beirne, curly red hair done up in tight ringlets, bounced off Athey's shoulder as she stepped on his shoe, knocking him into Dawley. Dawley's quick reflexes caught Athey before he fell.

Biddy, towing Tad Donnally along by the sling on his broken arm, was gone again before Athey had his balance back. "Decided to straighten up and fly right, he has!" she announced, waving her hand, and a diamond ring, for her friends to see.

Donnally gave Dawley and Athey a wary look as he disappeared into the crowd with his fiancé.

"Are you all right?" Dawley asked as she helped steady Athey.

"Yeah, thanks. You?"

Her hands were still on his arms as they looked at each other.

"Fine." She smiled awkwardly and pulled away. "Never did trust Donnally. Bad egg, that one. Maybe Biddy can make an honest man out of him."

"Unlikely." Athey straightened his jacket.

"Oh!" Dawley's countenance lightened. "I thought you might like to know Hackett says he's putting himself into a program. Gonna get clean and sober."

"Really? That's great." Athey's voice sounded flat as he realized his only excuse to see Dawley outside of work was drying up. "Not that I don't want him to, but why now?"

"He didn't like people not believing him when he said he saw a flying cow."

"Ha! Yeah. Well...maybe it was a dragon."

"Yeah... Radley?"

Athey blinked at the use of his first name. He couldn't remember her ever using it before.

"Yeah?"

"Do you ... wanna go get a bite?"

Athey hesitated as he met her eyes. "Yeah, I do."

Her phone interrupted the moment at the same time a buzzing came from his jacket pocket.

"Must be work," she said, sighing and reaching for her phone.

"Must be," he said, reaching for his.

"Hello?" she asked into her phone just as Athey realized it was not his phone vibrating, but rather the McDurn brothers'.

The number didn't have a name, so he didn't answer.

"Yes. Thank you." Dawley hung up and looked at Athey bemusedly. "Did you know Chief Inspector Yancey put in his resignation?"

Athey shook his head, but he wasn't surprised. Athey hadn't thought it good form to tell a constable how to write up an incident. It seemed Yancey's superiors felt the same way after Athey informed them about it.

"And," Dawley continued, her eyes wide, "I've been asked to apply for the position! Who'd have thought someone would have recommended me?"

"Why would anyone ever recommend you?" Athey had a hard time keeping the smile from his face.

"Oh! You knew!" Dawley lightly punched his shoulder then noticed the phone he was holding. "Is that the McDurns'? I thought it was broken."

"So did I. It seems to have come back on its own."

Athey checked the last few calls and messages. Nothing seemed related to the brothers' demise.

"Check for photos," Dawley said. "Maybe there's something there."

"It's a video. Eh! It's dark and the screen's too cracked. I can't tell what's going on."

Dawley leaned in, resting her cheek on his shoulder to look. "I wonder if it's worth taking to the lab and see if they could recover the information?"

"Oh, I'll be all right." Gianna's voice caught their attention as she walked by, arm in arm with Charles, her tears long dry. "Cows would fly the day they did something good for someone else anyway."

Athey looked at Dawley and put the phone in his pocket. "I don't know about you, but I agree with Gianna. Let's go eat—if we can find a place not too crowded."

MATILDA

FRANCES PAULI

About the Author: Frances Pauli is a hybrid author of over twenty novels. She favors speculative fiction, romance, and anthropomorphic fiction and is not a fan of genre boxes. Frances lives in Washington state with her family, four dogs, two cats, and a variety of tarantulas.

Matilda

Frances Pauli

"So, do we think this is a good idea?" The farmer ran coarse fingers down Matilda's neck and spat a mass of chaw near her hooves.

"Well...it's your cow." The veterinarian bent over in front of her, providing a close-up view of his posterior. He dug through his bag of supplies and Matilda regarded the target he made through long lashes. "But Macklemore up the street says his girls have never produced so well."

Matilda expressed her disinterest with a gentle release of methane.

"How well?" The farmer's hand dropped away. He bent to examine Matilda's udder. "Macklemore's using it, then?"

"Yup."

"Dose her up, Doc."

Matilda chewed her cud lazily, whisking her tail toward the occasional fly and softly releasing another fart. The farmer scratched her on the cheek, and she closed her eyes, leaning into it. The veterinarian moved to the other side of her neck, and something cold bit her just behind the jaw. Her tail flicked. Matilda stamped one rear hoof and mooed around the mouthful of hay slurry.

She had four stomachs. It was a strange thought, and it came upon her at the same instant the biting on her neck stopped. A slow burn replaced that, oozing outward from the injection site. *Interesting.* Matilda was certain a bovine shouldn't understand the concept of an injection site. Yet, the moment the thought appeared, she digested it, understood.

Bovine. Also a new thought, one she suspected came from the veterinarian. He bent over again, packing his equipment while the farmer stroked her neck in a slow circle.

"How long before we should see results?" His urgency, Matilda easily identified. He shifted his weight from one foot to the other and gave her a pat to hide his nerves.

"Next milking, I reckon." The veterinarian answered.

Matilda mooed and swung her head toward the farmer, dislodging his hand. His touch brought thoughts that made her muscles twitch, an eagerness that felt like little fly feet. She flicked her tail, stamped, and swallowed the cud.

Four stomachs. Strange to know that, to be certain the farmer only had one. When he tugged her halter, Matilda stumbled into him. Her tail swished. The farmer pulled her lead, and Matilda followed, thinking, *I have four stomachs*.

Thinking.

SHE HAD A CHILD SOMEWHERE. A WEEK LATER, THE FARMER TUGGED her back to the long yard beside the driveway. The veterinarian's truck parked beside the fence, and Matilda blinked her lashes at it, picking out the scrawl of symbols on the side that almost made sense now.

She remembered the children. *Yes, there had been more than one.* But she couldn't quite work out what had happened to them.

The farmer stamped his booted feet, and Matilda dragged her hooves through the mud. He reached to pat her neck, a long-ingrained instinct, but his hand pulled sharply back as the electrical tingles crackled between their skin.

This happened at every milking now, and though the process had grown uncomfortable, Matilda saw things in that contact. She learned things, picked them easily from the farmer's head.

Like the children. The calf—calves—that had been sold before she'd ever known them. *Sold.* Her hoof came down hard, inches from a rubber boot. She mooed, and the farmer tugged her head lower, stepping away from her side and clearing his throat.

"Bout ready, doc?"

Matilda felt the farmer's hunger. He leaned forward with it, brought his body close but didn't touch her again. She still heard it in his thoughts. Milk. He needed more of it, of her. The milk which should have fed her children.

"Macklemore reported some side effects." The veterinarian shoved his bag through the fence, climbing through after it. "He's worried. You notice anything with the old girl?"

"Seems fit as a fiddle," the farmer lied.

"Good." The veterinarian dug into his pack, found his drug and held it to the light, squinting. "Make sure you keep an eye on her, Bill. Let me know if you notice anything."

"Sure." The farmer's feet shuffled again.

Matilda reached for his thoughts, but without his hands on her they fluttered away. She caught an echo of fear there, and she pressed her question into the ether. *Where had the children gone?*

The veterinarian moved to her neck, and this time, Matilda tensed. Her muscles bunched as he lifted his needle to her skin. Injection. A thing like a bug that burns. Her tail slapped against her flank, and the needle broke the skin, shot her full of fire and deep thinking.

He'd mentioned side effects. As the fluid leaked into her body, she understood what that meant. The farmer knew it, too. His hands fluttered near her skin, not touching. He'd lied to the other man and...he hid things from her now, too.

She pushed outward, flowed like the milk-making serum, and found her answer. *Where had her children gone?*

The farmer cringed when she stamped her feet. He wrapped his thoughts in a blanket, but Matilda saw through it. The injection flowed beneath her skin, and its side effects opened another window.

SHE HAD A PURPOSE. MATILDA HAD THOUGHT ABOUT THE children all week. She'd thought, when the farmer milked her and his memories couldn't hide from her, not even with the gloves he'd started wearing.

You can't hide what you've done, Bill.

He led her to the long yard, and today, Matilda read the veterinarian's name on the side of his vehicle. She read his phone number below a poorly rendered image of a barn.

"How's she doing?" Doctor Jones asked.

"Fit as a fiddle and producing twice as much milk." Bill lied easily, just like slipping on gloves.

Matilda listened, flicked her ears to the front and pushed at her side effects to *hear*, to *understand.*

"I dunno, Bill. Maybe we should skip a week." The good doctor scratched his head. "Macklemore's taken the girls off it. Said the milk tasted funny."

"We haven't had any problems."

"To be honest, I'm thinking about killing the program. Too many complaints and you and old Matilda here are the only ones still with me."

"I need the milk, doc. I can pay you the difference if..."

"No. We'll keep her on it for now." Finally, the man moved for his bag. He withdrew the syringe, and Matilda leaned forward, seeking the injection with her whole body. "Listen, Bill. Just be careful and keep in mind that I may have to discontinue the drug."

"Sure, doc. I get it."

Matilda felt the needle prick and sighed. She felt the burn and understood that they meant to stop the injections. She only had a little time, but she had a purpose.

She had a week to plan her vengeance.

"ONE MORE, DOC. COME ON." BILL ARGUED WITH DOCTOR Jones, and Matilda waited with her breath held.

She was ready to kill.

The farmer spat and stamped his feet, and the veterinarian

shook his head. They argued, and Matilda feared they injection would not come.

"Just one more, doc." Bill pleaded.

Just one more. Matilda prayed.

Doctor Jones sighed and reached into his supplies. "The last one, Bill."

"Sure. Fine." The farmer said one thing, and plotted another in his mind.

Matilda focused on the good doctor. Her timing had to be just right, the perfect moment, the exact spot on the side of the head. *The temple.* She'd plucked that weakness from the farmer's fears as he sat milking so close to her hooves.

The cool needle found her neck. The hot serum washed magically through her blood, through her body, and into the milk she could make without effort now.

Doctor Jones removed the syringe, turned his back on the cow, and bent down over his bag. Matilda spun, jerking her head up hard and freeing the lead easily from Bill's tentative grip. She shuffled toward the veterinarian, aimed a hoof, and heard his skull crack at the impact.

His body slumped forward over his tools. He made no noise and no more thoughts. The veterinarian was an easy loss. He'd never planned to bring the serum to Bill's farm again. Bill had been cut off, and now, it was his turn to lose.

Matilda spun again, mooed deep from her belly, and came face to face with the farmer's shotgun. He'd backed toward the far fence, and he held the long barrel between them. It danced in his shaking hands, but the side effects told her, it didn't need to be accurate.

"Not so fast." Bill's voice shook too. "You think I'm stupid? You think I don't hear you, whispering in my head? Accusing me?"

Matilda blinked her lashes and watched the gun barrel. He'd kill her now. She heard that thought above the rest, but the rest just might hold an answer she could live through.

"Vicious beast." Bill spit on the ground and shook his head. "Your plans are in my mind."

But he hadn't had any injections. He had no side effects. Her thoughts reversed. The needle in her skin, the serum in her blood, the side effects in *the milk.*

"The milk." He nodded, and though he jerked the gun closer, his eyes drifted to her swollen udder. Bill had drunk the milk.

She could still make it. Matilda could make more milk than any cow in history. She pressed that thought at him now, and the barrel wavered. His fear of her warred with his greed, his love and terror at the new things he could do. How he knew when the salesman would take less for a tool. How he knew when the missus was in the mood, or when the kids were lying.

Matilda let the thoughts build, and when they'd swamped the fear with his new sense of power, she sent an idea of her own. A compromise. Something they could both live with.

"You're mad." The farmer laughed, but he lowered the gun. "You'd do it? And you can't hurt no one else."

Except he'd let her kill the veterinarian. He'd seen her plot, and he'd done nothing.

"Swear it," Bill hissed and waved the shotgun at the sky. "Swear you won't hurt no one. Never."

In her mind, Matilda showed him the promise he wanted. She threw a blanket over her plans, and gave Bill his confirmation. He was safe. Everyone was safe.

The farmer had taught her how to lie.

HER HEAD WAS FULL OF PLANS.

The farmer had milked her until her udder ached, but his thoughts were contented, full of chilling metal pails and mental magic. Matilda continued to read him anyway, kept half her attention on his musing just in case he hid something treacherous below all that self-congratulation.

She rode in the stock trailer, legs spread against the jerking of the floor, while Bill drove. In case he suspected her as well, Matilda filled the other half of her mind with images of the open hills ahead, with plans to find the range cattle, to mingle among them peacefully eating the long grass.

She could avoid the roundups now. Her side effects would make that easy. She could plan for the cold, had ideas about survival in the wild. The trailer rattled as Bill crossed the metal grates set into the road. Matilda felt, a cow with side effects could work out how to pass those as well.

Bill had her milk, enough that he was satisfied he could rule his little world. His mind churned with business deals and stock markets. He even flirted with the idea of politics. They were small dreams, but then, what would you expect from a creature with only one stomach?

As they neared the point of freedom, she found nothing sinister in his mind. He'd dismissed her just as soon as she'd agreed to cooperate. He would set her free. He would think he'd won.

Matilda tried to keep her mind on innocent dreams. She would have more children, and though she tried not to share the thought with Bill, she knew her future calves would have side effects as well. She'd have her progeny to talk to, to plan with.

Stuff that aside. Think of the grass and the hills.

Bill slowed the truck, called out from the driver's compartment. "Almost there, old girl."

Matilda mooed. She'd have time to think on it later. She'd have time. Let the farmer think his small dreams in his one stomach. Matilda chewed on hers, incubated them, digested four times over. Her offspring would rule his world.

She had a plan.

COMPANIONS, CLIFFS, AND A COW

R.J.J. GOUDE

About the Author: R.J.J. Goude writes YA and Middle Grade novels and short stories in various genres. She is from and lives in the Northwest with her husband and the kids who are still at home. She can be found running children around, reading and staring into space. Not to worry. Characters are plotting and dialoguing in her brain.

Companions, Cliffs, and a Cow

R.J.J. Goude

"So, do we think this is a good idea?" Howard stared down the side of the cliff clutching a weathered harness in his hand.

"Well...it's your cow." Fred widened his eyes at his long time friend and they both looked down at the ledge where Cornflower mooed mournfully.

"Dag gummet girl, don't ask for sympathy," said Howard, addressing the imperiled bovine. "You chasing after that devil mountain goat got you in this here predicament."

"Did she drop down there?" Fred's head swung back and forth taking in the cliff face.

"Nah, it's a far enough drop to that ledge. Fall like that, she'd be dead or badly injured."

"So...how'd she get there, and stay alive?" asked Fred.

"Love is a powerful force. In Cornflower's case, she'll follow wherever her love goes. Even prance along those narrow ridges you see there webbing the escarpment." Howard shook his head. "Her nimble suitor probably leaped to a higher trail and she couldn't follow."

"It's hard to believe she made it that far without falling." Fred stared at the ridge leading to the cow's ledge.

"Don't I know it. She's a fool, and that goat is going to be the death of her."

Cornflower hung her head and pushed back into the side of the cliff. A low, anxious grumble rumbled in her throat.

"Easy, girl. We're here to help you." Fred swallowed and patted his pocket. "And if you get too anxious, I've got something to calm you down."

"Thanks, Fred, for the thought, but she'll be fine once you lower me down to her."

"Uh...lower *you*...are you sure?" Fred glanced at his gangly arms. Howard seemed the better option for dangling a body over a cliff. Fred couldn't lift Howard as he was twenty years ago, let alone the extra pounds he'd acquired since.

"Yep. Better me repelling off the side of a cliff, especially given your...issues with anything with four legs." Howard raised his eyebrows at Fred, "Unless you want to cozy up to Cornflower down there on that itty bitty ledge?"

Fred craned his neck for another look, and gulped. His protruding Adam's apple danced.

"Didn't think so," said Howard.

"Well, unless you want to be dropped on your head, I need some help." Fred stared back and forth between Howard and the cow. Sweat sprouted on his palms as he thought of the distance.

Howard didn't argue. He searched the nearby, long grass and dirt. About two feet from the edge of the cliff he found a rock poking up from the ground and kicked it. "This'll do." He appraised Fred. "Wrap the rope around it, give you some leverage."

Fred inhaled and straightened his shoulders. "Okay, if you say so." He held up some rope. "Is this the one you're wearin' or is it the one you're holdin'?"

"Yours. Go ahead and give me the harness."

"Let's get going then. There's a chill in the air."

"You're right," said Howard. "Usually I'd say it's just your skin and bones talkin', but those clouds to the north have a look about them."

Howard dropped the harness for Cornflower and, after a couple of tries inserting his legs, got his harness in place and checked the carabineer. "All set here."

Fred stretched the rope out avoiding the tallest obstacles and draped it around the rock, looping the excess rope in a pile. "Ready."

"Well, here goes, nothin'." Howard turned around and planted his feet.

"Howard?"

"What?" He looked at Fred.

Fred looked at Howard. "Don't you think...uh...don't you think we should get..."

Howard lowered his eyebrows.

The suggested gurgled and died in Fred's throat. "Never mind." He shook his head and grasped the rope. He mumbled under his breath. "He's insane, doing this. We ain't young whipper-snappers. When was the last time he went traipsing over a cliff?" He tightened his grip and called out. "Ready."

Howard tugged the rope and Fred braced his feet.

Howard stepped over the ledge and Fred...fell forward.

Fred yanked the rope and slid his feet out and braced them against the rock.

"Howard?" Fred's voice trembled.

There was silence. Before Fred could call out in panic, Howard's reedy voice reached him. "Ya' Fred?" His voice had a higher pitch to it than normal, and Fred winced imagining the pressures exerted by the harness that had affected such a vocal change.

"How's it going?" asked Fred.

"Fine, Fred. Just fine." said Howard. "Just got here a mite sooner than expected. Do you mind if we take the rest of the way slower?"

Fred let out a slow breath of relief. "No problem. How much further?"

"Not much. I'm about a foot above Cornflower's head."

"Ready?"

"Yep. Lower away."

Fred gulped, willing his hand to unfreeze its grip on the rope. He released a breath and managed to ease it a smidge.

"That's it, Fred. Keep it coming." came the voice from over the cliff.

Fred's hands shook as he eased the rope forward. He stared at the rock, the one thing keeping Howard from falling on Cornflower's head. It looked kind of flat.

"Fred, when I said slower, I didn't mean slower than molasses."

Fred gritted his teeth. The muscles in his arms shook, but he somehow managed, hand over hand, to lower Howard. He was hopeful of managing a safe deposit of his burden on the ledge. At that moment, the clouds from the north chose to loose their rain upon the bovine-rescue operation. An icy rain. The rock didn't have quite enough grip on the rope anymore. It slid up over the smooth rounded surface.

Fred fought it, leaning back further, but the rope kept inching higher.

"Howard? You on there yet?" Widening his eyes and staring at the rope didn't stop it from coming free. Once it did, Howard's full weight yanked Fred toward the cliff.

Fred's throat and gut tightened as his body propelled forward. He face-planted into the pebbles and dead grass, but continued to slide on his forearms and belly and upper legs. He dug in his toes, attempting to slow down. He spit out the dirt and other foreign matter from his mouth, blinked, and had to blink again. The bright, white spots in the air were not warning him of a head injury. It was snowing.

"No. Higher than I—umph!"

Fred's forward momentum abruptly stopped.

"What the dag nubbit is going on?" Howard couldn't prevent a groan escaping this time. Bashing his head into Cornflower's was just too painful, and holding onto her neck like a koala was just costing too much energy to care about his dignity.

Fred crawled the rest of the way to the edge, peeked over and watched Howard through the snowflakes loosen his hold on Cornflower and gingerly place his feet beneath himself.

Cornflower shifted her feet.

Howard gasped and rubbed his head.

"Sorry about that, Howard. The rock failed."

"The *rock* failed?"

"Yeah. Rope slid right over it."

Howard blinked up into the snowflakes drifting down into his face. Momentarily distracted by them, he redirected his dazed expression to stare at Fred. "I knew I didn't like the look of them clouds."

"Is everything okay down there? 'Cause Cornflower is starting to look anxious."

The cow stomped and flicked her tail.

"Nothing to worry about. You'd be agitated too, if someone just hit you in the head."

Fred's eyes darted back and forth. "Who hit her?"

Howard stared up at Fred again despite the snow. "Fred?"

"Yeah, Howard?"

"Don't make me explain."

"Uh...yeah. Sure, Howard."

The stouter man rubbed his head, which gave Fred a clue what happened, but he wisely didn't say anything.

"I'm going to get the harness on her now." Howard planted his feet and took a deep breath.

Cornflower lowed and shifted her back feet.

"Yes, girl, I know. I want off here too." His stiff fingers worked the buckle open and he threw a strap over her back and began pulling the harness snug against her belly.

Cornflower shifted again, pushing Howard into the cliff face.

He pushed back. "Hey now, give me room." Once there was space enough to escape being pancaked, he moved to the edge side of the cow's fidgeting body.

"Howard, she sure looks uneasy. I'll toss this syringe down to ya." His cold fingers grabbed for it, poking his middle one on the sharp end. He jerked his arm and tossed the small device into the air. He fumbled for it, desperate to keep it from plummeting to the rocks below. "A-a-h... No!"

Fred dropped to his knees and peered over the ledge. The syringe was standing straight, ejection end down in Cornflower's hindquarter.

She jumped, knocking Howard off balance. He pumped his arms, flailing his body towards the agitated cow. She shifted and kicked. The rope attached to his harness tangled in her hooves.

"Fred!" Howard called, gesticulating at some hidden plan.

Before Fred could interpret Howard's gestures, the farmer slipped. He bent his body forward, slamming his chin into the ledge, but managed to stay conscious. He gasped and blinked from the pain shooting up his jaw, he engaged his arms just in the nick of time to prevent himself from sliding off. His fingertips gripped what they could.

Fred watched his friend's hold slipping.

"Hold on. I'm coming!"

"Don't. You. Dare." Howard huffed out with each breath. "Anchor me."

Fred jumped up, grabbed the rope and twirled around, hop-stepped it one direction and then another, searching for a tie off. Thankfully Howard couldn't witness his ineffectual jackrabbit dance. He may have let go and fallen to his death in despair.

Desperate on time, Fred wrapped the rope around a hardy-looking bush and secured it. He ran to the edge and skidded to all fours, anxious to see how his friend faired.

The tips of Howard's fingers were white with pressure, and they shook harder and harder with fatigue.

The snow now obscured Fred's view of Howard's struggle, but he could hear his grunts of exertion.

Fred squeezed the rope in both hands, and pulled upward, unsure of what else to do.

Howard's grip failed. He screamed, apparently of the belief that he was going to dash against the rocks below. The scream continued even after, moments later, he jolted to a dead stop.

Howard's sudden drop pulled Fred over and he plummeted head first for Cornflower.

A high piercing note echoed off the rock face.

Fred surveyed the scene, then shouted to his friend.

"Is that you Howard?"

"Who else would it be?" came the irritated response.

"Oh, good. It was hard to tell what I was seein'."

"Well, let me help you out then Fred." Howard twisted his body to angle back toward the cliff. The harness had a tendency to face outward. "You see an overgrown man hanging by his crotch, staring at rocks north and south."

"Oh, I thought the cliff ran east to west."

"No, dag gummit. South as in down. Below. As in, if I fall, my body will be bashed to bits on the rocks." Howard heaved a breath, trying to calm himself. "North, meaning above. Rocks above me, including your fool head. What in tarnation are you doing there?"

"I was holding the rope."

"The tied off rope?"

"Yeah."

"Did you have slack in it?"

"Of course, it needed to so I could get a good grip.

"Did you actually have it tied off?"

"Yep."

"Did it hold?"

Fred looked around. "Hard to tell...wait, here's the end. So, nope. Didn't hold at all."

"It's a wonder we're not dead."

"Not at all," Fred's lips stretched into a large smile. "Cornflower is laying on the rope."

"What?" Howard frowned. "What happened?"

"She's very relaxed."

"Fred. You didn't."

"Not on purpose. It was probably for the best though. Saved your life."

"Hmph!" What could he say to that. He was still breathing.

They watched the snow gently descend past them, some drifting on the rocks, leaving little mounds.

"Do you think Mabel will be mad?" Fred asked.

"I just hope she finds us."

"You didn't tell her where we were headed?"

"Of course I did, but whether or not she actually heard me is another thing entirely."

"Oh... Howard?"

"...what?"

"It's getting cold out here."

"Fred?"

"What?"

"Seeing as I'm dangling mid air filled with snow, I'm a little bit aware of the temperature."

"Sorry. It was just a concern for you."

"Oh..." Howard scratched his brow. "Just concerned for me and not yourself?"

"Nope. I'm not danglin' mid-air all alone."

"Not alone."

"Nope. I got Cornflower."

Howard shook his head, not willing to admit he would trade places with Fred faster than a Billy goat could chew through his rope. Cornflower was a big heater.

It stopped snowing. The quiet was only broken by the squawk of an occasional goose flying overhead. Until a new sound reached them. Voices.

A few pebbles pinged off the rocks.

"Do you see them anywhere? I thought this was where Howard was going to look for the cow."

"Nope. I don't see 'um."

"It would just be my luck to have to call the fire department to rescue them off the side of the cliff."

More rocks clinked down and one found Fred's head. He moaned. His noggin had already been a battering ram.

"Did you hear that?"

Fred rubbed his head and peered up towards the top of the ridge, into the faces of Mabel and Gretchen.

Mabel assessed the situation. Fred hugging Cornflower's body for dear life, sprawled across her back and her husband, further down, dangling. Legs and arms, shifting with the slight rotation of his torso, trussed in a harness.

The women shared a look.

Mabel sighed, "So, Gretchen, do we think this is a good idea?"

"Well...you know." She rubbed her mouth. "It *is* your husband."

"Yeah, we better call 'em and tell 'em they'll need a 'copter."

ENDING

LEE FRENCH

About the Author: Lee French lives in Olympia, WA, with two kids, two bicycles, and too much stuff. In addition to spending too much time on the Myth-Weavers game forum, she also trains in taekwando, keeps a nice flower garden with one dragon and absolutely no lawn gnomes, works an excessive number of book events, and tries in vain every year to grow vegetables that don't get devoured by neighborhood wildlife. She is an active member of the Science Fiction and Fantasy Writers of America and the Northwest Independent Writers Association, as well as serving the Olympia region as a NaNoWriMo Municipal Liaison.

Ending

Lee French

"SO, DO WE THINK THIS IS A GOOD IDEA?"

"Well..." The loaded question left me too nervous to give a straight answer. "It's your cow."

Mike adjusted his jeans, betraying his own discomfort. "She ain't no cow."

My relief shamed me, but I wanted to play a stupid game at least as much as he did, if not more. It beat talking about the real issue. "Sure. Couldn't be one."

"Nope." He took a drink of his beer, then pointed with the bottle at the animal in question, clearly visible through the transparent, signal-created fence. "Oversized goat."

"You sure?" I checked my own beer bottle—half full yet. Leaning against my parked hoverpod, I wondered when the buzz from the first bottle would kick in. This conversation had begun last night, and it needed alcohol. "Might be a de-horned rhino."

"Rhinos don't give milk." Mike stuck his second empty bottle into the sleeve on the old stump between us and grabbed his third beer.

"Sure they do, just nobody's stupid enough to try getting it."

"That's the damned truth." He popped the cap off his bottle. "You remember that time we found a cow in Porter's corn maze?"

"Yeah." I took a gulp from my beer. That had been quite a night. "Left for college the next morning."

Mike rubbed the embossed glass of his bottle with a calloused thumb. "Was a good night, though."

"The best." We'd stolen beer from my dad's stash, stumbled around in the dark like idiots to avoid the drones, and said lots of crazy things. Memories from that night... Guilt made me swallow the truth so I didn't have to face it.

I pointed to the nearby black and white animal. "You see some big difference between that corn maze cow and your oversized goat here?"

"'Course I do. That was a cow. This ain't. She don't do cow things, so she ain't a cow."

My laugh came out half-choked. "Yeah, that's the only thing that matters. What she does. The whole cowness of her doesn't mean anything."

"It's like they say. If she walks like a cow and talks like a cow and looks like a cow, she's a cow. This ain't no cow."

"Cows don't talk."

Mike scowled. "Don't be a big-city smartypants, Mr. College Degree. You know exactly what I mean."

"Sorry." The apology tumbled out empty. I did know exactly what he meant, and it had nothing to do with cows or goats. Maybe I'd asked too much. Some bridges didn't reach, as my father liked to say.

He grunted, showing less disdain than he'd earned toward me. "They have goats at your fancy new job?"

I wanted to accept the olive branch he offered. Mike was always a better man than me. But I couldn't. My gut churned. "No. Noc Luna has apartments. Nothing bigger than an average dog allowed."

"Apartment." He rolled the word around like he needed to taste it to understand. "Sounds small."

"Compared to your house, yeah." I could have left it at that. But he needed all the information. Leaving things out devalued his choices. "No yard, either. There's supposed to be a small park, but I'm not sure what's in it."

"Jesus. Sounds awful. How'n hell d'you live like that?"

I shrugged. "It'll be bigger than my dorm room was. I guess you get used to it."

"Ain't no way I'd never get used to that. 'Specially if'n there ain't no blue sky."

And just like that, he'd made a decision. The festering ache and niggling fear I'd nursed for years flared. My eyes burned. I could probably argue about the double-negative, but it would piss him off and net me nothing. Maybe coming back had been a mistake. Dad had suggested as much when I turned up at home yesterday. Purple hair didn't play well in this neck of the woods. Neither did polo shirts.

The next sip of beer tasted like dust. All of this was my fault. Four years ago, I left and never looked back. Five thousand times since then, I'd considered coming home and never did. This trip had happened only because I knew traveling home would get impossible once I left for my new job on the Moon base.

"Mike, I—"

"Nope. Not a cow. Goat. You stick around long enough, you'll hear her bleat." He might as well have pointed a gun and told me to get off his property.

I checked my beer again, wanting to say things I hadn't said yet but too scared to let them loose in the world. In two days, I'd be on a one-way shuttle. Only the pilots came back from Noc Luna, and they had to stay in quarantine while on Earth. Once a body acclimated to the environment up there, a trip back home could kill.

Downing the last few swigs, I thought about the moment I'd made the stupidest decision of my life. Three and a half years ago, I came out of the closet to my parents via vidscreen. My new friends in Los Angeles had been mystified to discover anyone still kept it a secret. Why bother when no one cared?

Neither of my parents had said anything direct. They'd thrown subtle hints to convince me to cancel my trip home for the holidays. I should've kept it to myself. If only I'd kept it to myself!

I set my empty bottle on the stump, wishing I could trade places with it. The stupid bottle could go to Noc Luna for the incredible job. *It* could be an empty husk instead of me. "So. Goodbye, then."

Mike grunted, staring at his stupid goat.

Activated by a mental command to the transmitter implanted

in my arm, the dome of my hoverpod slid open. I hesitated. "Mike—"

"Dammit," Mike snapped. "Shut the hell up!" He threw his beer bottle at the sigfence. It shattered and splashed the oversized goat, startling her into mooing.

I jumped and cringed. Nothing he'd ever done led me to expect sudden violence. For a moment, I thought he might slug me.

His shoulders slumped. "I waited for you. You said you'd come back for the summer, but you didn't. I waited for you. Then you show up here after four years. Four damned years! And now you're leaving forever, and I should come with you? Pick up and leave everything I've ever known. For what?"

Tears rolled down my cheeks. I was the asshole and we both knew it, and I didn't know what to do about it except run away. "I'm sorry. I never meant—"

"Go to hell!" He jabbed his finger at my chest. I wished he would get it over with and stab me. "You at least man up and tell me to my face that you got someone else, or you used me, or whatever, but don't you stand there and pretend it ain't nothing."

I shook my head and couldn't look him in the eyes. "I'm sorry. I thought— I don't know. I guess I thought it'd be like...like in the movies."

"You're a damned coward," he spat. "And a dumb fool. I don't know what I ever saw in you."

How could I respond to that? He deserved a real answer, not a blank apology. I wiped my face and forced myself to look at him. We'd met so long ago it felt like ancient history. My fifteen-year-old self had been miserable before seventeen-year-old Mike came along and made my whole world make sense. I owed him everything—my grades, my new job, my sanity, my life.

My darkest day had led to my brightest night because of him. An answer was the least I could give him. Even if I didn't want to admit to anything out loud.

"I can't take the way Dad looks at me. He's my father, and I'm his failure."

"Jesus H. Christ in a bucket ah turnips." Mike huffed and walked away.

"Wait!"

"What for?" he called over his shoulder. "You ain't worth it."

I clamped down the urge to taunt him for walking away. I'd done it first. He had every right to return the favor.

Mike stumped inside his house and slammed the door so hard I flinched.

"Wait because I can't do this without you anymore." No one heard me but the cow. Goat. Whatever. I climbed into my hoverpod and hugged my knees to my chest. My wrist itched. Pushing aside the decorative band I always wore, I stared at the old scar it concealed.

If I wanted to, I could fix the ugly line. These days, lasers and synthaskin covered something small like this with a ten minute procedure. No more reminders, no more memories, no more Mike. Like scrubbing away a stain, I could erase the past.

The memory of him keeping pressure on the trauma patch flooded my head. He'd murmured soothing words and held me in his arms. Blood had smeared his white t-shirt and the plaid flannel he wore over it. I'd passed out. When I woke, he'd rocked me in his father's easy chair, and I'd used his shirt as a tissue.

"I've always been the weak one," I whispered to the hoverpod. The truth ached.

I thought about going back to LA. My new employer wanted me. The shuttle ride promised spectacular views. When I got to Noc Luna, everything would fade away in favor of the future. I'd do a job that mattered.

Alone.

The stupid cow-goat-whatever mooed.

"You ain't thinking about doing nothing stupid, right?" Mike leaned against my hoverpod. The flannel he wore had the same pattern as the one he'd worn that day. " 'Cause I seen this movie afore, and it don't end well." A trauma patch peeked out from his breast pocket.

I sniffled. He'd come to make sure he didn't have to deal with a dead body. Now that he'd turned me away, I felt strangely free to say things. "There was never anyone else."

"No, I didn't reckon so."

"I tried to save enough to get you a vidscreen and connection. But I needed to eat."

Mike nodded, and I couldn't tell if he'd expected that kind of stupid excuse or not. He took my hand and peeled my wristband off. Like he used to do so often, he rubbed his thumb over the scar to help me center. I'd never needed that in LA. Or had I? Maybe I'd been holding back a lot more than I thought.

"You coulda sent a letter."

"I was scared."

"Of what? Me?"

Wiping my face, I blurted out, "I don't know."

"Bull puckey. You know. You just ain't willing to say. C'mon. You already done told me it's about your daddy. You told him, right? And he weren't real impressed. Said some stuff. You dove into your books and learning and stuff to distract yourself. Thought about visiting me, but knew you'd have to see the old man.

"Now that's all done, so you come home, thinking the music is gonna start up and we ride into the sunset." He brushed strands of purple hair out of my face. I let my eyes flutter shut and sighed. "Except your daddy said something new. And you forgot about the part where you explain to me why I oughta trust you after you done run away and never come back until now. Not even a quick message or nothing. You got any idea what I thought? That ever cross your mind?"

He knew the answer.

"I'm such a worthless bastard," I choked out.

"Those words mighta come up a time or two."

I tugged at my hand, ready to leave and undo the safety protocols on my hoverpod. Opening the hatch at top speed would take care of everything.

Mike sighed and held on. "I know what I said last night. And

I'm sorry I let myself get carried away on sight of you. Nothing ain't never that easy, and you know it as well as I do. I ain't selling my cow, I ain't giving up my house and garden, and I ain't coming with you. That don't mean I don't care. Come on back inside and stay for a coupla days. We'll talk. I can see you ain't never really thought about this stuff a whole lot, and maybe that's kinda my fault."

This man shouldered blame for my failings. Mike qualified for sainthood. I didn't. Not even close.

He let go and stepped back, giving me space to decide. This life had gone so horribly wrong. I could live on the moon, but I couldn't go back and prevent myself from screwing up everything. Another apology tried to force its way out. I swallowed it. Those words meant nothing.

"She's not a cow. She's a goat." I didn't know why I said that.

The corner of Mike's mouth quirked up. "I dunno. She might be a de-horned rhino."

I tried to smile. My face hurt. My everything hurt, inside and out. "Find someone worth it."

Mike sighed and shook his head. He knew. He always knew. "Come back inside. Please."

"You should've let me go the first time." I'd caused him enough pain for two lifetimes. At my command, the hatch slid shut.

He thumped a fist on the hatch, his brow drawn with concern. "Saving your life weren't no mistake! Dammit, you idjit, let me do it again."

The hoverpod rose and retracted its landing struts.

"I love you," I whispered.

I left him behind.

FREEZER CAMP

ELIZABETH R. ALIX

About the Author: Elizabeth R. Alix has been writing creative fiction for most of her life, taking detours into professional archaeology and parenting, both of which have provided much fodder for writing. She currently lives in eastern Washington and is working on The Maple Hill Chronicles, a series of three books about ghosts and magic.

Freezer Camp

Elizabeth R. Alix

"So, do we think this is a good idea?" the farmer's daughter asked anxiously.

"Well, it's your cow," her father replied with a perplexed shrug.

"Thank you, Daddy, you're the best." She hugged her startled father and removed the halter from her 4-H heifer, Baby, in a shower of glitter. Taking her big, beautiful, white face between her hands, the girl said, "You've got this."

In a rare moment of peace earlier that summer the farmer and his hired hand were leaning on the fence of the pasture watching their livestock. It was a gorgeous, mild, blue-sky day, and the cows were feeling frisky, gamboling about and kicking up their heels. All of a sudden, a brown and white heifer ran at the far fence and jumped straight over into the next pasture. "Damn. That's the third time this week," the farmer said, shaking his head.

"Freezer camp this fall?" The hired man thoughtfully chewed a stalk of grass.

"Prob'ly gonna to have to. Can't be runnin' all over the county looking for 843."

"What about the others?" The hired hand flicked the fuzzy seed stalk as he indicated each one. "860's a kicker. I still have a vicious bruise from the last time. And 845 spends half her time bellowin' for no good reason."

"I know it. The new neighbors called to complain again about the noise two nights ago." The farmer rubbed the stubble on his jaw and sighed. "The missus is on my case about 821 eating her roses. She chased it out with a broom again yesterday." He shook his head. "Maybe they're all defective one way or another. Maybe they should all go to freezer camp."

His daughter's white 4-H project, auspiciously named Baby, looked up from her grazing, gazed at them for a moment with remarkably intelligent eyes and then ambled off toward the other cows.

"Huh, been doin' this for forty years and sometimes you'd think they understand you," the hired man commented, shifting the stalk from one side of his mouth to the other.

BABY WANDERED CLOSER TO HER MOTHER, KICKER, AND HER friends Holler, Rosie, and Dandelion. "Hey, what's camp?"

Dandelion looked up, yellow pollen coating her lips like powdered sugar. "I don't know. Didn't your human go to camp last week?"

"Yeah," Baby remembered. "She seemed real happy when she came back, so it must be a fun place."

Rosie grinned. "I bet it's got acres of flowers!"

"Alfalfa!" Holler said dreamily.

Butterfly looked over the fence from the other pasture and said, "Maybe there's fresh green grass on *both* sides!"

"Dandelions," Dandelion sighed.

"Pears," Kicker added with a fond look.

"What are pears?" Baby asked, cocking her head to one side.

"The girl gave me one before you were born, and it was divine."

"Moooo, I hope she gives me one!"

A week later Baby, Holler, Kicker, Butterfly, and Dandelion were at the fence watching the hired man putting a rope halter on Rosie. As she was led up the gangway into the slatted truck, she turned and grinned. "I'll see you at camp!"

"Wow, lucky her." Dandelion called, "Save me some!"

The gate on the back was latched and the truck drove away.

Baby noticed that her girl was a little sad that night and rubbed her soft nose against her until she smiled again.

"HUMANS DO THE STRANGEST THINGS," KICKER SAID ONE afternoon. It was the middle of haying, so all the cows were closer to the house than usual. But instead of working today, the humans were gathered around the back of the house, eating and drinking. "They ate outside last year, too. Later, they shot off lights that made noise and sparkled like giant flowers in the sky. It was real pretty."

"Mama, I can't wait to see that!" Baby said excitedly.

"You'll have to wait till dark." She and the other cows grazed their way to the far side of the pasture, but Baby lingered near the fence. Her girl came by with long orange sticks that smelled sweet and tasted crunchy and wonderful. Baby thought they must be pears. She was plucking at long grass stems when the farmer's wife came out of the house and the foul, smoking box was opened.

Cooked meat was piled on a platter and put on the table where people loaded up their plates, squirted on red, yellow, and brown stuff and began to eat.

"These are amazing, Maggie!" everyone said.

"Well, they should be. That damn cow ate enough roses and garden produce to taste like a whole cornucopia. If you hadn't take her off to freezer camp, I wouldn't have any garden left this year."

"Mother, hush! You're upsetting Baby!" the girl said reprovingly.

"Don't be ridiculous," her mother snorted.

Baby trotted away from the house to the far side of the corral. "Mama! Mama!" she shouted.

Kicker looked up surprised by the panic in her offspring's voice. "What's the matter, dear?"

"Mama! They're eating her! They're eating Rosie!"

The others gathered around, and Baby told them what she'd overheard. "I don't understand. My girl loves me! She would never do that!"

Butterfly rolled her eyes wildly and mooed, "That's it! I'm

gonna jump away from here! I don't wanna be turned into foooooood!"

Her panic was contagious. "Neither do I!" Holler trumpeted. "I need to sing! I'm a natural born singer."

"I can't help it if I get a little testy when they grab me too hard in milking. I have sensitive teats," Kicker said soulfully.

Baby was getting over her shock and lowed softly to calm them. "They said Rosie ate too many roses and got into the garden. So, maybe only bad cows go to freezer camp."

Butterfly rolled her big brown eyes. "But I'm a free-range girl! I need my space! I don't want to be tied down to just one pasture!"

Baby soothed, "We don't mind if you can jump fences, Butterfly, but the farmer might. So, guys, don't be noisy, don't jump, and, Mama, don't kick."

Butterfly looked panicky at the thought of being trapped. The rest looked mournful.

Baby looked at her friends. "It's only for a little while. I'll think of something. Meanwhile, be good."

THAT NIGHT IN HER STALL BABY RACKED HER BOVINE BRAIN FOR hours, then cried herself to sleep, unable to think of anything to save her mother and her friends. The next morning the farmer's girl came in as the sun cleared the horizon to feed her, brush her, and clean out the stall.

She noticed that her white heifer was not her usual bouncy self. "What's the matter, Baby? You look down this morning." Turning on the little music player that hung from a strap on a nail, she hummed along while it played her favorite music.

"Baby," the farmer's daughter said as she brushed the white fur into velvety softness, "you're going to be the prettiest cow at the fair this summer. We'll win first prize for sure! I've never won first prize and that blue ribbon would look mighty nice right up there, don't you think?"

Feeling better, Baby rubbed her soft nose against her human in agreement. When their favorite song came on, they both hummed along. The girl laughed, "You sound pretty good, Baby! Too bad they don't have a talent contest for cows."

Later that day, Baby lay chewing her cud with her friends. They were all worn out with the effort of going against their inner natures. It was hard being good. They just wanted to be themselves.

"I wonder if we could convince the humans that you're talented, not annoying?" she mused out loud.

THE REST OF THE SUMMER WAS MOSTLY UNEVENTFUL. THERE were some strange occurrences, though. The farmer caught sight of 843 jumping fences, and she'd evidently taught 850 how to do it too. It was odd, though. They sometimes jumped back and forth over the fence as if they couldn't make up their minds before settling on one side or the other and grazing for a while. 845 bellowed all summer like a sick trumpet. The farmer would be glad when the fall came, and his field could be quiet again.

Gates and stalls were mysteriously unlatched. The new neighbor's son, hired for the summer, was blamed for it, though he staunchly denied it. Eventually he had to be let go since he never seemed to learn.

Rex, the farm dog, spent a lot of time dashing around and barking. Sometimes he spooked the cattle. At night he seemed to do it for no reason at all, and the farmer had to throw his shoes at the pesky dog to quiet him.

The hired man returned to the bunkhouse one night after a late night with his buddies at the bar and was arrested by an impossible sight in the moonlit field. He rubbed his eyes and concluded he was drunker than he thought. Cows just didn't do that.

The farmer's daughter continued to love and coddle Baby,

dreaming of first prize. When her CD player disappeared, she blamed her little brother for it. Their parents diverted his allowance in punishment, and he had to buy her another. Strangely, Baby had taken up humming.

A WEEK BEFORE THE COUNTY FAIR, BABY MADE A FUSS IN HER stall, mooing and kicking. She waited patiently until her girl came out to see what was wrong.

"Baby, what—" she started to say. Baby gave her a blast of her soulful brown eyes, nuzzled her hands, and shouldered gently past her through the open door. "Hey, come back!" Baby looked over her shoulder putting her all into a "follow me" look.

The girl put her hands on her hips, and said, "I don't know what's gotten into you, Baby." She shrugged fondly and followed her to the far end of the pasture. Baby brought out the music player from its hiding place and put it on the old tree stump they'd been using. Everyone took her place and Baby pressed 'play.'

When the farmer's daughter got over her shock and amazement, a huge grin lit up her face. "We'll get first prize for sure! You need to dress it up a bit, though, and I have just the thing."

THE 4-H KIDS, MOMS, DADS, AND FRIENDS WENT STILL AS FIVE cows walked out on stage at the county fair. The previous performance had been a precocious ten-year-old playing banjo. It was a hard act to follow, and Baby felt a little self-conscious. Her girl had invited her friends to the cow barn after the judging, and Baby, Kicker, Holler, Butterfly and Dandelion were now wearing more glitter, mascara, and ribbons than she had ever thought possible.

Baby took a deep breath and walked to center stage with

Butterfly and Dandelion flanking her left and right; Kicker and Holler who were bigger completed the "V" behind them.

The sweet strains of violins filled the night and people stared as the heifers began swaying their tails in time to the music when the keyboards and drums started playing a catchy disco beat.

"Do the shake, dooo the shaaaake!" the men sang. "Do the milkshake, the milkshake, the milkshake!" Holler mooed passionately on the chorus.

The heifers stepped in time to the music, crossing one hoof over the other to the left and then to the right in formation as they bobbed their heads.

"When they come home from school, and they want something that's cold to drink..."

Baby and the others turned in unison and swayed their hips, their udders swinging rhythmically. When the chorus came around again, Baby and Kicker turned to face the audience as Butterfly and Dandelion split, going up the center and around the back to opposite sides of the stage.

"When you're at work, and it's time for a coffee break...treat yourself to a big, thick and frosty shake."

On "big, thick and frosty shake" Butterfly and Dandelion sailed gracefully over Baby and Kicker, landing with a solid thud.

The stage, built every summer for the fair, was made of good two-by-fours. but wasn't built to take five hefty babes dancing rhythmically. However, no one could hear the creaking over the music, the laughter, and the clapping.

When the big finish came, "Yeah, do it, do it, do it, alriiight..." Kicker and Holler lay down on the platform, and Dandelion and Butterfly put their front hooves on their broad backs. Baby, the lightest of them, was carefully preparing to be the top of the pyramid when Rex finally broke loose. Left in the truck, tormented by the music that had driven him mad all summer, Rex wormed his way out through the half open window and raced between people's legs. He charged up the stairs, barking madly.

Alarmed, Kicker and Holler tried to scramble to their feet.

Dandelion and Butterfly lost their balance and Baby fell. The tortured beams below them gave up in a shower of splinters, and the entire stage disappeared with a crash.

The hired hand shook his head. “Damn. That was the best milkshake I’ve ever seen.”

WHEN THE WEATHER COOLED, THE GIRL WENT BACK TO SCHOOL. She’d finally learned to accept congratulations for training the remarkable, talented cows that had brought the house down at the fair. She missed Baby and the others, but even daddy wasn’t a miracle worker. From time to time she touched the blue ribbon hanging proudly beside her bed. In the spring she’d put it in Baby’s old stall and tell her new 4-H heifer all about the fair. The best thing was that every hamburger lifted her spirits and made her want to sing and dance. It was something about the glitter.

THE COW AT THE END OF THE WORLD

JOYCE REYNOLDS-WARD

About the Author: Joyce Reynolds-Ward is a speculative fiction writer who splits her time between Enterprise and Portland, Oregon. Her short stories have appeared in *Children of a Different Sky, Steam. And Dragons, Tales from an Alien Campfire, River, How Beer Saved the World 1, Fantasy Scroll Magazine, and Trust and Treachery among others. Her books include Shadow Harvest, Alien Savvy, Netwalking Space, Pledges of Honor, Challenges of Honor, and Klone's Stronghold*. Joyce recently completed editing her first anthology, *Pulling Up Stakes*. Besides writing, Joyce enjoys reading, quilting, horses, skiing, and outdoor activities.

The Cow at the End of the World
Joyce Reynolds-Ward

"So, do we think this is a good idea?" Loki scowled at the long-horned chestnut-colored cow chewing her cud. She blinked big brown eyes reproachfully at him and nudged his hand, opening her mouth wide before emitting a low moo.

"Well...it's your cow." Coyote laconically leaned back against the fence. "But for the record, no, I *don't* think just putting her back where she came from works. You said she was contained, but she managed to get out. Who says she won't do it again?"

"She couldn't do it by herself. She had help. She couldn't just break out of Buri's creation on her own."

"And that's the problem," Coyote sighed. "You can't just silver-tongue your way out of this one, buddy. She tried to eat Earth's reality, and we don't know who broke her out of confinement. What's to say whoever freed her won't try it again?" He crossed his arms. "Why not butcher her and throw a big party for all the superheroes and deities we can get to attend? I think that's the safest thing to do."

The cow flipped her ears back and shook her head, giving Coyote a baleful glare.

"Now, now, sweetheart, he didn't mean it," Loki crooned to the cow. The intensity of his scowl at Coyote matched the cow's glower. "You think you can b-u-t-c-h-e-r her? Audhumla is most definitely *not* anyone's cow, much less mine, and she's *very* powerful. I've not the faintest clue how we'd manage to k-i-l-l her without her regenerating right back." The cow nudged Loki's hand, rubbing against his fingers. Absently he scratched the long bones of her nose.

"All things are possible. You should know more about how to deal with her than me—I'm not the one coming from a tradition of the primeval cow," Coyote retorted, grinning as Audhumla eased closer to Loki, eyelids drooping and relaxed. "After all, didn't she lick your ancestors into being from a block of salty ice?"

Loki pushed Audhumla away as she got careless with the tip of one horn. "Careful, beast. If she belongs to anyone now living it would be Odin. It was his grandfather Buri she licked out of the ice—if you think that she's Norse—and no, Odin's *not* my brother. Or father. Or anything else. I have no kinship to Buri."

"Then maybe Odin should take custody of her. He does still have an interest in her, right?"

"There are—complications. He's just as likely to accuse me of letting her loose. Besides, he gets careless, too." Loki scowled as Audhumla circled around him, opening her mouth and lowing again, then sidled over to present her withers to him for scratching. "Just because she's not featured in tales of Ragnarok doesn't mean she doesn't have a role." His expression grew dourer. "After all, Fenrir and Jormungand's restraints fail at the end. Audhumla has the potential to be more dangerous—she could destroy the world once and for all. I don't trust Odin's fetters. Buri's the one who bound her in the first place, and he had access to primeval magic that Odin lacks."

"Well, we could talk to the Egyptians. Didn't Ra use magical beer to stop a destructive manifestation of Hathor?"

"It would take more than beer to stop Audhumla. And Set is still upset about our last prank, so I'd just as soon stay clear of the Egyptians. Besides, I'm not certain they could control her, either."

"We've got to do something with her. I'm still in favor of a big barbeque," Coyote said. He stretched. Audhumla lowered her head and shook her horns threateningly at him again.

"I keep telling you, I'm afraid she might regenerate. Like Thor's goats." Audhumla turned her head and gave Loki a searching look, then a soft bellow. Loki grimaced and pulled an ice ball out of his pocket. She opened her mouth wide and he tossed the ice ball into her mouth. She began to chew, then opened her mouth for more, batting long eyelashes at Loki.

"We're going to have problems when you run out of those ice chunks," Coyote observed. "Then what?"

"I'll think of something."

"And how soon will that be? How many more do you have?"

Loki cleared his throat nervously.

Coyote eyed him, recognizing a fellow Trickster's tell. "How many more do you have?" he repeated. "Or are you running out?"

"Eh, well—I am running low on them."

"All right. So, do you have an idea better than putting her back where she came from?"

"We could return her and set a trap," Loki said. "Catch who released her and find out what they used to spring her."

"Now you're talking," Coyote said. "I like that idea. Thinking for once." He ignored Loki's grimace and whistled for their horses. Loki's eight-legged mare, Little Sleipnir, mostly white except for the red patch covering her ears and poll and big red splotch on her chest, trotted over to Loki, pinning her ears at Audhumla. Her brother, Coyote's horse War Bonnet, a four-legged red stallion with white markings that were the reverse of Little Sleipnir's, ambled over to Coyote, ignoring Audhumla.

Coyote swung up on the stallion and patted his neck. "Back to work, Bonnet," he said. The stud snorted and tossed his head, pawing impatiently. His sister nipped at Bonnet and kicked at him with her outside right hind leg.

"Stop that, Little Sleip!" Loki scolded as he mounted. He spun her to face Audhumla and the paint mare dropped her head, pinning her ears flat against her head, now focusing on the cow. Coyote didn't bother tightening his reins but urged Bonnet forward. The stallion's ears flicked back and he lowered his head to match Little Sleipnir's posture.

"Maybe we should rope her," Coyote suggested. "If she takes off, it'll be another big chase."

"Won't be a problem if you get where you're supposed to be to keep her from taking off," Loki said.

Coyote shrugged. "It's your cow. Not my problem if you want

to chase her over all creation." He let Bonnet sidle sideways. Little Sleipnir marched toward Audhumla. The cow lowered her head defiantly. Bonnet edged forward. Audhumla bellowed and whirled away from Little Sleipnir.

Loki looked up at the sky. "Heimdall, a hand here?" He waited, raising his hand as a prism of light wrapped around it. Then he snapped his fingers. A bright flash of magic illuminated a rainbow-colored pathway in the starry dark ahead of them. "That's where we need to go. It's not the Bifrost, but it'll work."

"Get that?" Coyote asked Bonnet. The stallion darted forward when the cow would have headed in the wrong direction. They got her headed back toward the pathway, Little Sleipnir and Loki foiling another attempt to get away. Audhumla bellowed again, then set off at a lumbering gallop down the pathway. They rode up on her flanks, pushing her along the rainbow pathway amongst the stars.

Coyote had just started to relax when a shimmering, stocky, winged figure with orange hair materialized on the pathway in front of Audhumla. She skidded to a stop, bawling. Then she tried to whirl back but both Bonnet and Little Sleipnir blocked her.

Magic flared from the bright figure, breaking the pathway. "How DARE you interfere with my plans!"

"Lucifer, just what are you up to?" Coyote sighed. "And why?"

Lucifer fluttered his wings. "I need her to bring about the war in heaven. I want Armageddon to begin. No one is taking me seriously, and that is going to stop! I have the best plans for the world ever. It's going to be so great. I'm going to win Armageddon! I'll win it so big it'll never happen again!"

"Really?" Loki shook his head. "I've been through a dozen Ragnaroks, Luci. They aren't as much fun as you think they are. We Tricksters never win. Haven't you figured that out yet?"

"That's enough, Liesmith!" Lucifer pulled himself up, wings beating faster until it seemed they should be able to lift him off of the rainbow pathway, his orange hair blowing from side to side.

"You may have gone through your end of the world multiple times, but mine is overdue!"

"I'll loan you the ending of one of my worlds," Coyote offered. "I went through a Ragnarok with Loki. He's right, they're overrated. Come on, man. Us Tricksters have to stick together. Better to drink beer and have fun rather than get into all that business of rolling up the old world and laying down the new. Lots of work. Never goes right again in the end. Like Loki said, we never win anyway. Easier to just stay with a single reality."

"No." Lucifer stamped his right foot, growling. "I. Am. Tired. Of. My. Role. I want a reboot! I should have been the first and foremost! I want to depose Michael. And—and—HIM! Slimy little schemer—he—he—he..." His face turned red and a hissing sound replaced what words might be coming out of Lucifer's mouth.

Loki and Coyote exchanged looks. "Sounds like he's having a crisis," Coyote said.

"He just needs to get drunk and get into a flyting duel with Jesus," Loki said. "I could coach him on that."

"Strong drink can lead to bitter words." Coyote shrugged. "Trading insults—that's what flyting is, right?—while drunk always helps purge any hurt feelings I have." He grimaced. "Though the aftermath sometimes is enough to make me want to go through a world's end. Almost as painful. Let's go get drunk and do flyting with Jesus. Sounds like fun."

"I do NOT need to do flyting with—with—HIM!" Lucifer yelped. "I've read the Lokasenna. I don't want to end up being tied to a rock while a serpent drips venom on my face like they did to you, Loki. Besides, I have neither sons to contribute entrails to bind me nor wife to hold a bowl to catch the venom. Let's cut to the chase and have the end of the world."

"Maybe you need a wife and sons," Coyote muttered. "What is it with your particular pantheon that you're all celibate? Man, that just makes the frustrations worse. If you don't want to do the Norse thing, I'll take you to a winter potlatch or two. No—how about a good sweat lodge? With peyote. That'll get the spirit up in you!"

"No, no, no!" Lucifer's face crinkled up and was almost as bright orange as his hair. "I want Armageddon. NOW!" He stomped his right foot again. "And I don't need to be hanging around in smoky longhouses with pounding drums and eating foul-tasting mushrooms. What good is seeing funny colors and making a fool of myself?"

"This is really getting tiresome," Loki sighed. "He's like all that pantheon, Coyote. No fun at all."

Audhumla tossed her head and bellowed. She pawed at the rainbow path and tossed her head.

"Even the cow's sick of his temper tantrum," Coyote said. "I'd say we found our culprit. So what should we do now?"

Before Loki could answer, Audhumla launched herself across the gap in the pathway. She lowered her horns to grab at Lucifer. He gulped and began to run, lifting his robes high as the cow gave chase. Loki and Coyote exchanged another glance, and shrugged, then urged Little Sleipnir and Bonnet along in pursuit.

Lucifer stumbled. Before he could get up, Audhumla stomped on him. Then she reached down and bit off a chunk of wing. Lucifer screamed. She took another bite. Coyote and Loki reined in their horses and watched as Audhumla continued to eat Lucifer.

"Should we save him?" Coyote asked Loki.

"He wanted an Armageddon," Loki said. "I suppose Audhumla has decided to provide it for him."

"Yeah, but now we need to tell Michael." Coyote shuddered. "No way am I going to talk to Jesus himself, especially when someone that key to their mythos just got eaten by a Norse cow." He brightened. "Hey, maybe we should get Hathor or Set to relay the news."

"I'd go through Peter instead," Loki said. "And this won't last forever. She'll process him through, and he'll regenerate. Maybe he won't be so grumpy in a new form. That one was getting tiresome."

"But what if she shits him out where we put her? Won't he just break out again and let her free?"

"We've got a long, long way to ride yet, and she'll probably shit him out before then," Loki said. "Just make sure that Bonnet doesn't step on him when she does."

Audhumla finished, licking her lips and sniffing out the few scattered feathers from Lucifer's wings. Then she heaved herself down. A blissful expression crossed her face as she began to chew her cud.

"Looks like we'll be here a while," Coyote said. "Cow, buffalo, I know when they want to flop and digest." He dismounted and loosened the cinch on Bonnet's saddle, then unbridled the stallion. He grabbed a nosebag out of his saddlebags and hung it on Bonnet's face so he could eat. With a flick of his fingers he produced fire. "I've got some prime brew in my saddlebags, Loki. Care for a drink?"

"Don't mind if I do." Loki pulled a pouch out of his saddlebags. "How about some cards?"

Coyote frowned. "You cheat."

"So do you."

"How about dice instead?"

"Yours are loaded."

"And your cards are marked. Let's make a new game in memory of Luci and use them both." Coyote extracted a jug from his saddlebags.

"I think we could do something with that."

The Tricksters settled by the fire.

Coyote uncorked the jug and took a deep draw. "To Luci, and may his next incarnation be less of a pain to deal with." He passed the jug to Loki.

"To Luci, and may he finally be less of a killjoy," Loki said.

And so they sat, passing around the jug and arguing over the cards and dice. Audhumla chewed her cud while the horses crunched their grain.

There were worse ways to celebrate the end of someone's world.

THE COW JUMPED OVER THE MOON

WILLIAM GRAVES

About the Author: William Graves, a Texas native, writes fantasy, scifi, and horror. He has a bachelor's in philosophy and an M.A. he'd rather not talk about. He spends his days writing, grooming his magisterial beard, and brewing beer.

The Cow Jumped Over the Moon
William Graves

"SO, DO WE THINK THIS IS A GOOD IDEA?" SHEP ASKED, concerned.

"Well, it's your cow." Lemmy's response was gentler than Shep expected from the big man. "But it's got to be done. I wish it didn't, but there's no other way. She's one of the last ones left. If we don't send her tonight, it don't bear thinking what'll happen."

Shep kneeled down. Before him, an alien-looking spaceship, all sleek, foreign angles, rested on the ground. It had been crafted of some black metal that earth's scientists had yet to identify. It had pre-positioned itself pointing at the alien base so recently established on the Moon.

And within it, Shep had already strapped and secured his cow Penelope.

Shep, his son Jeremiah, his farmhand Lemmy, and Penelope all stood in Shep's back pasture in the dead of night. The grassy plain spread in all directions around them. Normally windy as all hell, the night was strangely still, as though the weather itself knew how hard this would be for Shep and didn't want to make a fuss.

"Just send her already," Jeremiah said. Shep's son stood off to the side, arms crossed, resolutely not looking at his father. He wore his last set of clothes—jeans and some t-shirt with a band's logo Shep didn't recognize. He'd given the rest of the clothing he'd brought to the few refugees in town. The boy had made his drive home four days ago, a single day before the aliens appeared and the government closed the roads.

Shep swallowed back years of a strained relationship and tried to extend an olive branch. "Son, will you help me?"

Jeremiah gave him a withering look. "She's. Just. A. Cow."

Shep glared at his son. "That's *enough*. She saved your life, for Chrissakes. Show some damn respect, boy." The younger man didn't respond, as if he didn't want to remember.

But Shep remembered. Penelope had, of her own volition, rushed into a burning barn to pull a crying, soot-covered seven-year-old Jeremiah to safety when the heat had been too much for Shep or his wife, Faith. Penelope had become Shep's only companion after Jeremiah went off to Texas A&M and the good Lord took Faith home. For the last few years, he and his favorite cow had just been two dried-up old timers walking the farm together.

And now... Now he had to send her to moon. To *them*. He looked up at the moon though his eyesight was blurred with tears. It was half-full but in the part that was normally dark he could see lights.

"It's not fair," he said, voice thick. "What the hell do they want with cows?"

Lemmy knelt next to him. Shep had always thought Lemmy looked too full, like a pillowcase stuffed with too many pillows. He had a knobby face and too-broad shoulders. Lord knows the man's strength had helped these last months on the farm, what with the world practically falling apart, but it'd always looked funny to Shep. But Lemmy'd a soft spot for Penelope, so Shep never said anything. "I don't know, Shep," he said. "But we don't got a choice. You know what happened in Dallas."

Dallas had kept its cattle. Had called the alien demand for all bovine life "silly."

A giant crater now marred Texas.

Shep stroked Penelope's snout and scratched behind her ears as tears trailed down his cheeks. The old girl moved her head gently into his hand and *mooed* softly, as if to tell him everything would be all right. Shep had always sworn she was almost as smart as a human. She was certainly as caring as any friend. "I can't do it," Shep whispered. Jeremiah scoffed.

"Let me," Lemmy said. The two men stood. Shep held Penelope's big, sad eyes for as long as he could before Lemmy began to close the canopy. Penelope *mooed* one last time as the hatch closed around her and Shep had to forcibly resist stopping

Lemmy to untie her. But Lemmy was right. If he didn't do this, who knew what hellfire the aliens would send down?

As soon as the canopy shut the ship hummed to life. A blue glow appeared underneath, and it rose a few feet off the ground. Its nose tilted towards the moon, the blue glow intensified, and with an electrified sound Penelope shot upwards.

Shep watched the spaceship ascend until he couldn't see it in the black sky, ignoring his son's impatient huffs. Then the three men turned around, got in the Ford, and rode back to the farm.

THE NEXT MORNING, HE HOPED TO REACH OUT TO HIS SON. He made grits, eggs, and bacon with sawmill gravy and biscuits. But the bacon came out black, and the grits ran as gloopy as mud. The gravy clumped and the biscuits were rocks. Faith had always been the cook. Not that his cooking mattered. Jeremiah never came down from his room. Shep eventually threw the whole mess away and came out to get some thinking done.

That afternoon found Shep wandering by himself along the north fence, about a mile from the house. This was one of the walks he'd often taken with Penelope. You could see for miles in all directions over the gently undulating Texas plains. The sky was blue and the sun shone its warmth down on him, though way off on the horizon he could see an angry, black stormwall headed this way. It looked sure to be a window-shaking thunderstorm, but it was a way off yet.

Some thunder sounded just fine to him. He felt the loss of his best friend like a wound gouged in his gut. Sure, it wasn't anything like being nearly unmade after his wife, but a hole had still opened up in his heart. He looked at the sky to curse the moon, but it wasn't there.

His son simply infuriated him. Always had. The two of them had never seen things the same way. He'd been an irresponsible boy, never helping around the farm like he ought. But that was the way it was with fathers and sons, right? Shep's own old man had been a lazy drunk who couldn't help but immediately spend every cent he ever earned. Usually on more booze. Nearly ruined the farm, that man.

Shep had saved it when he took over. Only seventeen and he'd managed to make it one of the more profitable family farms in the state. In the country, actually And all he'd wanted from his own son was an ounce of responsibility. Just an ounce. At least he'd actually expected something of the boy—not like Frank Shepherd Sr. had of him.

But Jeremiah had spent his youth shirking his duties around the farm, failing his classes, and playing those moronic video games. How he'd managed to get into Texas A&M Shep had no idea.

Stop it, Frank, Faith's imagined voice said inside his head. He still heard her, sometimes, even four years later. *He's just a boy. You need to be gentler with him. There's more in his head than you think. But he's not you. And you're not your father.*

She'd told him that sort of thing a lot, any time he'd gone hard on the boy. But dammit, she was right, wasn't she? Infernal woman. She'd always known just what to say to completely upturn his own thoughts. He'd lay them out, all nice and neat like china on the supper table, and she'd just come along and overthrow the whole damn thing, shattering any semblance he had of ever being right.

He smiled at the thought. She'd always been quite particular about her place settings. She'd hate him even thinking about breaking her grandmother's precious depression ware.

But she *was* right, even if she was only a memory now. Jeremiah might have stuck around because of the aliens and road closures, but he'd leave eventually. And probably for good. Shep should at least try one last time before then. He turned back towards the house.

Jeremiah was finally up. He stood in front of the fireplace, so he didn't hear Shep enter from the kitchen door. He was looking at an old photo of his mother hanging on the wall like he was saying goodbye to it. Hazy, yellow sunlight shafted in from the windows of the two-hundred-year-old farmhouse. The sunlight made the scene look like something out of a vintage sepia-tone photograph. He heard the television. Jeremiah had the news on—a report about whether or not the government had deemed it safe for people to drive.

Shep opened his mouth to say something then saw the duffel bag at Jeremiah's feet. "You're leaving." He meant it to come out as a question, but as it left his mouth it took on the harsh tones of an accusation.

Jeremiah turned towards him, and Shep could tell from his face that his son had misinterpreted his question as uncaring. "Don't be too upset. I'm sure *Lemmy* can take care of everything. You should probably just go ahead and give him the whole damn farm."

"Lemmy?" Shep asked, genuinely confused. "What's your problem with Lemmy?" First Penelope, now one of the more reliable farmhands Shep had ever had? What exactly was Jeremiah's problem?

"Forget it," Jeremiah said, picking up his bag and heading towards the door.

"Stop," Shep said. Jeremiah didn't slow. "Son, please," he said, softer, "I want to talk."

Jeremiah stopped and faced him. He didn't say anything.

"Look, I don't know why you've always had such a problem with this family. With—" He hated to say it, hated to admit this sort of vulnerability, "with me. I know you never had an ounce of interest in this farm. But times are different now. The whole world is in danger. First aliens show up and aim guns bigger than skyscrapers at us, then they take my Penelope—"

"Enough with the damn cow, Dad!"

"What's your problem with Penelope? She saved your life! And now Lemmy? That man's been nothing but kind to you. What's the matter with you? You've always had a problem with me and it's damn well time you tell me what it is." So much for not yelling. Shep felt his face redden with shame.

"What's the matter—what's the—" Jeremiah spluttered. His face twisted up in anger, frustration, remorse. He looked away, towards the window over the sink in the kitchen. He hesitated, like he was building up to something difficult, then pointed at the window.

"Fine," Jeremiah said. "I'm not coming back here so it doesn't matter anyways. You want to know what my problem is? I was playing right out there—around eleven or twelve—and I heard you tell Mom you didn't think I was good enough to run the farm." He spit the words like they were something he'd held in for years. "That I wasn't smart enough. Didn't have the right head on my shoulders. Thoroughly incapable. A waste. All I'd ever wanted was to be a farmer like my dad. But no, I wasn't good enough for you or your precious farm."

The memory slammed into Shep's brain. He hadn't said anything quite that harsh—but in a rare moment of clarity, he heard the decade-old conversation as his twelve-year-old son must have heard it.

He'd told Faith he was concerned that Jeremiah wasn't developing quite the right inclination towards running a successful family farm. It was hard enough what with all the corporate farms taking up so much space, but Jeremiah hadn't shown any of the steadfast calmness needed to successfully run a farm. The boy had been wild, never focusing on one thing for more than a moment, nothing like Shep had been at the same age. He was worried farming would be wasted on Jeremiah.

Faith had reamed him out good that night and he'd come around to her way of thinking—but that had been later. Nothing that Jeremiah could have heard.

All the pieces fell into place. Dear God, that was the same age Jeremiah had been when he'd really started pulling away from Shep. That was it—the linchpin. The moment his family fell apart. All because he couldn't keep his mouth shut when his son might overhear him being an idiot. Damn everything to hell. "Jeremiah, that—"

"Then when Mom died, I came to see you. Right out there in the barn. I came in to talk to you. You were just sitting there, mumbling to that damn cow. You'd barely look at me. I tried to bring up the past, but you wouldn't say a word to me. Just kept talking to the cow. Like I wasn't important."

Shep remembered. Sort of. He'd been in an alcohol-fueled blur for days after Faith had passed. Jeremiah had come to him... sometime after the funeral? Shep had been so drunk he could barely stay upright on the stool. He'd been using Penelope to steady himself. And, yes it was true, Penelope had let him vent and weep and rage. She was a damn cow, for Chrissakes.

But he'd failed to be there for Jeremiah when he needed him. Too drunk to listen, too drunk to even really recognize his son was there. The only moment Shep had ever truly been like his own father—and what a moment it had been.

"Jeremiah, please, I can explain. I wasn't—"

"You know what, forget it." His son shook his head and Shep could tell he was trying hard not to cry. He turned and opened the door. "Have a nice life." Then he was gone.

The sound of the door slamming was like a thunderclap. Shep stood there, shocked. Overwhelmed by what his son had said. Shep had never been quick on his feet with words—he'd always preferred a slower, more methodical approach—but dammit he wished he'd known just the right things to say. His own boy—the only child he had—had probably just left for good and all Shep could do was stand there with his mouth hanging open.

Go get him, Faith's voice said.

She was right. Again. He started towards the door but something in the corner of his eyes stopped him cold. The TV. It showed a picture of a nuclear explosion. No, a *live feed*.

The image cut back to the news anchor, a woman in her upper twenties. She looked shell-shocked. "What—Just—Ladies and gentlemen, I'm—I'm receiving reports of attacks. Washington DC, London, Paris, Tokyo, Beijing, Berlin, Moscow... all attacked by the alien weapon." She paused, staring at the screen, her eyes wide and terrified. "God help us all. They—They're telling me that you should all stay inside for the time being, stay—"

The screen turned to static. Then the power in the whole house went out. A second later the generator kicked in and the lights flickered back on.

He heard a strangled scream from outside.

Jeremiah.

No! Some paternal, protective instinct roared to life inside him and he bolted for the door.

There, only a few steps from his son's Camry, Lemmy had Jeremiah in a choke hold. Jeremiah looked terrified as he struggled to get out of the larger man's grasp, but Lemmy barely noticed. Miles in the distance, the black storm wall marched towards them, grown almost as big as the horizon itself. The wind was picking up.

"*Let my son go*!" Shep shouted, running forward. He was in a rage, unlike anything he'd ever experienced. Conscious thought barely entered his mind, but he knew one thing. As soon as he got to Lemmy, he was going to lay him out so hard he wouldn't wake up for a month.

"Stop," Lemmy commanded. He shook Jeremiah hard for emphasis, and Shep immediately brought himself up short. A slow, cruel smile crept up Lemmy's face.

The rage left Shep, replaced by a desperate need to save his child. "Lemmy, what are you doing? Let him go. I'll give you whatever you want."

Shep couldn't believe his own foolishness. He'd hired this man only three months ago, and here he was holding Jeremiah captive. He should never have trusted him. Jeremiah had been right. He locked eyes with his son. In that moment, he could only see the terrified seven-year-old on Penelope's back, flaming death burning behind him. "He's my son. Please, let him go. I'll do anything."

"There's nothing I want from your kind," Lemmy said, voice odd and deep, "except your extinction."

Shep saw plumes of dust some distance behind Lemmy and Jeremiah, down the long, dirt driveway. Someone was coming.

"Lemmy, look. We can work this out. Do you want money? I've stashed some away. It's yours. Just, please, my son. Don't hurt him."

Lemmy laughed. "Money. Tell me, how much do you think your son is worth? What's the price you're willing to pay?"

Shep didn't have an answer. What could you pay for something priceless? Jeremiah's terrified eyes wouldn't leave his father's. "I don't... Everything I have. I'll give you everything. The farm, all of it. Just let him go. Take me. Whatever you want, I'll do it. Take me instead. *Please.*"

Lemmy laughed again. "Such a sentimental species. Surprising, since you're monsters."

"Wh-what?"

"I'd rather just go ahead and kill you, but it has been decreed you're to know the weight of your iniquity before your destruction. Even now, across this horrible planet, the truth is being broadcast." Lemmy paused, then he began to *change*. He still held Jeremiah in his iron grip, but his lumpy, bulging body began to expand unnaturally. The process nauseated Shep. Lemmy's shoulders broadened and sprouted brown fur. He grew taller, towering over them, at least eight feet tall. More fur grew on his body, dark brown, pulled tight over too many bulging muscles. His head ballooned, then his mouth and nose pulled forward, elongating into a snout. Two massive horns jutted from the sides of his head.

He was... a giant bull. A bull-man. A bull's head and horns—though with intelligent eyes—atop an overly muscled, fur-covered body. He even had hooves. As he grew, he'd pulled Jeremiah off his feet, holding him across the shoulder and by the armpit so as not to immediately choke the boy out. Incredulity mixed with fear on Jeremiah's face at the sight of the brown, furry, bullish arms around him.

Lemmy began speaking and his voice was deep and melodious. "An age ago, my species seeded Earth with our DNA. A way to expand our empire and make use of this virgin planet. But later, when we weren't paying attention, *your* species showed up. You manipulated our DNA to prevent our descendants from gaining sentience, while at the same time seeded your own cursed DNA. We came back millennia later to find what? What do you think we found, *Shepherd?*"

Shep didn't know what the cow-man wanted him to say. He worked his mouth, trying to think of something, but nothing came. At that moment three trucks pulled into the driveway. He felt a momentary spark of hope, but six other bull-men, equally as large and menacing as Lemmy, got out and hoofed up to stand around him.

"We found horror and death, *human*. Our people diminished and enslaved. The milk of our mothers stolen. Our bodies ravaged, slaughtered, sliced up for human consumption." He breathed hard through huge, glistening nostrils, like he wanted to breathe fire.

"But the time of our revenge has arrived. We've taken back our people—where they will be uplifted, granted the sentience and intelligence you cruelly denied them—and now... Now we're going to slaughter every last one of you." He smiled a grisly, bovine smile. "Well, except the ones we take as slaves. And trust me, our chefs have created entire *libraries* of cookbooks to decide what to do with them."

This was crazy. Surely Shep was dreaming, right? There's no possible way this could be happening. He almost laughed. "Lemmy, this can't—"

"*That. Is. Not. My. Name.*" Lemmy snorted, the sound like a roar. It was matched by thunder in the distance. "The name given me by my fathers is—" He made a complicated *mooing* sound that no human tongue could ever reproduce.

Shep needed to save Jeremiah. However insane things might be, he needed to at least do that. But how? He couldn't overpower them. He'd stupidly left the guns in their case when he ran out here. Besides, there were seven of them now. He needed to keep them talking while he thought of something. "Why us? Why come to the farm? Why help me?"

"Our analysis showed you—a mass murderer—had little chance

of giving up those you considered your property. We sent agents to every slaver and butcher on the planet."

"Ah, I see." He was thinking furiously, but still nothing. "Well, you know that Jeremiah—"

"Enough. This conversation is over. You now understand your true nature. My duty is fulfilled."

He tossed Jeremiah on the ground. It had started raining and the dirt was turning to mud. His son tried to scramble away but Lemmy kicked him onto his back. Another of the bull-men wielded an alien device that looked an awful lot like a weapon. He pointed it at the prone Jeremiah.

"NO!" Shep shouted, bursting forward. He dove over his son. There was an amplified *zhoof* sound and hot pain exploded on the back of his left shoulder, the force of it spinning him in midair. He landed hard on the ground.

"Dad!" Jeremiah lunged towards where he'd landed. When he saw that Shep was still alive a look of rage came over his face. His son screamed an unintelligible battlecry and launched himself at the one who'd shot Shep.

The bull-man raised a hand and knocked him back like it was nothing.

All seven bull-men, including Lemmy, raised their alien weapons, but at that moment a sound like a hundred thunderclaps crashed overhead. It was too loud to be the thunder from the storm. All eyes, human and bovine alike, instinctively turned towards the sky.

A spot of bright white light appeared in front the storm wall. It was moving *fast* in their direction. In a matter of seconds, they heard the roar of engines and could see that it was a ship similar to the one that had carried Penelope away, only larger.

Oh no, not more of them. Were Shep and Jeremiah truly so threatening that these cow aliens needed to send a warship to make sure they died correctly?

The ship now hovered over them. Its nose angled towards the bull-men.

Laser bolts shot from it, throwing the bovine aliens in all directions. They cried out in pain, anger, and confusion.

What. The. Hell. What had just happened? Shep could barely form the thoughts before his son was pulling him to his feet and the two of them made for the house. Shep felt at his wounded shoulder. The shot had more grazed him than hit squarely. He was bloodied up good, but the wound looked clean and superficial. He could still move.

Two of the bull-men had died in the first barrage. The other five, including Lemmy, dove behind the trucks for cover, unleashing their weapons on the ship.

For a moment Shep's front yard was a wild display of rain and slashing white and blue lights as lasers fired back and forth. Shep took the moment of relative safety to hurry to his gun case which he'd moved into the living room after Faith had died. Quickly, he spun the combination into the safe. He handed an AR-style rifle and a few boxes of ammo to Jeremiah and armed himself with a 12-gauge he loaded with slugs. They took up position on the two front-facing windows.

The bull-men's rifles weren't doing much to damage the hovering ship, but they had the advantage of mobility. Surprisingly fast and agile for their size, they managed to skirt around the trucks, back and forth constantly, as the ship slowly and awkwardly adjusted its angles, trying to keep a line on them.

"You far left, me far right. Work your way in."

Jeremiah nodded. Father and son opened fire. Both first shots hit home. Shep only wounded his target—the one with the tan fur—but Jeremiah managed a headshot on the charcoal one. Shep fired again, taking his bull down.

The remaining five aliens turned their attention towards this new threat.

The ship above took advantage of that moment of distraction and blew them to hell.

A moment passed. Both Shep and Jeremiah were out of breath. Shep's heart felt like it wanted to smash its way out of his chest.

Jeremiah came over to him, eyeing his shoulder. "You alright, Dad?"

"I'll be fine." Jeremiah didn't look like he believed him. "Trust me. I promise. It's not as bad as it looks."

The ship was landing outside. Then, Shep noticed that one of the bull-men was still stirring on the ground, dark brown fur matted with blood.

Lemmy.

Something white and hot burst in Shep's mind and before he knew it he was stampeding down the porch steps, shotgun raised. "You tried to hurt my boy! *You tried to hurt my boy!*"

He was just about to fire when Jeremiah stopped him. "He's already dead. Look."

True enough, the light had gone out of the bull-man's eyes.

A hissing sound split the afternoon, and Shep smelled the gassy smell of something like fuel. A hatch on the ship slowly opened. Shep and Jeremiah turned to face their savior—though for all Shep knew, this could just as easily be another attack.

Out came Penelope. She trotted towards him.

"Penelope!" He couldn't believe it. Penelope! It was his cow! How was that possible? He ran to her, and Jeremiah joined him. He went to scratch behind her ears and she made a strange *mooing* sound. Then he looked inside her cockpit at the complex, if hoof-shaped, controls that only an intelligent bovine could possibly pilot. Jeremiah noticed the same. "Penelope," he said, "Um, can you understand me?"

The cow nodded.

"Did you fly that ship all the way here and kill those assholes?"

Penelope nodded again. She rubbed her head affectionately against Shep's chest.

"Remember what Lemmy said?" Jeremiah asked. "They're making the cows smart."

Shep didn't much care right now. He bent over and hugged Penelope, his friend, now his and his son's savior.

The rain was really starting to come down now. And—the thought returned to him—the world's capitals had been destroyed.

He turned towards the house. Penelope followed but Jeremiah didn't. "Dad, I do need to go. I, uh—there are people. A person. I need to make sure she's safe."

Shep met his son's eyes. For the first time that he could remember, the two men shared a look of appreciation and respect. Apparently, fighting for their lives together had done more than anything to start patching up the tatters of their relationship. "Keep the rifle and rounds. Go get her. I'm going to get some of the guys from town up here and we'll fortify. Bring her here. We'll keep you safe."

"I will. I'll be back as soon as I can." He held out a hand for a shake.

Shep pulled his son into a hug. A quick hug. Nothing too much. "Be safe. Get back here as soon as you can, boy. And stay ahead of the storm."

"I will." He smiled then got in his Camry and drove away.

Shep took Penelope inside the house. Didn't make much sense putting her in the barn now, did it? He got some gauze from the first aid kit and wrapped his shoulder. He'd have Jimmy, his doctor friend from in town, take a look at it tomorrow.

He got some pen and paper and sat down at the table. Outside had gone almost completely black with the storm. "Girl, do you want to help me?"

She *mooed* what was clearly a yes and came over. With the rage of the storm shaking the house, he and Penelope began to plan the fortifications.

The real war was about to begin.

ALL THINGS GOLDEN

OLIVIA BAXTER HUDSON

About the Author: Olivia Baxter Hudson lives with her family in the PNW. Her hobbies include gaming, hiking, sewing, and telling her cat to GET OFF things (usually the sewing table). She is fond of daffodils.

All Things Golden

Olivia Baxter Hudson

"So, do we think this is a good idea?" asked Axel, looking at the young bovine before him.

"Well . . . it's your cow," said Odie.

"Bull. It's a bull. You can tell by the bits between his hind legs," Axel explained patiently.

"Girl bits, boy bits, whatever," Odie said as he waved one dusky hand dismissively. "As far as I'm concerned, people just cover animals in spices and eat them."

Axel glanced at the circle of rocks that held the sooty remains of his campfire and thought longingly of what he would cook on it if he had the right supplies. Nearby sat his wooden spice box. Once, it had contained such delights as coriander and cumin. These days, it was used to hold only bitterwild onions foraged from the fens. Axel had become rather adept at the process of drying them out. His efforts at teaching Odie these same skills had not been as fruitful.

Axel chuckled at the irony of Odie's words and said, "Thought you were too delicate for such strenuous activities as cooking."

"That doesn't mean that I don't understand how the cow goes from moo-moo to yum-yum."

"You're not being very helpful, you know."

"I found the flowers, didn't I?" Odie protested, once again waving his hand in an overly exaggerated fashion.

Axel caught his breath as Odie's gestures sent a small zephyr of patchouli whirling around his head. He glanced around at the barren sandstone rocks and once again marveled at how Odie had managed to keep his delicate vials of perfume safe from the wild terrain.

Then again, Odie's small collection of infused oils could sometimes serve as a diversion from some of the less desirable campsite scents. These days, it was folly to waste precious drinking water on bathing. At least the slime from the mud fields could be buffed off skin; it crumbled once it was dry. But it did leave a lingering odor of rotting vegetation.

As if on cue, the little calf raised his tail and fertilized the clump of mutilated greenery that had once contained Odie's flowers.

"Sacred cow, indeed," Odie commented wryly, and then proceeded to examine his fingernails as though his opinion on the matter had been concluded.

He'll have plenty more to say on the matter, Axel thought. Odie's side of the conversation always cooled and warmed; like our desert sun returning at dawn.

He regarded the calf while Odie nibbled delicately at a hangnail.

Daisy, the milk cow, had birthed him a week prior. He would have been pure white were it not for a few patches of darkest auburn; the same color as Axel's own hair. On his back he wore the not-saddle that Axel had woven out of spare rags and ropes.

And then there were the daffodils.

Odie had stumbled upon them when they were mere budding shoots a fortnight ago. Axel had been excited to see greenery; after all, cow food was cow food.

But Odie had something to say on the matter.

"Don't let Daisy eat these," Odie had cautioned. "These are special."

And so, Axel had waited, and watched the rocks that surrounded his tent. In due time, the tiny flowers stretched and turned their heads to the sun as if they were chicks and she was their mother. They were delicate golden double-circles of softness, poking out from cracks in the sandstone in a hundred various places.

Odie had asked Axel all sorts of questions about the moist soil and whether he thought the rocks contained an underground spring.

Axel had fielded the questions to the best of his ability and marveled at how something as trivial as flowers could stir Odie's typically complacent attitude into curiosity.

He was nudged out of his reverie by the calf making a spirited attempt at suckling his fingers. Axel grunted with parental exasperation. Gently, he rubbed his moist hand behind one bovine ear and gifted the saliva back to its owner.

"They're holy, you know," Odie remarked, not for the first time. "Those flowers."

Axel sighed to himself. He knew that Odie hated to be ignored. But he ignored him anyway.

"We don't have to parade him through the encampment," Odie eventually continued. Axel silently noted that his tone had been modified from sanctimonious to merely peevish. "He's your cow, after all. I can keep him here while you go do your rounds with Daisy."

Axel gave Odie a searching look, then replied: "We went through all this trouble to cover him in flowers because you said it was a tradition among your people. A celebration, you said. A way of lifting spirits, you said. Now, you know that I like your ideas. I'm just worried that not everyone is going to be as receptive."

"The Holy Man hasn't here to shout at us since he ran up the mountain. You know half of them are more scared of what he says than what we do. Or what I am, for that matter."

"People tend to fear what they don't understand."

"People are assholes."

"That is fundamentally true, but you don't have to say it that way."

"Look, this was meant to be a simple prayer festivity. You've turned it into a war of perspectives."

Axel emitted a series of irritated grunts. He scratched his beard vigorously. He glanced from Odie, to Daisy, then to the calf, and then back to Odie. He rolled up his shirt sleeves and thought: What's the worst that could happen?

"Let's go spread some good cheer," Axel declared, and proceeded to untie Daisy from her hitching post.

❄

AXEL HAD ESTABLISHED HIS OWN CAMPSITE NEAR THE TOP OF A series of sandstone cliffs that, examined from a distance, could generously be described as a hill. The cliffs themselves had been softened by time and erosion, so the path itself was nothing more than a series of long, gentle traverses across the gritty surface.

This location was far removed from the only source of drinkable water, but it did offer an escape from the cacophony of the main encampment. Given that Axel had a set of young and sturdy legs, it had been a price that he'd been willing to pay.

Odie had been perfectly silent as they wound their way down the trail. Something as simple as a flower had finally tied his tongue. In his hand was the tether attached to the flower-adorned calf, who was ambling along contentedly by Odie's side.

Axel smiled as he watched this quiet comradery. Then he grimaced as he realized that the tranquility would not last for long.

There was a veritable sea of tents in the valley below, populated with a bustling throng of people. The noise they were creating crashed off the sandstone rocks in waves.

"What would you call us?" Axel wondered aloud. "Social exiles? Refugees?"

"You can call me anything you want to," Odie replied, as he dug inside his satchel. He retrieved his linen scarf and draped it over his shaven head. "Just as long as you don't call me ugly."

"Asshole?" Axel suggested.

"You would know," Odie said coyly. "Now shut up before Ada overhears you."

A tiny girl ran to meet them. Axel watched as Odie bent down and scooped her up.

"Would you like to say a prayer, Ada?" Odie asked, and handed her a flower. "And have a flower?"

"Why a pay-er?"

"It's like making a wish. For something you want to see happen."

"I want lotsa water. To play wiff."

"Would you like to pray for rain?"

"Rain?"

"Water that falls from the sky."

Ada's grubby little face broadened into a hopeful smile. "Yes! Yes!"

Odie handed her a flower and said, "Now you get this."

Ada regarded the flower thoughtfully, then stated, "Need'un for da baby."

Odie gave her a second flower and then set her down. Without another word, she dashed back to her tent.

Axel watched her go; remembering the two boys that should have accompanied her. Ada's older brothers had been the first to discover the unassuming bush with its waxy yellow berries.

The berries had been returned to the earth; inside two small caskets of dead flesh.

After the burial had concluded, the Holy Man had ordered that all yellow-berry bushes were to be burned immediately upon discovery.

It was the one decree he'd ever made that Axel had wholeheartedly supported.

A woman emerged from Ada's tent. Her belly was beginning to bulge with babe. She carried a wide-mouthed jug in one hand and a small brick of cheese in the other.

"What's with the daffodils?" she asked when she saw the calf.

"They're a tradition among my people," Odie explained. "I give you a flower, and you say a prayer."

Rachel brushed her frizzy hair away from her careworn face and regarded the colorful calf. "I don't know, Odie," she said. "Seems like nobody's prayers ever get answered around here. Why are you bothering with all this?"

"It's meant to be a thing of hope."

Axel watched Rachel's face soften under the glow of Odie's earnest expression.

"Can I have two, then?" Rachel asked. "For my boys. I will hope that wherever they are, they're happy."

Odie handed Rachel two flowers, and she handed him the cheese.

Axel asked Rachel for her container. Then he untied a small stool from Daisy's back and proceeded to go about the business of milking.

Another woman appeared from the neighboring tent. She was younger than Rachel; painfully young to be carrying such a swollen belly. Axel felt a pang of sympathy as he watched her waddle towards him.

She waved what appeared to be a lumpy log made of random cloth scraps at him and announced, "I've got your pillow ready!"

She's a sweet girl, Axel thought. Even if she can't sew.

But a trade was a trade. Axel smiled graciously and replied: "That's perfect, Martha. My neck will be much happier with me when I wake in the morning."

"Would you like a prayer flower, Martha?" Odie asked her.

"What's it for?" she asked curiously.

"It's a tradition among my people. I give you a flower, and you say a prayer."

Martha beamed at Odie, her dimples creating miniscule shadows in the morning sunlight. She took the flower he offered her and answered, "Then I will pray that Daniel always returns safely from his hunts."

"Got some dried venison, too," she continued cheerfully, and handed Odie a small package. "From the deer that Daniel bagged a couple weeks ago. Took forever to cure, but Phineas was there to help."

"Has Daniel been learning a lot from Phineas?" Axel inquired politely.

"Learning? How to hunt?" Rachel interrupted. "Probably. That and the art of wandering off into the wilds to go nap in a place where his wife can't nag him."

"But when he's here, you just kvetch about him getting underfoot," Martha playfully chided.

Rachel rubbed the little calf's head affectionately and declared, "Husbands are a lot like bulls, Martha. They hang around long enough to make a calf, then as soon as they're done, they run right back to their pastures."

RACHEL WAS POURING OUT MARTHA'S SHARE OF THE MILK INTO a pitcher as Axel and Odie proceeded down the trail. Here and there a child would run up to them, point at a flower, follow Odie's instructions about the prayers, and then wave their gifts in the air like celebratory banners.

Most of the parents would laugh with aloof amusement at their children's antics.

Axel silently noted which ones rolled their eyes at Odie behind his back.

The throng of children had mostly dispersed by the time they reached the rock outcrop that contained the spring, where the thrill of splashing in the water called them away.

Axel untied a tether on Daisy's back and pulled off a long home-made trough, which he wedged inside one of the cracks that the spring was forever attempting to escape. Daisy and her calf began drinking eagerly as the trough filled with water.

"I still don't understand why you bother with all that crap."

Axel glanced up. He had never bothered to learn the man's name; in his head he'd always referred to him as the dour man, who just happened to own the most forlorn-looking milk goat in the world.

Oy vey, Axel thought. I'm so tired of repeating this conversation.

"I'm trying to not sully up our only source of drinking water," he explained patiently.

The dour man spat on the ground and said, "Water is water."

"It's about hygiene," Axel replied. He could feel a twitch beginning on his left temple.

"So?"

"Well, to put it one way, would you kiss your goat?"

"Hell no. But what's that got to do with anything?"

Axel glanced at the puny pools of water below the rocky outcrop, where several herds of joyful children were splashing. Every few seconds, one of them would bend over and lift a handful of water to their mouth.

He then looked to Odie, who was holding his flask directly inside of a nearby crack.

In the meantime, the dour man had been eye-balling the calf. "You two the ones who been handing out flowers?"

"Yes," Odie replied stiffly. "They're prayer flowers. Would you like one?"

"Sure."

Axel plucked a daffodil off the calf's back and handed it to the dour man.

The man promptly fed it to his goat.

"Asshole," Odie whispered as they watched man and goat walk away.

"Yes," Axel agreed. "But you want to know the funny thing about assholes? They're very talented at surviving."

AXEL COULD SPOT ADINA'S TENT FROM A MILE AWAY. SHE WAS A lover of beauty in all forms, therefore it was no surprise that she had decorated her tent with remnants of bright materials. Children would come to her when they were bored, and she would hand them bits of charcoal and teach them how to draw pictures on the rocks. She made the best soaps from scratch, and she knew a great deal about herbs and natural medicines.

Axel had always harbored a soft place for her in his heart, despite some of their carnal differences.

The Holy Man, however, had vehemently disapproved of her primary source of income, and therefore regarded her with strong disfavor.

This had been the main source of contention between Axel and the Holy Man.

A scruffy man was exiting Adina's tent as Axel and Odie approached. He adjusted his waistband as he leered at the two newcomers.

"Next customers!" he shouted before walking away.

"Asshole," Odie hissed.

"Indeed," Axel replied. He could feel his stomach curdling with resentment. "But at least we know that she can handle them."

Adina was well-curved and full-lipped. And tall. Taller than most of the men in the encampment.

She appeared in a robe, dark hair plastered to her sweaty neck, and regarded the scene before her with amazement.

Odie smiled radiantly at her and said, "Care for a prayer flower?"

"This is new," Adina remarked with a small laugh. "But I wholeheartedly approve of anything novel around here. How does this work, anyhow?"

"I give you a flower, and you say a prayer," Odie explained.

Adina took the offered flower and pondered silently for a few moments.

"Let's see," she murmured. "I've got a tent. I've got food. I've got my herbs. I know how to entertain myself. And business has been better since the Holy Man's been away. I'm not sure what to pray for."

"That tomorrow looks just like today?" Axel suggested as he waggled his eyebrows at her.

Adina bubbled over with laughter.

"Well prayed," she agreed. She tucked the stem of the daffodil inside a loop in her robe, where it laid against her chest like a brooch.

"That looks fetching," Odie said. "Too bad you don't have anyone to dress up anymore."

"Once a handmaiden, always a handmaiden," Adina joked.

"We are what we are," Odie agreed.

Axel set his stool down next to Daisy. Adina sat herself upon it and proceeded to very delicately fill her own container full of milk. She downed the drink in three gulps, and then pulled out a small jar.

"A happy cow is a good cow," Adina remarked as she dipped her fingers in the jar. Daisy's teats were quickly covered in a soothing ointment.

Adina stood, and turned to Axel.

"Your turn," she announced. "Let's see those hands."

"Is this really necessary?" Axel asked meekly.

"Axel, there is not a single woman in this world who likes the feel of chaffed hands on her bosom," Adina chided. "Cows included."

Axel gave in.

"Did you ever have a coming-of-age celebration?" Adina asked him as she rubbed his hands with ointment.

"I probably would have, had I not lost my parents when I was young."

"But you're theoretically a man now?"

"I suppose."

"Will you come see me without your cows someday? Inside of my tent? For free?"

Axel could feel his cheeks stinging with heat. "You know I'm fond of you, Adina, but that's just not my thing," he sputtered.

"Pity," said Adina, with a playful wink. "You've got bigger hands than any other man in this tent-town."

Axel abashedly retied the stool to Daisy's back while Adina dug around in the pockets of her robe.

"A gift," she told Odie, and handed him a small stick of homemade kohl. "From one lover of beauty to another."

"ARE YOU GOING TO HAVE THE CALF . . . YOU KNOW . . . altered?" Odie asked several hours later, as they sat watching the cows graze. He had paused mid-stroke in front of his mirror of polished metal, kohl temporarily forgotten, as an older man fussed over a lamb that his sheep had unexpectedly birthed in the middle of a patch of crusty mud.

The ram of the herd was nearby, trying to make a new lamb with a different ewe. He had yet to gain satisfactory leverage due to the slick patch that the ewe was standing on. Such was a day spent in the mud-lands.

Axel looked at Odie and felt a twinge of sympathetic regret. "No," he murmured. "That won't happen."

Odie gave him a gratified nod and then returned his attention to his mirror.

"You know you look fine without all that," Axel told him.

"Don't judge."

"What? I said you looked fine without it."

"That's still judging."

"How so?"

"Think about it for a minute, Big Hands."

"Who's the asshole now?"

"What?" The shepherd had trudged closer, lamb cradled in a blanket.

"Not you, sir," Axel apologized. "Can we help you?"

"Got a little clean water to spare? For my rag?"

Axel obligingly wet the rag, which the man then used to delicately wipe mud off the lamb's eyelids. "Why's that calf covered in flowers?" he asked as he worked.

Odie explained, and then offered the shepherd a daffodil.

"No thanks," the man said with a grin. "I've found it's faster to take care of problems on my own. A man can grow old waiting around for gods to bring him what he needs."

And with that, he tottered away.

Odie handed the flower to Axel and said, "Well, if he doesn't want this, should we put it to use instead?"

Axel glanced to his left. In the distance, a tiny pond of exceptionally murky water was bubbling weakly. He felt his heart sink with the futility of the scene.

"Let's pray that someday these springs do more than just produce mud," he said, and gently tossed the daffodil towards the pond.

They ate their lunch in silence. The calf sucked on Daisy's teats. Daisy sampled the vegetation.

Phineas and Daniel appeared on the far side of the mud-field, each sporting a dead goose and beaming with manly satisfaction.

Axel and Odie waved a greeting. Daniel waved a goose at them and honked in a madcap fashion. Axel pretended to shoot. Daniel feigned his own demise. Odie giggled. Phineas shook his head. Daniel rose miraculously from the dead. They waved their goodbyes.

The sun crawled towards the west. Odie appropriated the pillow that Martha had made and proceeded to nap.

Axel watched a snail wind its way around a rock. It discovered a soggy blade of grass that had escaped Daisy's champing and began to nibble heartily.

A bird pounced upon it. Axel sat motionless as the feathered creature unceremoniously extracted the tiny gray monarch out of his calcium palace.

After the bird had flown off, Axel retrieved the shell and mused over the bits of slimy gore that had been left adhered to the beautiful casing. Then he glanced at Odie, and for the second time that afternoon, he felt another twinge of sympathetic regret.

Odie stirred, sat up, and drank from his flask. Axel handed Odie the snail shell, which Odie admired.

"Why did you come with us, Odie?" Axel asked. "You could be living in the lap of luxury right now."

Odie swallowed his last mouthful of water as he gazed off at the mountain in the distance. Then he shrugged. "I was bored."

The fens cooled quickly as the sun set. Already, crisp breezes teased their way through the slanted sunbeams. Axel found them refreshing.

Odie, however, removed his linen scarf from his head and wrapped it around his shoulders. "Think we can start a fire tonight?" he asked as they started walking the trail that led towards the encampment.

Axel grimaced. "I don't think we have any food that needs warming. Not sure I can justify using the fuel."

"Maybe if Martha or Rachel is cooking one of those geese, we can stop for a bit? Cozy up to their fires?"

"Ingratiating, aren't we?"

"I could give Ada a ride on the calf as a means of compensation."

"Oh, yes. And I'll just stand off to the side and reassure Rachel that she's not going to lose her only remaining child by course of falling off a cow."

"Bull."

"Whatever. My point is . . ."

A figure appeared in the shadows. At first, Axel watched as it scrabbled at the foot of a rock formation, When it saw the newcomers, it straightened and chuckled.

"Ugh. It's Aaron, isn't it?" Odie asked as he squinted into the gloom.

"Hush," Axel cautioned. "He's harmless. Just be polite and he'll eventually go away."

The outfit that Aaron wore must have been well-tailored and respectable in its prime. Now it hung from a bony frame in gray tatters, which danced forlornly in the breeze as its owner minced his way forward.

He was clutching a handful of mushrooms to his chest.

"Odion!" Aaron wheezed, drawling out the syllables of Odie's real name with a gleeful arrogance. "And . . . Axel."

He waved a mushroom at them. "Care for a bite?"

"No, thank you. Neither of us partake of those," Axel said, politely but firmly. He fought off a wave of nausea as he scrutinized Aaron's beard, where bits of fungus had cemented themselves to the unkempt bristles. "But I can tell that you have been enjoying a veritable feast."

Aaron began to snort with laughter, but then stopped mid-grunt as he spotted the cows.

"Golden calf," he hissed, his eyes bulging with amazement.

Axel looked at his young bull, who was standing inside the last remaining sunbeam touching that swath of path. In the light, the flowers that covered his back did appear to glow with a metallic radiance.

"Golden calf!" Aaron repeated loudly.

"I needed him to carry my daffodils," Odie began to explain.

Axel felt his skin crawl with apprehension. He shifted his weight and braced himself for whatever might happen next.

Aaron ran.

"GOLDEN CALF!" he shrieked as he barreled down the trail that led deeper into the fens. "GOLDEN CALF! GOLDEN CALF!"

Axel and Odie blinked at each other in disbelief.

"Should we go after him?" Odie finally asked. "He is the Holy Man's brother, after all."

Axel squirmed as conflicting thoughts harried his conscience. "Maybe not. It's getting dark. With our luck, you and I would get lost and then we'd all be in trouble. How about we go see Phineas and I'll talk to him about forming a search party first thing in the morning? You can warm yourself by the fire while I talk to him."

SOMETHING FELT DIFFERENT. SOMETHING WAS OFF.

Nervously, Axel led Daisy along an empty trail. Odie followed close behind, one hand holding the calf's tether, and one hand clamped tightly to his scarf.

Axel could sense a hidden panic trying to consume the evening air. He could hear a muted commotion in the distance. He could see an absence of figures minding the busy doldrum of the nearby tents.

There was no one at the spring.

Everyone hovered outside of Martha's tent.

The first thing that Axel saw was the backside of the crowd. Then he spotted Adina standing off by herself, a bundle of forgotten herbs dangling from her hand. She was wiping her watery eyes.

"I came when they called me," she rasped, after Axel had pressed her for news. "But there's no herb that will stop a woman from bleeding like that."

Axel turned and elbowed his way inside the crowd. A disaster lay splayed out before him.

Daniel was on the gritty ground, weeping inconsolably and cradling his head within his arms. Rachel knelt by him, trying her best to persuade him back into his senses.

Phineas stood nearby, looking utterly lost and trying his best to comfort a squalling babe. Ada tugged at him and whimpered.

In the shadows, the crowd hovered and bobbed like awkward chickens.

"What would the Holy Man do?" said one man. A woman nodded in non-comital agreement. "Holy Man, yes, Holy Man," another echoed. "Do something."

Axel felt the bile rise in his throat as people tittered around him. He leapt up upon the rock that Martha had playfully referred to as her "table," and cupped his mouth with his hands.

"The Holy Man is not here!" he bellowed. "But we are. There's a babe that needs to be fed. And I've got a milk cow. Will anyone trade milk for milk?"

Axel scanned the crowd. A woman carrying a babe of varying

age in each of her arms glared resentfully at him, and then stomped away.

"Anyone?" Axel repeated desperately.

He spotted the dour man in the crowd, still holding onto his goat's lead.

The dour man grinned shrewdly back at Axel, and then turned to face the pinch-faced woman standing next to him. She was holding onto a snotty toddler.

The dour man nudged her.

"What?" the woman shrilled. "You know I hate cow milk!"

The dour man grabbed his woman by the back of her neck and shouted into her ear. "Get him to turn it into cheese for us, you dumb-ass! Everyone knows that the dead girl's friend makes the best cheeses in this godforsaken tent-town!"

Stricken, Axel held his breath. He watched as Rachel rose to her full height, her legs bolstering her like the pillars in a tomb. In the light of the campfire, her eyes glinted with an angelic rage.

"Feed the babe, and I will give you plenty of cheese," she spat.

The woman set her toddler down. She collected the babe from Phineas, crudely motioned Axel off Martha's rock, sat down, and popped out a breast.

The babe was fed.

Axel grabbed Rachel by the wrist and pulled her off to the side. "I'll make sure that you get Martha's share of the milk. Every morning. I'll be here first thing," he told her desperately.

Rachel nodded. A tear escaped her eye as she rubbed her belly. "And I'll take over feeding the babe as soon as I can. I swear it."

Under a cold moon, Axel and Odie walked the cows home. Once they reached Axel's tent, Odie removed the not-saddle off the calf's back and shook the remaining flowers onto the ground.

"I suppose Daisy could finish these off?" he suggested.

Axel sighed. "I didn't have the heart to tell you this earlier, but cows aren't really supposed to eat daffodils. It can make them sick."

Odie paused for a moment. Axel braced himself for a lecture

regarding what Odie felt that he did or did not have the heart to hear.

Instead, Odie gathered the wilted flowers together, and walked them to a nearby ledge. As he let go, the wind took them away and scattered them across the sandy expanse that bordered the mud fields.

And then, with a heart-breaking silence, he sat himself down on a nearby rock.

There was nothing left for Odie to say.

Axel untied the small burdens from Daisy's back and made sure that both cows were settled for the night.

He retrieved the pillow that Martha had made for him and smiled bitterly at the haphazard stitchery. Sweet girl, he thought. He fixed the droop in the tent and tossed the pillow inside.

He gave his beard a good scratch.

Then he returned to Odie, who had been using his thumbnail to scratch bits of dried slime off the snail shell.

Axel regarded him for a moment, then bent over and kissed a tear off his cheek. "You're my favorite flower," he confessed.

They entered the tent together and crawled into the blankets, where Axel spooned himself around Odie's body.

As he ran his hand along Odie's arm Axel wondered, not for the first time, what the willowy Egyptian boy might have looked like had he never been castrated.

Odie stirred, and whispered softly over his shoulder, "Do you think the Holy Man is going to be angry?"

"What about?"

"Well, do you remember what he said about other religions?"

"Moses can say whatever he wants to as long as he doesn't touch you or my cow."

"Bull."

"Whatever. Go to sleep, love."

IMPERIAL BATTLE COW OF NEW BRUNSWICK

SANAN KOLVA

About the Author: Sanan Kolva cannot claim the title of cowgirl; however, as the granddaughter of Hula Joe, she can attest to the fact that he was a cowboy and did, in fact, escort a princess. Sanan's more mundane life lacks both cowboys and alien invasions, so she instead devotes time to writing epic fantasy novels as well as short stories in a mix of genres. "Winterlight" is the first book in a steampunk-esque series, The Silverline Chronicles. "Shrouded Sky" is the first book in her fantasy series The Chosen of the Spears, and Book 2, "Thorns in Shadow" is expected out later in 2018. Sanan can be found at sanankolva.com.

Imperial Battle Cow of New Brunswick

Sanan Kolva

"SO, DO WE THINK THIS IS A GOOD IDEA?" ALICE WHISPERED TO her friend.

"Well, it's your cow." Tammy's gaze fixed on the road and on Spike.

Alice opened her mouth to say that Spike was Father's cow, but the words stuck in her throat. Spike *was* her cow now and denying it wouldn't bring Father back. And if this worked, Spike would have some part in repaying the aliens responsible for Father's death.

A low buzz of insects hung in the air. In the middle of the narrow road, a lone bovine chewed on the hay and grain liberally scattered across the asphalt. Sixteen hundred pounds of retired rodeo bull, Spike cared little about the teenagers crouched in the brush, and even less about the distant hum of a float-car. He was king of his domain, and kingship had the perk of eating without interruption.

The float-car's hum drew closer. Alice swallowed hard. She had no idea if this would work. Beside her, Tammy fidgeted, braiding stalks of grass.

The float-car buzzed around the corner and drew to a halt. Alice could almost read the puzzlement as the vehicle bobbed in the air. Would they get out? Would they try to go around Spike? There wasn't a lot of space, with trees on one side of the road and a deep ditch on the other. Would they suspect?

A door on the float-car slid open and a gangly Pulsi stepped out. Alice couldn't tell if it was male or female. Like most of the aliens she'd seen, this one wore a full-body protective suit with a closed face plate. Supposedly, the Pulsi hadn't taken such precautions initially and had suffered serious, even fatal reactions to spider bites and bee stings. Apparently, aliens were allergic —who knew?

The one who stepped from the car eyed Spike, then looked back into the vehicle and gabbled something. Alice glimpsed two more Pulsi within. After a brief argument, the one who'd gotten out grumbled and walked toward Spike, waving its arms in a shooing motion.

Spike ignored the figure until it got close. Then the bull's head jerked up, nostrils flaring. The alien gabbled at him, waving its arms again to encourage him to move on.

Spike seized every opportunity to relive his glory days in the rodeo. He lowered his head, pawed the ground, and charged. The alien's gabbling rose to a shriek and it bolted for the float-car. Spike thundered in pursuit. The alien scrambled into the vehicle and slammed the door shut. Spike rammed the car. The bull staggered for a moment, shaking his head as the car bobbed erratically. Alice wondered if he would return to his meal.

Instead, the bull snorted and rammed the float-car again. The vehicle rocked. Another strike from the bull nearly tipped it on its side. Sensing victory, Spike hit it full force, horns catching the bottom edge. The float-car was meant for transport, not battle, and though it could traverse rough terrain without much issue, the technology keeping it afloat also left it curiously vulnerable when an angry bull took it in his head to flip it over. Alice had thought it would be too heavy and bulky for the maneuver, but Spike performed with all the flair of his rodeo days. He wheeled around and slammed his rear hooves into the car, sending it careening into the ditch.

Only then did the bull lumber back to his interrupted meal, chewing with great contentment on the sweet hay.

Alice and Tammy glanced at each other, then stared at Spike in awe. "I can't believe that worked," Alice whispered.

"Gives a whole new meaning to cow tipping," Tammy whispered back. "You'd think if they could make a car float, they could figure out how to keep that from happening!"

"Well, it happened." Alice scrambled to her feet and grabbed her lasso. "Get the horses. I'll round up Spike, and we can get out of here before they crawl out to see what happened."

ICAJUC CAUTIOUSLY OPENED THE FLOAT-CAR DOOR. THE VEHICLE sensors had been damaged and could only have shown a view of the ground anyway, since they were mounted on the roof. No sign of the savage beast. He forced the door open a little more, ignoring the anxious protests of his companions.

"We can't sit here forever! We're on patrol! If we're late again, who knows *what* punishment Commander Vishoquar will inflict!" Icajuc hissed at them.

That silenced them. Patrol duty was already one of the lowest assignments, grunt work that the commander deemed unworthy of troops with any skill. None of them wanted to know what would happen if they failed even as patrollers. Rumors of teams being fed to monsters of one sort or another had been circulating like a stench through the air ducts for the last few days.

The beast was gone. Icajuc crawled through the tall grass until he could stand upright. The road stood empty but for wisps of hay. He signaled the other two to join him. Wary, they checked the surroundings for fauna large or small. No horned beasts, no snakes, only the persistent droning insects, which couldn't penetrate their protective gear.

As a team, they heaved the float-car upright and back onto the road. The moment the vehicle was stable, they scrambled back inside, sealing the doors.

Mavakak dropped into the driver's seat and triggered the engine. The float-car shuddered, sputtered, and went still. Icajuc looked at him with alarm. "What's wrong?"

Mavakak punched the button again quickly. "Nothing, nothing, I'm sure."

The float-car's engine chugged valiantly. The vehicle lurched forward half a meter. The engine choked with an audible clunk and fell silent. Mavakak pushed the button again with rapid, panicked jabs. Nothing stirred.

Fear's sharp sting coated Icajuc's throat. He struggled to keep his voice steady. "Stop. It's not doing any good. What's the status of the comms? We need to call for a pick-up."

"Who put you in charge?" Sugawi demanded, her voice rising shrill.

You two did, when you voted that I had to chase off the beast. Icajuc fixed a hard look at her. "What's the status of the comms?"

She swallowed hard. "I... can't get a signal."

They were more than three hours from base. Walking back was out of the question. The cabin of the car grew still and silent. Stranded. Icajuc steeled himself. "We'll need to leave the car, then, walk to the nearest human settlement, and demand access to their communications equipment."

The others looked at him in horror. "Leave the car? We can't! It'd be much better to just send one. As a scout," Sugawi said in a rush.

"No." Icajuc refused to be set out on his own again. "We go as a team and protect each other."

"What if humans steal the car?" she argued.

Mavakak laughed sharply. "What good will *this* do them? You think these primitives can fix it? No point in waiting here. No one from base will come looking for us unless we're more than a day late. We might as well go outside and die there—I don't want this piece of junk to be my grave." The failure of the car seemed to have drained all hope from him.

"We won't die," Icajuc said. "Sugawi, what's left in the weapons locker?"

Her shoulders slumped. "It's empty. Right before we left, Commander Vishoquar requisitioned the remaining arms from all the patrol cars, saying they were wasted resources here, since the patrols are in vehicles, while her troops are in the open."

"We're doomed," Mavakak said, and this time, Icajuc was inclined to agree with him.

Instead of saying so, or cursing their commanding officer, Icajuc opened the tool kit and grabbed a wrench. "Take what you can. We'll keep to the road."

His companions looked at him like he was insane, but they complied. Poorly armed and entirely unprepared, they opened the car doors and ventured out into the strange and savage world.

The road sorely needed maintenance. The pavement was pitted and cracked, but Icajuc couldn't blame human incompetence for that, when the holes were clearly results of the initial bombardment of this area. The local flora had recovered well, filling gaps in the pavement and breaking it down further. The local fauna made itself scarce, to Icajuc's relief.

All the briefings they'd received before the invasion had promised that once the humans were subdued, the planet would be ripe for Pulsi taking. They'd never imagined that conquering the sentient inhabitants would be the *easy* part. Even that had been more complicated than it appeared. Targeted bombardments effectively crippled most of the military powers on the planet, aside from a few extremely paranoid and isolated groups, but guerilla resistance persisted. Making matters more difficult, and further infuriating Commander Vishoquar, rumor said since the ascension of the new Battle Queen, some within High Command expressed opinions that brute force and violence were not the best methods for subduing human resistance. Icajuc kept his thought—that any option which kept him from being attacked while trying to do his job was good—firmly to himself.

They walked in near silence for half an hour, moving slowly and cautiously. Finally Sugawi pointed out a long drive and a house surrounded by fields. "There. Maybe it won't be occupied, and we can use their communications equipment to call the base."

They started up the drive. As they neared the house, Icajuc glimpsed movement in one of the fields. He froze, then caught both of his companions by the arm. "Hurry."

They didn't protest, though both looked toward the spot. "What—Oh no," Mavakak whispered.

The horned beast raised its head, watching them, but it didn't charge or leap the fence to attack. They gained the porch intact, short of breath and on edge. Icajuc moved to the door to knock.

On the other side, something growled, then barked.

Icajuc jumped back. Though humans had tamed the cousins of wolves, the canines offered little welcome to the newcomers to the planet. "I think it's occupied." But he didn't leave the porch—not with the horned beast out in the field waiting for its chance at them.

Footsteps approached the door, and a female human spoke. The canine growls grew less pronounced. The door opened. A human female in her teens looked through the screen down and her face drew in a sharp scowl. "What do you want?"

Face-to-face, Icajuc's translation program worked correctly—or seemed to, at least. He hesitated. It was appropriate to demand to speak to the head of the household, but he wasn't certain if that was her or not. She seemed young, but he didn't want to offend her when they needed assistance. "I need to speak to the one in charge of this house. Is that you?"

She folded her arms across her chest. "Well, since your people killed my parents, yeah, it is. What do you want?"

"Our vehicle was damaged. We require use of your communications equipment," Icajuc said.

"Damaged by that beast outside," Sugawi added in a low voice.

The human looked to her, one eyebrow rising. "Oh, you guys met Spike, huh? Well, must have been fun."

Icajuc thought that was sarcasm. He hoped it was sarcasm. "Not particularly. We prefer to avoid a repeated encounter."

"I bet." She snorted and finally opened the door. One hand hooked through her canine's collar, restraining it. Icajuc gave the snapping white fangs wide berth as he hurried inside. The canine continued to growl until the human dragged it into another room and closed the door. "So, here to borrow the phone, huh?" She pointed to a receiver on the wall. "You know the number you want to call?"

Sugawi picked up the receiver and studied it for a long moment before nodding curtly. "Of course."

"Good. Last time one of you tried to make a call, it took five tries for them to figure out they had to push the *big green button* to make it connect."

Sugawi found a tight smile. "Of course. Surely all know that." She jabbed at the receiver before holding it to her ear.

The human sighed. "Sit down already. You want water or something?"

"I want to know why that beast lurks outside your residence." Icajuc glanced around the room, guessing it served as a kitchen. He pulled a chair from the table and sat, watching the human.

"Spike? Spike isn't lurking, and he's there because he lives there," she said. "That's his field, and he's earned it."

"Earned... it?" Mavakak repeated uncertainly.

"Damn right." She folded her arms again. "Spike is a champion. Prize rodeo bull. He's earned retirement and, let me tell you, it cost a pretty penny."

The translation program helpfully tagged the phrase as a human colloquialism for "very expensive" before Icajuc made a fool of himself by asking the worth of a pretty penny, and how one distinguished it from an ugly one. But the rest of her words rendered an image unlike the one he had understood about the governmental system of this region. "Your people use beasts as champions?"

"You must be joking," the human girl said, voice flat. "You have no idea, do you? Do you know how many of our figures of legend have battled and bested savage animals? Do you even know what a rodeo *is*?"

"Um... no," Icajuc admitted. "That wasn't included in our briefing."

She gave him a look half disgust, half pity. "And you think you can take over our planet without even knowing *that*?"

He fumbled to regain control of the conversation, though he

wasn't certain he'd ever had it. "Well, how many of *your* leaders have managed this feat?"

"Not many. Probably why so many of them are utter crap at the job," she said. "I can't even *remember* the last time I heard of someone grizzly wrestling."

Icajuc paled. "Grizzly? The massive furred...um...bears?"

She nodded. "Yep, those."

"Hand-to-hand combat? With those monsters?" She couldn't be serious, could she? It had to be some wild exaggeration.

"Well of course. How else would you expect a good Canadian to prove their worth, if not grizzly wrestling?" she demanded.

"I don't know a good Canadian from a bad one," Icajuc answered.

"By grizzly wrestling, obviously! Or at least by riding the rodeo circuit." She pointed to a framed photograph on the wall, depicting a human clinging with one hand to a bull like the champion Spike. The image captured the bull mid-buck, and the human looked about to fly from the beast's back. "Same in the States, too. We call the folk who can ride the bulls 'cowboys' or 'cowgirls', and you don't get to claim a name like that unless you've earned it."

His mind whirled. "I have heard of these cow-boys in your entertainment shows, but I have not seen them completing such challenges."

She rolled her eyes. "If they've claimed the title, they've already *completed* the challenge."

"If one of our leaders were to defeat this challenge, they too could claim the champion's title?" Icajuc asked. "And would earn the respect of your kind?" He grasped desperately for something they could bring to turn away Commander Vishoquar's anger.

"I think anyone around these parts would tip their hat to someone who could ride Spike," she said.

Mavakak gave Icajuc a long, cautious look. "You're not suggesting Commander Vishoquar should attempt such a challenge, are you?"

The look Icajuc gave him was bland. "Surely the commander would welcome another method of subduing this land, given how heavily armed she insists the ground troops must be, and their inability to spare even the most basic weapons to patrols such as ours."

Icajuc realized he'd forgotten to deactivate his translator when the human paused, eyebrow rising. "They send you guys out without *weapons*? Seriously?" She shook her head. "You get on the bad side of someone in charge?"

Sugawi gave up pretending she knew how to operate the human communication device. "Our commanding officer determined that patrols in float-cars are unlikely to encounter situations where we would need heavy arms."

"Oh, so they did leave you with *some* weapons," the human said.

"No," Icajuc admitted. "The officer two levels above *her* earlier reclaimed most small arms from our teams, on the theory that the heavy arms in the car weapons lockers would serve any need we had for weapons." Should he tell this to a resident of this conquered planet? Probably not, but he didn't dare voice complaints within the base, where whispers of dissent reached a commander's ears at the speed of light.

"So, basically, you're in bureaucratic purgatory." Her expression grew thoughtful as her gaze settled on the photograph on the wall. "You guys think your commander would take Spike's challenge? Maybe the ride would shake some sense into them."

Was she serious or not? Icajuc wasn't certain. "I... don't know. If... when we return to base, I will present the matter to her."

The human looked over her shoulder to Sugawi, who had returned the communications handset to the wall. "No luck contacting your base? Frankly, they aren't inclined to answer calls from us locals most of the time." She pushed back from the table. "So I guess that means you need a ride."

All three perked up. "You have the means to do so?" Icajuc asked.

"Yeah, we can pile in the farm truck. The suspension is crappy, but it'll get us there. Might even be able to hook up the hitch to tow your car."

Mavakak shook his head quickly. "No need. Just returning us to base will suffice."

Icajuc nodded in agreement. Returning to base in a human vehicle would be embarrassing, but they would never live down having their car dragged in by one.

As the human, Alice, warned, the drive back to base was bumpy, and the truck cramped. Alice suggested a couple of them could ride in the open bed of the truck, but no one volunteered to risk stray encounters with Earth wildlife, instead making do in the confines of the cab.

Along the drive, Alice regaled them with tales of warriors of the past, from exploits of Annie Oakley to the more recent Hula Joe, who escorted a Crow princess ("The tribe, not the bird!"), as well as some local celebrities. Her passengers questioned her about the rodeo and other traditional battles of humans against the beasts of their world. Icajuc wasn't certain he believed all her stories—some of the creatures she described matched none of their zoological database, and even considering the many strange beasts on this planet, he couldn't quite accept the idea of the jackalope.

Alice dropped them off at the first checkpoint, well before they reached base. "Your guys don't like us locals getting too close. Good luck and all."

"What's the best means of contacting you should our commander agree to battle?" Icajuc asked quickly.

She wrote several lines on a scrap of paper. "There you go—address and phone number. Call before showing up, so I can get the dogs inside."

He accepted the information and gave her a quick, polite bow. "Thank you for your assistance."

She had an odd expression for a moment but nodded. "Sure, no problem."

"I THINK THEY ACTUALLY BELIEVED ME," ALICE SAID TO THE steering wheel. "They seriously *believed* that." She felt a little guilty now. The three aliens had felt more like lost tourists than otherworldly invaders, and if what they said was true, whoever was in charge was treating them like cow pies.

"Also, who sends out a patrol, but won't let them have weapons?" She shook her head. "I thought our bureaucracy was incompetent! Hah. I hope they *do* convince their commander to challenge Spike. He loves novice riders. Especially cocky ones."

Alice stomped on the accelerator, and the old truck roared in response. Time to get home and make some calls. This might not be cowboy country, but they were going to have a rodeo.

COMMANDER VISHOQUAR GLARED FURIOUSLY AT THE HAGGARD patrol and slammed her fist against the desk. "You call *this* a report?"

Before she could work into a fiercer frenzy, Icajuc cleared his throat. "Commander, our report is an accurate statement of our findings. Which aspects do you wish clarified?"

"What is this nonsense about 'challenging' the beasts of this province?" she demanded. "Our survey of this planet revealed nothing of the sort."

"The same survey that failed to report the existence of bears, wolves, and bees?" Sugawi muttered.

The commander fixed a hard look on her but did concede the point with a slight motion of her head. "And what do you propose we should do with this information now?"

"The human Alice is caretaker of one of these battle beasts." Icajuc wished he dared speak as boldly as Sugawi, but Commander Vishoquar blatantly favored her female underlings. "If you, or one of the other commanders, agree to the challenge, she will arrange it."

Commander Vishoquar's eyes narrowed on him. "Have you spoken to anyone else about this? Who told you about the Battle Queen's decree?"

When did she think they'd had time to talk to anyone else? "Once we returned to base, we wrote up our report and submitted it to you, Commander. To my knowledge, no one else has read it." *She doesn't believe it. She'll refuse.* Icajuc swallowed hard. "Commander, no one has spoken to us about new decrees from the Battle Queen. We never hear about her decrees until you inform the base."

Commander Vishoquar glared the report once again, face set and hard. "Her Excellence the Battle Queen has ordered that we are to establish 'rapport' with the humans to properly understand the nature of this planet and has forbidden bombardments until further notice. I have personally received orders to lead this initiative, as well as instructions forbidding retaliatory actions against the local population should initial efforts prove unsuccessful. Now you bring me a report where this human claims that to earn the respect of her kind, I have only to ride the beast for eight seconds? Hah! What kind of challenge is that?"

"Presumably, the one before grizzly wrestling," Icajus said.

"And none of you attempted—no, mere patrollers wouldn't dare aspire for something so far beyond their reach. Just as you will not dare repeat a word of this outside my office." Commander Vishoquar's eyes gleamed now, and Icajuc saw the lure of victory catching her. She stood abruptly. "You will not share this report with anyone else. I will ensure the information is properly disseminated to those who require it. Inform the human to prepare the beast. His challenge has been accepted."

One call to Alice unleashed a barrage of preparations

for the rodeo. Icajuc found himself thrust into the role of mediator between the base and the humans. He didn't understand the purpose of half the items the humans insisted were necessary, but he did his best to arrange the release of materials to them.

Commander Vishoquar demanded status updates daily, if not hourly. She'd already begun planning how to use her new status, assuming it already won and in hand. Icajuc was not surprised at her attitude, but he was surprised by the humans' eagerness. Had they been waiting for someone to understand their customs enough to realize the need for the challenge? Or were they mocking the event? He couldn't tell.

Regardless of motives, the mood of both humans and Pulsi improved, and the two, invaders and locals, tolerated each other better than Icajuc had ever seen. A festive mood cheered the atmosphere. He wasn't certain what Commander Vishoquar had told the other officers or her superiors, but even they appeared enthusiastic about the event.

The greatest difficulty Icajuc encountered turned out not to be the materials the humans required, but the uniform. Alice provided him with a description of the required clothing. Commander Vishoquar took one look and chased him from her office, roaring profanities and maligning the lineage both of him and of every human in the province. Icajuc hid for several hours before risking a return venture. To his relief, Commander Vishoquar had calmed, and her displeasure took the form of petty, overly specific requirements for the uniform rather than outright violence. While Icajuc wasn't certain it was *possible* to find the required plaid shirt in violet and peach, he put out the request to the humans. Rather to his surprise, he was assured it would be no problem, and that it was far from the worst request they'd received.

He wasn't certain whether the answer made him less worried, or more.

The day before the challenge, Commander Vishoquar deigned to accompany Icajuc to the arena. As human workers completed finishing touches, she frowned at the wooden walls plastered with faded advertisements, scowled at the racks of metal bleachers, and demanded, "*This* is a fit battleground for a challenge?"

Alice, showing them around, met her gaze evenly. "Well, normally we'd have it at one of the official arenas, but you guys *bombed* them. So, unless you want to put this on hold and provide people to rebuild them, this is what we've got."

Commander Vishoquar scowled, but accepted the sharp retort from another female, even a human one, that she would never have allowed from a male subordinate. "Very well. It will suffice, this time."

"Good. I'd hate to disappoint Spike by delaying the big event," Alice said. "I hope you're prepared—I know he is."

Commander Vishoquar straightened. "I am entirely prepared."

Alice grinned, and Icajuc didn't think her expression altogether friendly. "Glad to hear it. See you tomorrow, then."

The two women parted. Icajuc watched them, both of them confident and self-assured, and he wondered which of them would suffer defeat.

COMMANDER VISHOQUAR GLARED INTO THE MIRROR, THEN turned her burning gaze on Icajuc. "This is ridiculous!"

"It's the traditional garb of those who accept the challenge, Commander," Icajuc told her diffidently, not daring allow even a hint of humor in stance or voice. "The measurements are compliant with those you provided, as are the colors."

She looked comical in denim pants, the best approximation their fabricators could manage for cowboy boots, and the plaid shirt in a hideous blend of peach and purple. The brimmed hat sat awkwardly on her head.

"If this doesn't work, I'll nail your worthless hide to my office wall," she snarled. Without waiting for a response, Commander Vishoquar stormed from the dressing room to await the final call.

Icajuc seized his opportunity to escape into the stands. The bleachers were packed with humans and Pulsi alike. Everyone who could find an excuse to leave the base and attend had done so. Icajuc started to squeeze between people to find a spot. To his shock, when his fellows noticed him, they voluntarily shifted to make room—even the front-line soldiers who normally ignored or scorned lowly patrollers. A cheer rose from the humans as the preliminary challenges began—human children wrestling sheep.

Sugawi waved him over to join her and Mavakak. "Can you believe it? Look at this crowd!" She slapped Icajuc on the back. "I don't know how you pulled this off, but good job."

Icajuc swallowed hard. "The commander will kill me if this doesn't work."

Sugawi shook her head. "Idiot. It's *already* worked. Our soldiers and humans are talking to each other, and no one's attacking anyone. It's what the Battle Queen wants!"

"But if Commander Vishoquar loses..." Icajuc began. "What will happen if she orders Spike executed? Or the humans?"

"While you've been running all over organizing everything, High Command has been making *very* clear announcements that any form of retaliation will be considered treason and punished by execution." Mavakak glanced to either side and added in a whisper, "There's a bet going. There are soldiers—*soldiers*—wagering that Commander Vishoquar will lose. Even some of *them* don't like her! No one will hurt that bull or his human."

"Really?" Icajuc whispered in disbelief. A weight lifted from him. He wondered whether the ban on retaliation would extend to him as well.

Humans ran into the packed dirt arena, arranging barrels around the ring. The buzz of excitement grew, then rose higher when the tight corral shook and trembled, heralding the arrival of Spike. Alice stepped into the ring, every centimeter a cowgirl. She raised a hand, and the crowd roared. She waited for the noise to die down, then spoke into a microphone.

"Thank you everyone for joining us today to witness this event.

If you're local, of course, you all know Spike." She waved toward the chute, and the humans cheered, stamping feet to make the stands tremble.

Alice continued. "If you're not from around here, you might never have met Spike. He's the meanest, nastiest bucking bull in this province. Champion of dozens of competitions, once witnessed by the Queen herself, I give you the Imperial Battle Cow of New Brunswick!"

Humans and Pulsi cheered together, hooting and shouting.

"The challenger, of course, you all know. Ready to risk life and limb in the arena, our first Pulsi to attempt to claim the title of cowgirl, the one and only Commander Vishoquar!"

The human cheering was less enthusiastic, but the Pulsi covered their lack. Icajuc watched the pen. Spike snorted and tossed his head as Commander Vishoquar straddled his back and gripped the rope.

Alice darted from the ring. The buzzer sounded. The gate opened. Spike surged into the ring, pivoted, and bucked.

Icajuc knew he would never leave this planet. He might not even leave the stands alive. But he knew, without a single doubt, that for the rest of whatever life he might have, he would treasure the memory of that moment—the graceful movement of the champion, the precise leap, and the scream of shock and terror as Commander Vishoquar flew from the bull's back to land face-first in the dirt.

Alice, just outside the ring, smirked, her revenge complete. The Imperial Battle Cow of New Brunswick reigned supreme.

THE LLANTHONY LIVESTOCK LITIGATION

FROG AND ESTHER JONES

About the Authors: Frog and Esther Jones are a husband-and-wife writing/editing/publishing team living deep in the rain forests of the Olympic Peninsula. They are primarily known for their running urban fantasy series, *The Gift of Grace*, and they appear in many anthologies other than this one as well. They can be found online at www.jonestales.com.

The Llanthony Livestock Litigation
Frog and Esther Jones

"So, do we think this is a good idea?" asked Camy, her bright wings bringing her to rest atop the massive beast's rump.

"Well," said Canhem. "It's *your* cow." The young male sprite picked up a stick from the ground just behind the bovine and hefted it over his shoulder, deftly avoiding his fluttering wings.

"They're *all* my cows," said Camy, her voice rising in both pitch and tempo as she gestured across the green hillside toward the herd of cattle. "Whenever I want them to be."

"Yes, love," said Canhem. "So where's the harm in a bit of fun with one or two?"

Camy settled down on the bovine's haunches and pondered this. She shook a strand of her long, red hair out of her face and folded her shimmering wings behind her. "I'm just not sure we've thought this through," she said after a moment.

"Um, love?" said Canhem. His bare chest rippled with the effort of lifting the small branch, and his wings began to raise both sprite and stick off the ground. "You're Camymddwyn and I'm Canhem. We're sprites, and our job is mischief and mayhem. So, no. We haven't thought this through at all. It honestly makes me concerned that you *want* to."

Camy shrugged. "That's all well and good where the Cymri are involved. But I'm worried about the cows."

"Ha!" said Canhem, beginning to fly forward, stick outstretched like a tiny lance. "The *cows* should be fine."

And with that, he buried the rough length of wood firmly into the bovine anus before him.

The cow reacted both immediately and predictably. The big animal lurched forward in a mad dash. Camy fell for a moment, then caught herself on her iridescent wings. Hovering in mid-aid, the two sprites watched as one bovine's madness spread through the herd, turning a once-docile mass of cud-chewing tranquility into a rolling wave of panic, galloping down the hillside in a mud-churning flurry of hooves and insanity.

"See?" said Canhem. "Now *that's* a good day's work."

THE NICE THING ABOUT BEING OTHERWORLDY CREATURES OF magic—or, at least, one of the nice things—is that the cruising air speed of a sprite is far faster than one might expect given their diminuitive physiology. So as the stampede approached the construction site around Llanthony Priory, the two sprites sat perched atop the half-built stonework of their target.

"You know," said Camy, "it's pretty impressive what these people can put together when they decide on a goal."

"You know we're here to *oppose* this building, right?" responded Canhem.

"Well, obviously," said Camy. "But still. You have to admit, awful lot of effort to bring all this stone here and stack it up like this."

"Oh, aye," said Canhem. "Their God keeps having them *build* things. Build the churches to bind their beliefs. Build the fences to cage the beasts, build mills to harness the river. They build their weapons out of iron, *iron,* to aid them in killing both each other and us. And everything they build drags them further and further away from who they were."

Camy looked down at the stonework. The massive priory had rooms, but no ceiling as yet. And all around it, the builder's huts and a small chapel to the God of the Normans and the Saxons stood. Those huts were little more than sticks, with a thatched roof. Looking up the hill at the bovine tide on the way with her far-seeing eyes, Camy didn't put a lot of odds on anything *but* this stonework surviving.

"Well," Camy said, "that's all true. But if they're willing to put that much effort into constructing things, maybe we should learn to reach into their buildings. After all, there's only so much we can do to stop it."

"But, these are the *Cymri*!" said Canhem. "They are *our* people! Ever since the alliance of Pryderi and Arawn, the Cymri have been our allies among the mortals. And now, they begin to turn away from us to this Saxon God. This Norman God. And *this* is Calan Mai. Today, of all days, the straw men should be hanged. The warriors of Winter and Summer should duel. We may not be able to stop their building, but we can at the least remind them *who we are*."

Below the two sprites, the workers bustled, pointing up at the hillside. The distant thunder of hoofbeats grew louder, joined by maddened lowing and the occasional clank of a bell. Workers fled or ducked into the unroofed stone walls as the wave of angry beef bore through their tents and over their personal belongings.

God was displeased.

Brother Cledwyn did not know *why* the Lord of Lords had chosen to visit his wrath on the monks of Llanthony. He found himself especially confused as to why it would happen *today* of all days. Was this not the Feast of Saint Bertha of Kent, the holy Lady responsible for bringing the Word of the Lord to the British Isles in the first place? Why, on her feast day of all days, would Saint Bertha turn her back on her people?

Brother Cledwyn could not fathom it, and tried only for a moment. The ways of God were mysterious, and if He should choose to test his followers with a stampede of black Welsh cattle, Brother Cledwyn could but persevere. He pressed himself to the unfinished wall of stone sheltering him from the raging herd, pulled the long string of wooden beads from his waist band, made the sign of the cross, and began to pray.

"Credo in Deum Patrem omnipotentem, Creatorem caeli et terrae—"

As he prayed, a high-pitched, female voice sounded out of nowhere. "What're *you* doing?" it asked.

He ignored it. "*Et in Iesum Christum, Filium eius unicum, Dominum nostrum, qui conceptus est de Spiritu Sancto—*"

"Those are really funny-sounding words," the voice said.

Was this the holy Saint Bertha, speaking directly to him from heaven? Had he been rewarded for his faith? He continued his prayer. "*natus ex Maria Virgine, passus sub Pontio Pilato, crucifixus, mortuus, et sepultus, descendit ad infernos, tertia die resurrexit a mortuis, ascendit ad caelos, sedet ad dexteram Dei Patris omnipotentis—*"

"You know, it's really rather rude to talk to someone else while I'm here."

This could not be Saint Bertha. That holy lady would never interrupt someone in prayer like this. And no women had joined the Brotherhood in their labors to build the Priory of Llanthony, so that could only mean one thing. The Devil was afoot and had driven these bovines down to stampede amongst the Brotherhood. Now all made sense, for he and his brethren were clearly being tested like Job, as a plaything between God and Satan. Like Job, Brother Cledwyn resolved to meet this test.

"*—inde venturus est iudicare vivos et mortuos. Credo in Spiritum Sanctum, sanctam Ecclesiam catholicam, sanctorum communionem, remissionem peccatorum, carnis resurrectionem, vitam aeternam. Amen.*"

"Ooo, an 'amen.' I know that one," continued the voice of Satan. "That one means you're done, right?"

Brother Cledwyn ignored the voice, moving onward to the bead above the cross and continuing to chant. "*Pater Noster, qui es in caelis, sanctificetur nomen tuum. Adveniat regnum tuum—*"

"Oh," said the Devil. "You're doing the bead thing. I've heard of this. It'll take a while, won't it? I mean, the cows are long past by now, but if you're going to keep sitting there and mumbling weird words, I can wait. Go on."

Brother Cledwyn did not believe the Devil would react so passively to these prayers. After all, Brother Cledwyn had been taught that prayer horrified the Devil, driving him back before the power of Almighty God. He expected Satan to continue her interruptions, to pester him away from the Peace that was God's.

Instead, he circled the Rosary without further interruption from the feminine voice. The only sound to reach his ears came from his brethren, each in his own prayer to God the Father.

The power of his prayer victorious, he put aside the temptations of the Dark One. He focused only on the holy blessings that were his and his brotherhood's. His mind focused, cleared, and prepared itself for the labor of cleaning the camp after the evil works which had been wrought upon it, and his spirit celebrated once again the greater task of constructing the Priory.

"*—Per eundem Christum Dominum nostrum. Amen*," he finished, and opened his eyes.

Before him, standing upon an uneven stone in the rock wall, stood a small figure with iridescent wings and a shining nimbus.

Brother Cledwyn's spirit soared.

HER LOVER HAD FLOWN OFF IN A BIT OF A HUFF BEFORE THE strange man had finished with his hand on the cross, leaving Camy alone to watch the robed Cymri men.

This Saxon God seemed like a pretty demanding fellow. Camy stood upon the wall and watched the Cymri pray, eyes closed, to their deity. She couldn't fathom why they repeated the same words over and over again, but as she didn't understand the Roman language they spoke she couldn't comment on the contents.

She tried, early on, to get one of them to speak back to her, but the Saxon God apparently demanded absolute obedience and attention. She knew she shouldn't be surprised about this; the Saxon God had always been something of a domineering stick-in-the-mud, and he apparently demanded the same from his followers. But rudeness did not necessitate rudeness in response, and Camy's curiosity got the better of her.

So she leaned herself against the rough-hewn stone of the Priory wall, and waited for the man to circle his beads.

And as she watched, she became fascinated. Because the prayer *did* seem to be having an effect. The man's muscles relaxed, and his breathing evened. The corners of his lips began to turn upward, and his eyebrow unfurrowed into an expression of peace and relaxation. Camy looked about the ruins of the tent city and saw the same effect on the other men. Slowly, one at a time, they began to rise to their feet.

And the man before her stood and opened his eyes.

He took a step back from Camy, his eyebrows flying up. Then he fell back to his knees and pressed his forehead into the ground. Camy, confused, flew down to ground level to stand next to his ear.

"Hello?" she asked tentatively.

"Oh holy messenger, forgive my behavior should it affront you."

"Um..." said Camy, not sure how to respond to this. "Well, we did figure the stampede would be a lot more upsetting than this. Canhem's going to be more affronted than I am about that, though. I'll pass your words along?"

"Canhem? An angel of mayhem?" asked the man.

"What? No!" she recoiled. "Canhem's like me. Can't you even recognize a sprite?"

The man raised his torso up from the ground, resting himself in a kneeling position, and looked squarely at Camy.

"You are not an angelic messenger of the Heavenly Father?"

"Ew. No," said Camy, her face contorted in disgust. "What a terrible life. No genitals, complete servitude. No thanks."

"So you *are* a devil," the man grabbed his cross again, holding it in between Camy and himself.

"Were you not listening?" asked Camy in an irritated tone. She flew up and lighted upon the cross itself. "I'm not an angel, and I'm not a devil. I'm a *sprite*. Camymddwyn is my common name. You can call me Camy."

"Mischief?" asked the man.

"If you're going to use the *Saxon* tongue for things, yes. It felt like a good enough moniker. Now, I've given you something to call me. It's only polite you return the favor, you know."

"If you *were* a demon, you'd likely lie to me about it."

"Maybe," said Camy. "I don't know much about demons. Hmm, let's see...could a demon do this?"

Camy swung her right leg in an arc as she crouched with her left. She hooked her right ankle behind the cross and spun, sliding down and spinning with a dancer's grace to end resting her buttocks upon the cross-beam of the icon, her arms embracing the top of it. She reached into her memory while embracing the cross, then repeated the sounds she'd heard the man making earlier.

"*Credo in Deum Patrem omnipotentem, Creatorem caeli—*"

"Agh!" shouted the priest, and he shook her free of his cross.

"Could a demon do that?" Camy asked him, hovering now with slow flaps of her wings.

The robed man sat, staring. She'd flummoxed him with that move; that was good. "I, uh...no," he said. "I don't believe one could. Are you really a Christian?"

"A follower of your Saxon God? Hardly," said Camy. "I told you, I'm a sprite."

"But you just said you believed—"

"Did I?" asked Camy. "I really have no idea what those Roman words mean. I remembered the sound of you saying them, is all. Now, since you know I'm not a demon, can I *please* know what I should call you."

He stared at her for a moment, and Camy could not tell what thoughts went through his head. Finally, he seemed to relent, and he half-smiled as he said, "I, uh, I'm Brother Cledwyn of Llanthony Priory. Or, at least, I will be once we build Llanthony Priory. So, if you are neither angel nor demon...what are you?"

Camy rolled her eyes with an exaggerated head motion. She sighed deeply, then said, "Have you not been listening to me at *all?* I'm a *sprite.*"

"Yes, of course I've heard you say that. But, well...what's a sprite?"

"Are you not Cymri?" Camy asked, her voice rising with her exasperation. "You know the meaning of my name, and of Canhem's. Do you no longer tell the tales of Arawn's kingdom?"

"Arawn? You mean, the faeries? Those are just peasant superstitions, tales for mothers to tell their children. There is only One True God," Brother Cledwyn kept talking. Camy gave him a flat and increasingly angry stare, but he did not appear to notice as he continued to ramble. "Stamping out that kind of superstition is the reason we're building this Priory here in Wales. The Word of God must—oh," he cut off suddenly.

"And the lightning strikes at last," said Camy through clenched teeth. "You know Arawn's Court is fully aware of your intent to "stamp out" any belief in us. Although," she paused to look about the destroyed remnants of the monks' tent city. "I think the stamping has gone *quite* the other way for the moment."

"Fairies are real?" Brother Cledwyn asked.

"Flying *right* in front of you," said Camy. "Right here. That you even have to *ask* shows me how in violation of the pact between Arawn and Pryderi you are."

"Pact?" said Cledwyn. "I don't remember any pact."

"Look," said Camy, her irritation at this clueless, insulting human in front of her hitting its peak. "There's a pact. You're in violation of it. And for so long as you continue your disrespect of Arawn's Court, Canhem and I are tasked to make your life miserable. Your little string of beads can't save you or your Priory. Only your compliance."

And with that, Camy flitted off to join Canhem.

BROTHER CLEDWYN TOOK A LONG TIME TO WRAP HIS HEAD around what had just happened.

It couldn't have been a demon. No demon would be able to touch a holy cross while reciting the Apostle's Creed, regardless of whether she understood the words or not. Still, that left the problem of who this sprite was, and what pact she referred to.

Around him, his Brothers were beginning to pick up the remains of their tents. The canvas had been ripped apart by hooves, and no other shelter save the unfinished walls of the Priory remained.

"Brothers," he called. "Let us gather for a moment and discuss the situation."

"The situation?" said Brother Anarawd. He was a great, black-bearded fellow, with broad shoulders and a deep voice that would normally have been soothing. "God has shown his displeasure with us. The only question remains whether we suffer here or attempt to journey to shelter ere night falls."

"It's a seven-mile walk to Abergavenny," said Cledwyn. "Mid-day is already past us, and we are without horses or even a donkey. I do not believe all the brethren can make that journey before the fall of night."

"No," said Brother Anarawd. "Likely not. But there's a small farming village not half a mile up the mountain from us. Hasn't a name, but the folk have come down to trade their eggs and milk a time or two. Mayhap they'd be willing to extend a hand."

"Up the mountain?" asked Cledwyn. "That's a pagan village, isn't it?" He could not stop thinking about the little sprite, and her anger with him. "Are we certain we'll be well-received there?"

"Folk seem kindly enough," said Brother Anarawd.

"They're pagans, though," said Cledwyn. "Do you actually think they'll provide succor to us?"

Brother Anarawd shrugged at this. "Don't see why not. They think us curious, but they seem like good folk. Might be God has sent us this test as an opportunity, to let us go and speak with them about the Holy Word."

Should I tell them? thought Brother Cledwyn to himself. The other brothers would likely discount his vision of the sprite, might even go so far as to accuse him of some form of witchcraft, though he rated that unlikely. Still, didn't they have the right to know that it was not God, but Faery, that had shown its displeasure on them? And given that, that a pagan village could present problems?

But Abergavenny lay too far away. The Brothers had nothing with which to survive here. They would walk to the pagans, and would pray to Almighty God for protection.

"HA!" SAID CANHEM. "LOOK AT THAT, THEY'RE RUNNING. RIGHT to our *actual* people, no less."

"Yes," said Camy. She'd calmed down since talking to Brother Cledwyn. After all, it wasn't *his* fault he'd never been taught the Pact. Sure, the man had been nothing but pig-headed, but still he'd been willing to listen.

"And on Calan Mai! Let the Straw Men be formed!" shouted Canhem.

"Straw men?" she said. "They believe in their God, and they believe in suffering for their God. Do you really want to give them that kind of suffering?"

"Oh, pish," said Canhem. "I doubt that once the straw man is alight that these brothers praise their God. And I certainly don't think he does anything about it. It's Calan Mai, and this is the time for such celebrations!"

Canhem's tone of voice struck Camy as giddy, verging on joyous. Camy, though, wasn't so sure. She remembered the look of peace on Brother Cledwyn's face as he prayed to his bead-thing. He'd just been overrun by a stampede, he and all his brethren's makeshift homes had been destroyed, all their belongings crushed under the hooves of Canhem's vengeance.

But she hadn't seen anger.

Camy prided herself on being a connoisseur of human anguish. She had seen humans yell, and scream, and tear their clothes, and gnash their teeth in response to her and Canhem's ministrations. Brother Cledwyn hadn't expressed any of that. No frustration, no rage; just a calm acceptance. He'd even *blamed his God,* and then prayed anyway. She couldn't put her finger on why, but she found herself growing more impressed with the pious brother.

So she couldn't bring herself to join in Canhem's glee at the thought of Brother Cledwyn burning in a Straw Man. Instead, she became lost in her thoughts, struggling to reconcile two contrasting worlds. She wished for a solution before Canhem reached the village, but could not think of any.

THE VILLAGERS MET THE BROTHERS JUST DOWNSLOPE OF THEIR small collection of homes. And Brother Cledwyn didn't see food and blankets among them, but rather bows and spears.

"Ho!" shouted Brother Anarawd. "Is Bran among you? Him that brings the eggs and cheeses to trade with us?"

A grizzled-looking pagan in his mid-thirties stepped forward. He wore rough-spun clothes and carried a crude yew bow with a hunting broadhead.

"Ho, Anarawd. I'm here, but you've come to us on Calan Mai. It's not a day for trading eggs."

Calan Mai? thought Cledwyn. *The First of May? They still celebrate the old holidays here. To us, it's the Feast of St. Bertha. To them, it's Calan Mai. And that means—oh. Oh, no.*

He tried to speak, but could not beat the booming voice of Brother Anarawd. "Calan Mai? A pagan holiday? Well, regardless, it's not trade we're seeking, but succor. A herd of cattle—likely belonging to one of you fine folk—took fear and destroyed our homes."

"Aye," said Bran calmly. "At the behest of the Tylwyth Teg, no less. Mischief and Mayhem have passed a bit of Arawn's judgment on you."

"Well, of course we believe differently; we feel our God is testing us," said Brother Anarawd. "But this is no time to debate theology. We are without shelter, food, or—"

"Ain't about theology," said Bran.

Cledwyn cringed.

"It's about you pissed off the faeries, and we're not terrible keen to do the same. Mayhem himself brought the word, and we've little choice in the matter. First time in my life we'll have real Straw Men on Calan Mai, but that's the way of it. You calm down and cooperate, we'll get you senseless first."

Anarawd's face grew ashen as he processed Bran's meaning. Cledwyn closed his eyes and bowed his head in prayer. As he chanted the words to his God, his mind raced back, through his past. Back before he'd been given to the Brotherhood, back to his sheep-herding father and all the old tales. The pact with Arawn, the Fair Folk, Calan Mai—there had to be something to stop this tragedy.

Then he had it.

"WAIT!" he shouted, and as he heard his voice joined in the cry by another, higher-pitched and feminine. He opened his eyes and raised his head to see the small, glowing figure hovering between the pagans and the Christians, her eyes locked with his. She gave him a smile, then gestured for him to speak first.

Cledwyn cleared his throat, then raised his voice.

"We seek Judgment before the Stones!"

Brother Cledwyn had gotten it right!

Camy heard the invocation of the Stones and could not believe it. She hadn't thought Brother Cledwyn knew enough of the Tylwyth Teg to invoke, assumed she'd have to do it for him. But he'd known. Somewhere, under all those layers of Roman chanting and prayer beads, somewhere Brother Cledwyn was, in fact, Cymri.

Hope blossomed within Camy.

"Judgment before the Stones?" asked one of the other brothers, a black-bearded man of significantly larger stature than her Cledwyn. "You would submit yourself to a pagan ritual?"

"Have faith, Brother," said Cledwyn. "Did not Elijah challenge the prophets of Baal in their own ritual? Judgment is for the Lord our God, and it will be His whether we stand before a Stone or an Altar, will it not?"

"You are willing to go before the Stones?" she asked aloud, so that both the groups of Cymri could hear her. "It is the judgment of Arawn you seek, then, and not your Norman God."

Grumblings from some of the other brethren at this, but Brother Cledwyn simply smiled at her. "My faith says otherwise," he said. "Lead on."

Camy's frustration warred with her amusement at this man. Even here, even now, the brother exuded a sense of calm acceptance. Canhem wanted him to burn, but Camy simply wanted him to bend. The fate of the priests, as it always had been, would be for the judgment of Arawn.

The trek to the Judgment Stones that lay uphill of the village took but minutes. The three Stones themselves had been laid in a small circle; Bran and Brother Cledwyn sat upon two, and a third remained empty.

For a short time.

The air began to shimmer over the third stone, and out of the air itself stepped Arawn. Camy saw that he had chosen, this time, to appear as a man, more slender than any human in proportion. He wore intricate armor of boiled leather, dyed to a glossy black, that interlocked and moved quietly in perfection. A black cape flowed off one shoulder only, and a long witchwood sword hung at his hip. He quietly moved to sit upon the Judgment Stone.

Camy took a deep breath, then flitted to alight on his right shoulder just as Canhem arrived and lighted on his left.

I have been called in Judgment. Arawn's mouth did not open, and no noise issued forth. But Camy heard his words nonetheless, and based on the ashen faces of the Llanthony Brotherhood, they did as well. *And I have answered, for my servants do not agree.*

Camy looked away from her lord, blushing slightly. At best, this sort of intervention between her and her partner ranked as one of the more embarrassing moments in her life.

Speak your case, Mayhem, said the Lord of Annwyn.

"My Lord," said Canhem, "These men, who used to be Cymri, are building a place to worship their Norman God. They have turned from their compact with you and seek to turn other Cymri away from us. It is Calan Mai, and we can stop this now."

"No," said Camy, "We can't."

All eyes, save those of Arawn's, turned to her.

"We can't stop them. They've won. We can burn these unarmed brothers, sure. But what happens to Bran and his people when the steel-suited ones find out and bring cold iron to purge us? We once reigned over all this island, and now we have these mountains in Cymru, but nothing more. We can't stop them."

Do you argue, then, to not punish a violation of the pact where we see it? said Arawn. *Even should we agree that the steel-bearers cannot be resisted, why should we leave such an insult unanswered when it is in front of us?*

"Exactly!" cried Canhem. "Exactly my point. The Pact is broken, and the oathbreakers must pay."

"My lord," spoke Bran, and Camy took a deep breath at the sound of a Cymri entering the discussion. "What you say is true, but I would tell you that these Brothers have been nothing but kind to us, even though they worship the Norman God. They have traded in good faith, they have never spoken in ill will toward us. Aye, they've sought to turn us to their God, but only by words, not steel. Surely this counts for somewhat. Let them re-swear the pact with you, take the damage to their homes as their punishment, and continue living."

The Lord of Annwyn sat long in silence. Camy felt her nerves sing while the King of the Faeries determined the fate of Brother Cledwyn.

"My king!" said Canhem, interrupting the silence. "These monks will continue to break the oaths their forefathers made, even after today, should you let them live. They will return to their Priory, and they will begin their work anew."

Is this true? asked Arawn, for the first time turning his head to stare directly at Brother Cledwyn.

"Yes," said Brother Cledwyn, his voice still calm and accepting. Camy gawked at the strength to look Arawn in the eye and admit something like this.

"Yes," said Brother Cledwyn again. "Yes, we will continue to build the Priory, for that is our holy mission from our God. And we will continue to educate all around us in the Word of our Lord, for so we have been instructed. If that alone is enough to burn us, then by all means burn us. We shall join Saint Stephen and face your flames as he faced the stones. I am sorry, my lord, but I will tell the truth. My faith is with God in Heaven."

Brother Cledwyn's voice trembled as he said this. Behind him, the other brothers shook as their leader pronounced what certainly must be their death sentence, but none gainsayed him. Camy could not cry, could not breathe, could not act for what seemed an eternity after such a stunning display of faith.

"Lord," she said at last, "must the Pact be exclusive with their actions? Do you see their strength, and how it drives them?"

"*Ego sum Dominus Deus tuus qui eduxi te de terra Aegypti de domo servitutis non habebis deos alienos coram me*," said the black-bearded Brother.

"I am the Lord thy God," translated Brother Cledwyn, "who brought you out of the Land of Egypt, out of the house of bondage. You shall have no other gods before me." He took a breath at this, then continued. "And so we are commanded. We *cannot* worship Arawn, even though he be real, and seated before us. We are commanded to worship one god alone."

The Pact is not one of worship, nor do I lay any claim to Godhood, said Arawn. *I am a King, and I demand fealty, not piety. Worship whatever God you choose to believe in. But you* shall *respect my people, and work in tandem with them. You shall light the straw man in remembrance of them, and you shall tell their tales. You shall feast on Calan Awst, burn the fires on Calan Gaef, hang the straw man on Calan Mai, and dance the Mari Llwyd during Alban Arthan. You shall bring no steel into the Rings, nor refuse hospitality when asked of the Tylwyth Teg. Does your God forbid these things?*

THE PAVED STREET BEFORE THE CHEPSTOW MUSEUM HAD BEEN cleared of cars, and crowds of people gathered, waiting. On top of the small, half-circle awning, Camymddwyn and Canhem perched.

"A thousand years," said Canhem.

"Not quite a thousand, yet," said Camy. "Still, you have to admit it's largely worked out. In a choice between extermination and adaptation, I think we chose correctly. I mean, look what happened to the *Irish* fey when Fionnbharr went all nutty."

Down the street, a parade of horse-skulls began to move. Men carried the grim things on poles, cloth draping down to cover all but the bottom portions of their legs. The skulls bounced up and down, lit by the streetlights above them. Here and there, one of the Grey Mares would dip, approaching the face of some small child, who would recoil and squeal in terror and delight.

"The Mari-Llwyd," said Canhem. "Still dancing, after all this time."

"Aye," said Camy. "They worship their God, and they respect their otherworldly King. The Pact holds."

Canhem shook his head and smiled. "That it does. But still, we are who we are. Shall we go have some fun?"

BLIND DATE BLUES

MADISON KELLER

About the Author: Madison Keller is the author of the epic fantasy Flower's Fang series of young adult fantasy novels, the humorous fantasy Dragonsbane Saga novella series, as well as numerous short stories. Madison originally hails from the great state of Utah, but for the last eight years they have made the Pacific Northwest their home. When not writing Madison enjoys bicycle riding, sewing, and playing Dungeons and Dragons with their pals. They live in Oregon with their partner and their pack of adorable Chihuahua mixes.

Find out more at http://www.flowersfang.com.

Blind Date Blues
Madison Keller

"So, do we think this a good idea?" Sam said, propping the phone up with her shoulder while she held a dress in front of her reflection. The red complimented her dusky brown fur and eyes, but it was too revealing for a first date.

"Well," Parker said. Sam could practically hear the shrug. "It's your cow."

"He's a bull, Parker, not a cow." Sam rolled her eyes.

She dropped the dress and picked up another one. This one was a cotton sun dress with a red paisley pattern. She held it up and twirled in front of the mirror, using her wide, flat tail to stop her momentum. Perfect.

"I still can't believe you are going on blind date," Parker chided. "And a *cow*, at that."

In the background, his cubs began singing. "A beaver and a cow, sitting in a tree, k. i. s. s.—" There was the sound of a door slamming and the singing cut off.

"They better not do that during the date," Sam growled. She clicked her phone over to speaker-phone and laid it on the bed so she could pull on the dress.

"Don't worry, we got them a sitter."

Sam laughed as she picked up a brush and began resettling the fur that had been rumpled by the dress. "They must be furious that you're going to the carnival without them."

Parker paused. "We, uh, didn't tell them where we were going."

"They're going to smell it on your fur when you get back," Sam warned in a good natured tone.

"I know." Parker sounded resigned, but then his voice perked up. "Anyway, we'll pick you up in ten minutes." Parker hung up without saying goodbye.

Sam turned and regarded herself in the mirror once more. The sleeveless dress hit her about mid-thigh, with crisscrossed straps over her shoulders that left her arms and upper back bare.

It looked good, but it was missing something. She went over to the closet and regarded her hat boxes. She had a cute straw sun hat with a fabric band and bow that matched the dress, but a hat would be impractical on the rides and prone to be blown away or lost. Still, it was too adorable not to wear.

She grabbed a pawful of bobby pins from her bathroom on the way out. Parker's wife Stacy could help her pin the hat in place.

Rather than leave through the underwater entrance to her lodge, she climbed the ladder set in the corner of her living room and exited via the hatch in the roof.

Parker's mini-van turned into the Lake Bybee's parking lot as Sam stepped off the dock.

THEY ARRIVED AT WATERFRONT PARK AS THE GATES FOR THE Portland Rose Festival opened for the morning. The Festival grounds took up the entirety of the west side of the waterfront along the Willamette River. Parker dropped Stacy and Sam off by the gate before driving off to locate parking.

The waterfront was particularly pretty this summer morning. Seagulls glided overhead, white specks against the blue sky. A northern breeze ruffled Sam's fur, the cold air taking the edge off the heat.

Despite the extra pounds she still carried from her last pregnancy, Stacy walked like a dancer, skipping and hoping along in a way that Sam could never hope to duplicate. Sam waddled off, which wasn't very fast on her stubby little webbed feet. In water, she always felt graceful and dexterous, but on land she felt awkward and disproportioned. Especially while walking next to the nimble raccoon woman.

Once at the gate, Sam's date was easy to spot. The tan-furred

Texas Longhorn relaxed against the fence in a casual-yet-confident pose, muscled arms tucked into the pockets of his jeans, one leg extended and the other bent back to rest against the fence.

His cowboy hat did nothing to hide the two long horns that curved out from his head. It was pulled down low over his forehead to shade his eyes against the bright morning sunshine. He wore jeans and a white, embroidered western shirt, and together the entire outfit screamed cowboy.

"There he is," Sam said, pointing out the bull lounging by the gate to Stacy. "My date, Oscar Widehorn."

Stacy's eyes widened. "He's a bull? But, he's so short!"

True to his word, Oscar stood barely taller than Sam's own two and a half feet. Even more amazing, he looked exactly like his online profile picture.

Oscar straightened from his slouch as Sam and Stacy approached and tilted his hat back. He flashed them a wide grin as he waved them over. "You must be Samantha."

"I am." Stacy hung back while Sam went over to Oscar and offered him her paw. Oscar's hoof-like finger tips were rough on her webs, although his grip was surprisingly gentle.

When Oscar drew back from the shake Sam gestured to Stacy who stepped up next to her with a smile.

"Oscar, pleased to meet you. I'm Stacy, Parker's wife. I'd like to say Sam told us so much about you, but, well, she didn't."

She must not have heard her cubs singing, or maybe she thought it had been a joke.

Stacy shot Sam a dirty look. "I'm sorry I'm a bit flustered. I admit I thought you'd be a beaver."

To his credit, Oscar took Stacy's sniping in stride. He nodded, his expression serious. In a deadpan voice he said, "I get that a lot."

Sam laughed but Stacy scowled.

"What's so funny?" Parker asked, coming up from behind them to stand next to Stacy.

"Just a slight misunderstanding," Sam said, smiling at Oscar. "Anyway, Oscar, this is my partner, Parker."

"Pleased to meet you," Oscar said politely to the raccoon. "Samantha's told me a lot about you."

Parker's black eyes lit up. "All bad things, I hope. After all, I have a reputation to uphold."

"You'd be surprised." Sam cut in, flustered. "Shall we go in?"

"Of course, m'lady." Oscar held out his elbow to Sam.

Sam suppressed a groan at the antiquated wording and overly condescending manner. He'd been so sweet and soft-spoken online that caught her off guard. However, to be polite she reached out and took his elbow. It was a bit awkward; he was short for a bull, tiny even, but he was still a bit taller than Sam.

Inside the festival grounds Sam waved to a pair of on-duty PPD patrolmen watching the incoming attendees. One of the pair was Theo, a lean otter who'd grown up in her Lake Bybee neighborhood.

Theo puffed up his chest and gave her a sharp salute. His partner, a porcupine and a long time veteran of the department, smiled ruefully and shook her head at Theo's behavior before turning her attention back to her duties.

"So, Oscar," Stacy said, dragging Parker forward so that they walked on Oscar's other side. "What do you do for a living?"

Sam cocked her head to look up at him, also curious about the answer. Online, he'd told her that he'd moved to Portland from New Mexico to take a position at a local startup, but had been a little vague about what exactly that position was or what company.

Oscar hesitated and glanced at Sam. "I'm working as a lab technician right now while I finish getting my Oregon certifications," he said after a pause. "I graduated last year with a Ph.D in chemistry, but some of my New Mexico certs didn't transfer."

"So Lab Technician isn't the job that brought you up here?" Sam asked. Her eyes had widened as Oscar had spoken. Like Theo, she'd gone straight to the academy after High School and never looked back. Oscar's admission made her doubt that she was good enough for him.

"No, but it's only going to be for a few more weeks at most." Abruptly he shifted direction, turning towards the rows of carnival games.

Sam let go of his arm and jumped back, trying to keep her feet out from under his clomping hooves. She steadied herself with her flat tail, or she would have fallen over. At least Oscar noticed her distress and stopped.

"Ah, sorry," he said, having the grace to look embarrassed, with ears and tail drooped.

"It's fine," Sam said. "But we need to buy tickets before we can play the games." She pointed a webbed finger towards the closest ticket booth situated at the beginning of the midway. It had a sign over the top that read "Tickets Sold Here" and was painted a bright yellow.

They walked over as a group, where Oscar graciously offered to buy enough tickets for all of them.

"Thanks, but I'm not interested in games, just food." Parker said, his whiskers and nose twitching. Sam smelled it too, the aroma of fat and fried sugar wafting over from the line of food carts nearby.

"How about we meet up in half an hour? Then we can go on the rides together," Stacy said to her and Oscar, but her head was swiveled around staring at the food carts. Raccoons, honestly.

Sam hesitated. She wasn't sure about being left alone with Oscar that long; it defeated the purpose of the double date.

"Sure. Meet back here in thirty," Oscar said.

Before Sam could protested Parker and Stacy were off.

Oscar handed Sam some of the tickets as they walked into the midway. "Anything catch your eye?"

Sam stopped to consider the arrayed games and then pointed to the Shooting Gallery. This particular one had air rifles and targets shaped like birds. The banner at the back read "Shoot

Ducks to win!" Homely tchotchke prizes hung from the ceiling and down each of the poles in front.

Oscar's muzzle wrinkled in a horrified expression and he snorted. "Wouldn't you rather play Skeeball, or, oh, I know!" he flexed his arm for Sam, causing the muscles to swell against the fabric of his white button up shirt. "I can impress you on the Strongman Game."

"Oh, c'mon." She gestured to his cowboy hat, Western shirt, and jeans. "Surely a strong cowboy like you isn't afraid of me beating you in a shooting contest?"

Oscar pouted and batted his eyelashes at her. They were very long, thick eyelashes. She caught herself admiring them and chastised herself. This date was going downhill fast; he might be attractive but that was about it. She wondered where the funny, thoughtful guy that she'd chatted with online for the last two weeks had gone.

"Fine, Shooting Gallery. But Strongman Game next," Oscar said.

"How about the Shooting Gallery winner picks the next game?" Sam lobbed back at him.

He deflated a bit, but nodded. "Best two out of three."

Sam agreed, so they made their way over to the Shooting Gallery booth and each gave their tickets to the mongoose behind the counter.

"You get ten shots," the mongoose said, stepping aside. "If you can hit seven targets you win the smallest prize." When he finished his speech he hit a button on the side of the target area and the little ducks began bobbing and weaving about on the backboard.

"Ladies first," Oscar said, pressing one of the air rifles into her paws.

Sam lifted it and took a moment to become familiar with its weight and heft. Then she raised it to her shoulder, sighted down the barrel at the wooden ducks, and pulled the trigger. Pop-pop-pop. Each shot found a target.

"Wow!" the mongoose exclaimed when she was done. "You hit ten out of ten. For that you can pick one of the medium prizes."

Sam selected a garish orange and purple plush raccoon to give to Parker's kids. When she was done she stepped back, hugging the ugly thing to herself, and gestured to Oscar. "Your turn."

He picked up the rifle and held it awkwardly as he aimed towards the little bouncing ducks. The air rifle popped several times. Sam watched the board expectantly, but none of the ducks flipped back.

"That's odd. It worked for me," she said when Oscar was out of shots and all of the targets were upright. "Best two out of three, right?"

Oscar pulled his cowboy hat down and turned away. "No, it's fine. You win. I forgot you were a cop when I made that bet."

She smiled. "I guess I do have a bit of an unfair advantage, but I thought with you growing up on a cattle farm that you'd know how to shoot."

Oscar shrugged his broad shoulders and glanced over at her, eyes wary. "Never much good at it. In any case, you won our bet. So what game do you want to try next?"

"Now I feel bad, taking advantage of you like that!" Sam slapped her tail on the grass, sending up a little puff of dust. "How about you show me the Strongman?"

Oscar's face lit up, and he gave Sam a little smile. "Alright."

The employee manning the Strongman Game, a bighorn sheep with curling horns that towered three feet taller than both Oscar and Sam, was calling out to passerby's as they approached. "Step right up, test your strength! Show your lady you're a man and not a boy!"

He spotted Oscar and Sam and pointed a finger at Oscar. "You there, pocket bull! This is your chance to show your girl there that you're only tiny in size, not spirit."

Oscar grinned and winked at Sam, and gave the sheep a ticket. The sheep stepped aside and pointed to a line of rubber mallets of various sizes lined up near the Strongman's striker plate. Oscar selected a mallet with a handle almost as tall as himself, grunting with effort as he hefted it over his shoulder.

The sheep bleated with surprise but recovered and began heckling. "Oh, tiny here thinks he's a big bull. Let's see if he can pull it off!"

Oscar staggered as he stepped over in front of the striker plate. He lined up, gripping the mallet with booth hooved hands. He lifted it off his shoulder and up, his arms shaking with effort. As he swung he slightly turned his head, and the rubber edge of the mallet caught on one of his horns. His blow went wide, barely hitting the edge of the striker.

The little puck jumped up, and the bulbs on the sides began to light up. One. Two. Three. Sam counted the bulbs; fifteen total lined each side.

"Better luck next time," the sheep said, casually picking up the mallet and placing it back with the others.

Oscar huffed. One back hoof pawed at the ground making round little divots in the grass. "Again." He handed the sheep another ticket.

"Oscar, really, there's no need to—" Sam began, but cut off when Oscar glared at her.

Sam sighed and hugged her garish plush raccoon to her chest as Oscar selected a mallet. At least he chose a slightly smaller and lighter one than before.

This time his blow hit the plate dead center. The little puck flew up, and Sam was sure it was going to ring the gong at the top. Two bulbs from the top it plummeted back down.

Oscar's eyes narrowed and his chest heaved as the bighorn sheep took back the mallet.

Sam waved to get Oscar's attention before he could insist on another try. When he glanced her way she pointed towards the food carts. "Time to go meet Parker and Stacy."

Oscar didn't say anything as they headed back to the midway's entrance.

"Good job with that second hit!" Sam said, trying to cheer him up. "Only two away from the bell."

"Stop making fun of me," Oscar growled.

Sam slapped her tail on the ground. "I'm not! I was complimenting you. You know those things are calibrated to challenge even bigger animals. Trust me, I'm impressed you hit it hard enough to get that close."

Oscar was silent the rest of the way back to the meeting spot. His expression was distant, and she hoped he was mulling over her words.

Parker and Stacy were waiting for them when they exited the midway. Parker carried a paper plate that contained a piece of fried dough bigger than his head.

"Want some bear claw?" he said, thrusting the plate towards them. Then he spotted Sam's plushie. "Nice raccoon, Digger."

Sam grinned back at him. "Thanks. I'm thinking of making it my next partner. At least then I'd get some peace and quiet in the office."

Parker held a paw in front of his eyes and squinted through his fingers. "You planning to blind the suspects with it before you question them?"

She laughed. "It is pretty brightly colored, isn't it? But I thought your kids might like it."

While she and Parker bantered Oscar tore two pieces off the bear claw. He offered one to Sam, who tucked the plush under an arm to take it from him.

Overhead a gull cawed and a second later a feral seagull was beating her about the head and face with its wings. Sam screamed and dropped the plush raccoon to swat at the bird.

In the chaos she saw that Parker and Stacy had somehow managed to protect the rest of the bear claw from the thief. So the bird turned and snapped its beak down on the piece of bear claw she held, ripping it free of her paw before launching away with a screech.

The gull's feet hit her hat as it winged away, tearing the bobby pins free of her fur. The breeze caught the wide hat and lifted it up way and into the air.

"My hat," Sam cried and grabbed for it, but it the wind twisted it up and out of her reach.

"I'll get it for you!" Oscar cried, charging after it.

Sam waddled after him, cursing her short legs. The breeze carried her hat over the midway games and towards the river. Oscar galloped through the growing crowd, mooing loudly to clear himself a path.

The hat fluttered over the last row of games, clearing the eight foot high chain-link fence that separated the festival from the river and walking path.

Sam emerged from between two of the carnival games in time to see Oscar shaking scraps of chain-link from his horns. There was a hole torn in the fence where he'd charged right through it. Someone behind her called for security, and someone else for the police.

"Oscar, stop! It's just a hat!" Sam yelled, but Oscar either didn't hear or ignored her.

The breeze shifted to blow downriver, blowing the hat south above the sidewalk. A railing along one edge kept pedestrians from falling into the river, forty feet below.

Roller skaters, bikers, and walkers were out in force today on the path, taking advantage of the perfect Portland summer day. The hat floated overtop their heads, oscillating gently in the breeze.

Oscar charged after it, letting out a rumbling sound more like a bark than a moo. Heads turned and eyes widened as people saw the enraged bull charging towards them.

A bicycling rabbit directly in Oscar's path let out a high pitched scream and jerked his bike to the side, causing him to crash into a nearby bench. He pitched head-over-heels into the grass.

A skunk couple pushing a stroller with their backs to Oscar let out startled yelps at Oscar's bellow. The skunk mother lifted her tail at Oscar as he charged by and greenish-yellow goo sprayed out, splattering all over his right side.

Oscar didn't even seem to notice or slow down, but the rest of the animals on the trail fell back gagging and retching. The breeze carried the scent away from Sam, for which she was grateful.

Beavers were neither fast nor graceful on land. Sam stopped running, since she was never going to catch up with Oscar.

She'd halted before she reached the skunk couple, but already her eyes were watering from the pungent stink. Not all the spray had hit Oscar. The sidewalk was going to need a thorough cleaning before people would be willing to use this path again.

By now, most of the pedestrians had fled. In the distance, Oscar still chased after her recalcitrant straw hat. He was fast, but the breeze was faster and the hat danced about in the air a finger's length out of Oscar's reach, despite his impressive jumps.

The hat fluttered to the side and drifted lower. Oscar saw his chance, lowering his head and pumping his legs as he prepared to make another running jump.

"Oscar, no!" Sam cried, able to anticipate what would happen.

Oscar's legs bunched and he bounded up, high into the air. His hooved hand closed over the rim of the hat just as he cleared the railing. An expression of comical surprise crossed his face as he plummeted out of her field of view.

Sam cursed and darted for the railing. The bars were far enough apart here that she was able to squeeze between them, rather than having to waste time climbing over.

Oscar had fallen in a ways downriver of her, and the rushing water would quickly sweep him downstream. She didn't know if he could swim or not, but there was no time to wait to find out.

Out of the corner of her eye she spotted Theo and the porcupine officer coming up behind her.

"The longhorn I was with earlier fell into the river. Call for help," Sam yelled at them. She turned and dove into the water without waiting to hear their reply.

She was much faster in the water than on land. She pointed

herself downriver and shot through the water as fast as she could swim.

The river was murky and visibility was down to only a yard around her. She never thought she'd be grateful for the nauseating odor of skunk spray, but the stench was bad enough that it overpowered the rest of the river scents. She followed her nose until she spotted him.

Oscar was actually swimming rather well, paddling his arms and legs to keep his head above water. He fought against the current towards the shore without much success. Not that it would matter much if he got there; at this point there was still a sheer wall with no way out of the water.

Sam surfaced and swam over to him. "We can't get out here, we have to go further down," she called at his back. "Past the Hawthorne Bridge."

Oscar didn't even turn her direction and she cursed herself. Of course he wouldn't know which bridge she meant.

"See the bridge downstream?" she yelled, splashing water at Oscar's face to get his attention. "We need to swim under it to get to a beach."

"No," Oscar grunted, responding to her at last. "Ladder."

Sam followed his gaze, squinting against the spray. A series of darker gray lines stood out against the gray of the cinderblock waterfront. She looked between the ladder and Oscar, calculating. He wasn't going to make it to the ladder at his current rate of progress; he'd be too far downstream, and he wasn't a strong enough swimmer to make any headway against the current.

There was nothing for it, she'd have to help him. She spared a second to think about the best way to accomplish that. Maybe if she swam up to him at an angle, pushing against his back?

"Here, I'll help push you. Otherwise you aren't going to make it," Sam said, already swimming towards him.

"I don't need your help," he grumbled, but didn't object when Sam's paws hit his back.

Together they managed to make it to the ladder. Oscar got a

hooved hand around the bottom rung. He got one elbow up over the rung and hung there, panting hard. Sam treaded water at his side.

"Do you need me to help boost you up?" Sam asked. She really wanted to swim away; the skunk odor was almost overwhelming this close, but Oscar looked exhausted and she didn't dare leave him here. Muted sirens came from somewhere up above.

Oscar swallowed and lifted his other hand out of the water. Clutched in his fingers was her straw hat. "I retrieved your—" he gasped. "Your hat."

Sam couldn't help it, she laughed. "Thank you." She took it and perched the soggy thing on her head. She was sure she looked as bedraggled as Oscar, but it was the thought that counted. This wasn't really the time or the place to have this talk, but it would give Oscar a chance to rest and recover for the climb up. "I appreciate it, I do, and you seem like a sweet guy Oscar, but you're trying too hard."

Oscar seemed to deflate, slumping down over the rung and hunching his shoulders. "I really like you. You're a tough-as-nails cop, and I'm," he kicked a hoof into the cinderblocks. "I wanted to impress you."

"By acting like a tough guy?"

Oscar nodded. She only now noticed that he'd lost his cowboy hat at some point. He looked better without half his face hidden in shadow. But, something seemed different. She squinted at him as she tried to pinpoint what.

Sam sighed. "I liked you online because you weren't like the other guys. You were funny and sensitive, and," she paused. "Wasn't your fur all tan before?" It still was, mostly, except for a misshaped patch of white around one eye and a white triangle in the middle of his forehead. She'd only ever seen that mark on horses before, but the way he deflated further made her hold her tongue on commenting on that fact.

"I guess that batch wasn't as waterproof as I thought," he muttered, mostly to himself.

"Batch?" She was thoroughly confused now.

"Hey, Detective Digger!" The yells came from above.

Sam craned her head back. A brown, round head poked out above the ladder. She couldn't make out features, but she recognized the Otter's voice.

"Theo!" She yelled back. "Stay up there, we're on our way up." She turned to Oscar. "Perhaps we should finish this discussion once we are back up on dry land."

He grimaced and snorted. "If you insist."

With a grunt of effort he grasped the ladder and pulled himself up to get his hooves on the lowest rung. When he was a few feet up Sam started up after him. The water dripping down on her from Oscar stunk of skunk. She grimaced as they hit. She was going to have a nice long tomato juice bath when she got home.

Halfway up, Oscar's exhaustion became evident. Even from below she could see the tremor in his arms and legs.

"You can do it," Sam called up. She yelled encouragement to him for the remainder of the climb.

By the time she pulled herself up over the top of the ladder Oscar was sitting on the sidewalk, wrapped up in a shiny thermal blanket. A fluffy, white, flat-faced Persian Cat EMT was shining a light into the shivering Oscar's eyes and asking him questions.

Theo, along with the Porcupine officer, and two more EMTs, a Human and an Opossum, stood well back from Oscar. All held their hands or paws over their noses. She guessed the cat must have drawn the short straw, or maybe he'd volunteered. She'd heard those flat muzzled animals sometimes had a poor sense of smell.

Theo let out a squeak of relief as Sam climbed onto the sidewalk. She flopped out on her back, enjoying the warm sun on her fur. Theo and the human EMT approached her. The human shook out a thermal blanket, but Sam held up a paw and pushed it back at her.

"I don't need it. My fur kept me warm," Sam said. She was interrupted as Theo flung his arms around her. He gave her a quick hug, before wrinkling his muzzle and jumping back.

"You *reek*," he told her, covering his nose with both paws.

"Thanks for noticing," she responded dryly. She pushed herself to her feet and waddled over towards Oscar. Theo and the human EMT hung back, unwilling to get closer.

Oscar looked miserable. He was shivering under the thermal blanket, and his fur was plastered down, making the white patches even more noticeable. At Sam's approach he hunched his shoulders, pulling the blanket tighter around him.

Waves of stink rolled off him, so strong she almost imagined she could see them. A glance at the cat EMT's serene expression told her that her guess about him lacking a sense of smell had probably been correct.

"How is he?" Sam asked, addressing the cat.

"Chilled, but he isn't hypothermic, at least." The cat straightened up to address both Sam and Oscar. "He's still in danger of pneumonia if he inhaled any of the water when he fell in."

"Does he need to go to the hospital?"

The cat rubbed his chin thoughtfully. "We can take him if he wants to go - we could warm him up a lot faster there - but it isn't strictly necessary, no."

"No hospital," Oscar said through chattering teeth.

The cat shrugged. "Fine by me. Keep the blanket." He turned away and together the three EMTs trudged off across the grass to the ambulance parked on the nearby street.

"Sam," Theo called.

Sam turned to look in his direction. He'd lifted a paw from his nose and was gesturing to her. Sam looked down at Oscar. "Wait here, I'll be right back."

Oscar sighed and nodded, resignation in his eyes. Good enough for her. She waddled over to Theo and the Porcupine.

The Porcupine officer held up a yellow ticket book. "Will you have the cow fill this out and bring it back?" She wrinkled her nose and shuddered, making all her quills clatter together. "I tried to go over and present it myself, but, goddess help me, the smell..."

Sam sighed and took the proffered book. "He's a guy, so he's a bull, not a cow," she told the Porcupine, who shrugged.

The top form was filled out with a ticket for reckless behavior and vandalism. Sam carried the book over and waited while Oscar entered his information into the form. When he was done she returned the book to the Porcupine officer.

Job done, Theo and the Porcupine took off, Theo offering her a little wave as they left, and Sam returned to Oscar.

Pedestrian traffic had resumed on the waterfront, but Oscar's smell meant that everyone gave them a wide berth, leaving a clear space in a wide circle around them.

Sam relaxed back on her tail and crossed her arms as she regarded the bull.

"You make a horrible tough guy," she said at last.

Oscar boomed out a laugh and shook his horned head. "I know."

"You were so sweet online. That was what I liked about you. So, why'd you'd think that act would impress me? Plus," she gestured to his face, "why the fur make-up? And why so evasive about your job?"

"Truthfully? Back home the cows all kept telling me to be more of man. I came to Portland to get a fresh start, to get away from all that." A massive sneeze shook his body. "Excuse me. Anyway, when you said you wanted to meet in person, I panicked. I remembered the cows and that you were a cop. I didn't want to disappoint you, too." He fell silent.

Sam waited a moment for him to begin speaking again. When he didn't she prompted, "and the rest?"

"It's embarrassing. This," he ran a hooved finger up his nose to touch the white triangle. "Is a horse marking, not a cattle one. I used to get teased about it relentlessly until I started covering it up.

"Buying fur dye was how I discovered my love for make-up," he batted his eyes at her. His lashes were longer and thicker than most cows she'd seen and she finally put together why.

"You have on mascara, too?" Sam blinked.

He chuckled, a low rumble that vibrated in Sam's chest pleasantly. He had a nice laugh. "Yeah, the water-proofing on that, at least, worked as I intended."

" 'As you intended' makes it sound like you made it yourself." Sam couldn't help but smile back at him.

He glanced away. "I did. It's a test batch. I, uh, didn't lie when I said I was a lab tech. I helped start *Swimming Beautiful*."

"The local fur cosmetics company?" Sam said. They were the brainchild of Portland's hottest new breakout entrepreneur.

"Yeah," he was still talking to the ground, occasionally glancing at her with his big brown eyes. "Specializing in products for Aquatics."

"But," Sam protested, "that company was started by a Nutria."

Oscar brightened. "Yeah, she runs the business side of the things, the marketing and the like, and I design the product formulas. I got my degree in Cosmetic Chemistry. She approached me before graduation. I wrote my Ph.D thesis on ways to waterproof fur makeup, since I was frustrated when mine kept getting washed away during my work on the farm."

"That's amazing." Sam smiled at his obvious enthusiasm about makeup.

"You don't mind?" He was staring at her wide eyed now.

"Why would I? Honestly, right now you're impressing me far more than your antics earlier at the Shooting Gallery and the Strongman Game," Sam said. Here was the bull she'd been chatting with online, who was sensitive, smart, and enthusiastic.

Oscar grimaced and looked down at his sodden and bedraggled self, clothing splattered with green skunk spray. "I really messed that date up, huh?"

"Just a tad." Sam straightened, putting her paws on her hips. "I happen to have tomorrow off work, too, so I expect you to pick me up tomorrow afternoon for a first date-do-over."

Oscar's smile could have been seen from the moon it was so bright.

"But," she held up a paw. "There is one condition."

His smile dimmed, but he looked more amused than anything. "What's that?"

"No carnivals!" Sam slapped her tail forcefully on the sidewalk to make her point.

THE ELFIN COW

DEBY FREDERICKS

About the Author: Deby Fredericks has been a writer all her life, but thought of it as just a fun hobby until the late 1990s. She made her first sale, a children's poem, in 2000.

Fredericks has six fantasy novels out through two small presses. The latest is *The Grimhold Wolf*, released by Sky Warrior in 2015. Her children's stories and poems have appeared in magazines such as *Boys' Life, Babybug, Ladybug*, and a few anthologies. In the past, she served as Regional Advisor for the Inland Northwest Region of the Society of Children's Book Writers and Illustrators, International (SCBWI).

The Elfin Cow
Deby Fredericks

Pawl the Butcher went to stand at the pasture fence, where Farmer Clydno gazed over his herd of cattle. After a moment, he asked, "So, do we think this is a good idea?"

"Well, it is my cow," Clydno pointed out.

His daughter burst from the house, crying, "No, Father, no!"

Young Gwynedd was as pretty as she was kind-hearted. The skirt of her woolen bedgown flowed behind her, and a lacy cap covered her braided hair. Pawl cast a sympathetic eye upon her.

"Men have to eat, miss."

With a heavy thud, he set his great hammer on the trestle table set out in the yard. Opening his bag, he laid out a selection of keen knives.

"That's right." Clydno cast a greedy eye toward the pasture.

Anwyn, the white cow, ambled up to the fence. Her ears were pointed forward with friendly interest. She was round as a ball of butter after having been fattened all summer for her appointment with the butcher.

"This isn't right." Gwynedd's two hands knotted in the paisley shawl that covered her shoulders. "Think what she means to us."

Clydno caught his breath as anger surged in his breast. The girl meant well, but she was too young to remember the hard years gone by. He straightened his shoulders and glared at her.

Off down the valley, the lake of Llyn Barfog glistened under a bright morning sky. The hills of Wales were turning yellow with fall, but he could never forget their emerald brilliance on a cold spring morning ten years ago.

There had always been rumors in their village of Dyssyrnant. It was said that a clan of beautiful ladies lived beneath the waves of Llyn Barfog. In the pub, late at night, hunters claimed to have seen these women of elfin beauty dressed all in green. A pack of moon-white hounds was ever with them. Or sometimes men told that their uncles, or their grandfathers, or such like, had glimpsed a herd of pure white cattle grazing along the lake shore. Gwarthe y Llyn they called them, the cattle of the lake.

Clydno had paid no mind to such stories. He was a practical man, and what's more, a desperately poor one. Forever he seemed to be mired in the struggles of life. His farm stood on rocky ground, so that he must scrape for any bit of wheat or a few potatoes to feed his wife and young child. His chief wealth was a handful of nut-brown cattle passed down from his father, but with such poor grazing they gave him little enough meat or milk.

That early spring morning, he'd gone to the lake to catch a few fish. Instead he caught a stroke of luck. One single white cow wandered along the shore, lowing plaintively.

"Well, aren't you pretty?" the farmer cried.

Indeed she was — in the way of a cow — wide and sturdy, with a broad brow and no horns on her head. Not a single dark hair soiled her swan-white hide. Even her great eyes were silvery gray.

It seemed this cow had always been well treated, for she came right up to Clydno. When he crooned to her, she followed him all the way back to his pasture. The other cows gathered quietly around her, as if a queen walked among them.

"She must belong to someone," his wife, Gwernen, had said.

"I know, my dear." Clydno had sighed, for it would pain him to let this good fortune go. "At least we'll have the extra milk until her owner turns up."

In good faith, Clydno did pass the word in Dyssyrnant that he'd found a stray cow. All the neighbors came by to admire her and exclaim over her beauty.

"Gwarth y llyn," they cried. "An elfin cow. The ladies of Llyn Barfog have favored you."

"She's just a cow," scoffed Clydno.

Since none of the neighbors could fairly claim her, the white cow stayed on with Clydno's herd.

He called her Anwyn, meaning *blessed*, and indeed she brought many blessings to the struggling farm. For one thing, she soon dropped a bull calf. Her milk was plentiful and rich. Even with a calf to suckle, she gave enough for the family to drink and still allow Gwernen to make butter and cheese.

Days turned into weeks, and Gwernen's cheese was the prize of Dyssyrnant. On market days, much coin jingled in Clydno's pocket. He bought a tall felt hat for Gwernen and a china doll for young Gwynedd.

Weeks turned into months. All about the farm, things that had been crooked were straightened up, and whatever was crumbling got patched. Months turned into years. With a young bull cavorting among them, the rest of the herd dropped their own calves in time. Every last one of them was white.

TEN YEARS ON, CLYDNO WAS THE MASTER OF A PROSPEROUS farm. In town he boasted of his large cattle herd. Each cow was as gentle and productive as Anwyn. The house and cow byre were well built and maintained. Though Gwernen had passed on, Gwynedd had grown up strong and healthy because of Anwyn's good milk. She wore sturdy wool instead of shabby cotton, and her cheeks glowed with beauty.

Only now, her fair brow creased in a frown and tears glimmered in her eyes.

"Don't do it, Father! Not to dear old Anwyn."

"Now, now," he tried to console her. "You can see that we need to make room for next year's calves."

And the butcher added, kindly, "It's only sense that the oldest go first, miss."

Gwynedd wiped her eyes and frowned. "It is wrong to scorn a gift from Llyn Barfog."

For the first time, her father scowled back at her. "Nonsense! It's just a cow."

He'd been all summer fattening the cow. The profits he expected from sale of so much beef jingled enticingly in his mind. At last the day had come. The butcher was here, with all his tools, and whatever regrets Clydno had, his pride awoke in him. Anwyn was the best thing that ever happened to him, and no one was going to deny him even one bit of his good fortune.

"Go in the house, daughter," he ordered curtly. "My mind is made up."

Despite Gwynedd's weeping, the cow was led out and tethered in place. She bawled mournfully while Pawl tied on his apron and rolled his sleeves back. He raised up his great hammer and swung with all his might. The hammer struck Anwyn fair and hard between her eyes.

But when the blow fell, she did not. A great shriek of pain and betrayal echoed over the hills. Then the weapon rebounded and flung both men off their feet. They tumbled backward and knocked the table flat. All the butcher's tools went flying.

Gwynedd stood trembling and blinking. And then, it seemed a vision appeared to her. Far across the valley, a woman dressed in green stood high on a hilltop above Llyn Barfog. In a trumpet's voice she cried out.

"Come, blessed Anwyn, strayed from the lake. From the Gwarthe y llyn you have been lost. Arise now, and come home!"

The elfin cow reared back, snapping the ropes that held her. She bolted through the pasture, bawling to her kindred with the summons of her kind. As one, the cattle took up her call. They stampeded through the pasture, mad with fear, then followed as Anwyn crashed through the fence. Across the hills they streamed, until they had all disappeared from sight.

Gwynedd ran to see if the men were all right, and then she gave chase, but in vain. The swan-white cattle were gone. Even the third and fourth generation of Anwyn's line had gone with her in her flight. Only a handful of cows were left, and they had all turned black as the soot in the fireplace.

Pawl the Butcher lay for a long time, feeling the earth spin beneath him. As for Clydno, he wailed with despair when he saw what had happened.

"Alas! I am ruined. We may as well drown ourselves in Llyn Barfog, rather than live in poverty again."

So saying, he struggled to his feet and limped in the direction of the lake. Again, his daughter ran to stop him.

"Father, no! Do not lose hope. We have as much as you had before — a handful of cattle, and pasture to graze them. Let us be glad for the mercy of ten good years, and resolve to somehow regain the favor of the elfin ladies."

What choice was there, truly? Once again Clydno scraped in the dirt for a bit of wheat or a few potatoes. But the village of Dyssyrnant never again saw the likes of that elfin cow.

ALL DONE

PROGRAMMING LOYALTY

THOMAS GONDOLFI

About the Author: Thomas Gondolfi is the author of the *Toy Wars* series, and the *CorpGov Chronicles*. He is a father of three, consummate gamer (board or role-playing) and loving husband. Tom also claims to be a Renaissance man and certified flirt.

Raised as a military brat, he spent the first twenty years of his life moving to a new place every few years giving him a unique perspective on most regions of the United States.

Educated as an electrical engineer and working in high tech for over twenty years, Tom has also worked as a cook, motel manager, most phases of home construction, volunteer firefighter for eight years, and even as the personal caregiver to a quadriplegic.

Thomas founded TANSTAAAFL Press four years ago in the Pacific Northwest. TANSTAAFL Press now publishes the novels of four authors and will begin an anthology series later this year.

Programming Loyalty
Thomas Gondolfi

"SO, DO WE THINK THIS IS A GOOD IDEA?"

"Well...it's your cow."

"We wish people would stop calling them cows. They are Cybernetically Optimized Warriors," the prince barked, retaining the royal 'we.'

The prince leaned back on his temporary throne, his robes filthy from six days without a change.

"Yes, your highness," the chamberlain replied humbly. "But as you have been overseeing the cow —" The chamberlain caught the storm building on the prince's face. "— I mean Cybernetically Optimized Warrior program, you know more about it than I, sire."

The prince stood and paced the panic room. He toed the stacked remnants of meals. "Do we have any choice, my friend?"

"I hoped that your loyal forces would once again take the palace and rescue your highness." The chamberlain stood straight and tall. He managed to retain his dignity in spite of his fear, wrinkled clothing, and the soot smudges on his face.

"We agree that we did hear combat the first three days, but no longer."

"I agree, your highness," the chamberlain offered. "Our cameras and all other access to the outside have been compromised, so we don't know what is happening now."

The prince walked over to a thick glass cabinet to stare at the sleeping construct within. The chamberlain shuddered. What the case held could no longer be considered human. The multifaceted, electronic eyes covered most of the upper half of the thing's face. A red crested helm covered its oversized metal skull. The gold, mechanical arms bulged, merging with gray, pallid flesh of the chest. The legs of what had once been a man had been replaced by mechanical monstrosities twice the size of the originals. One could make out dozens of healed surgery scars across the torso and up the neck. These were the tortures the men had to endure to become C.O.W.s. This is what the prince had made out of his elite troopers.

"We did well on this one," the prince remarked. "What was his name?"

"Beant, your highness."

"What an ordinary name for such an exquisite creation," the prince said, fondling the case as if it were a woman he intended to bed. "But you haven't yet answered us, chamberlain. Do we release Beant to free us?"

"We have food to last us months but we are now out of water, prince."

"But we have cases of champagne!"

"I'm sorry, your highness, but alcohol dehydrates. It won't keep us alive."

"Then why did they stock this shelter with it?"

"I believe you ordered it, sire. I seem to remember you threatening the head engineer with having his daughters defiled if he didn't make your favorite refreshment available."

The prince smiled. "Yes, I remember that. A good man, that one."

"That may be, your highness. I believe that we can go a week without water. After a week we will have hallucinations and other debilitating symptoms." After days of terror the chamberlain carried only resignation delivering such bad news. In the past he would have worried about being beheaded. There was no headsman within the bunker. "But to answer the question you have of your servant, I think we have to expect no different behavior from this Cybernetically Optimized Warrior than any of the others."

"Yes," the prince said. "But we programmed them with loyalty to our lineage."

"That didn't exactly work, did it, your highness?"

"We are not pleased with the outcome. But this – Beant – was stored here after twice the indoctrination and infused with more combat capability to save us than all the others. He was the most loyal."

"Weren't they all indoctrinated, sire? Weren't they all loyal before they were mutilated?"

"Yes," the prince whispered. He snapped, "How could my own warriors turn on me?"

"It is incomprehensible, your highness," the chamberlain said managing, with his lifetime of practice, to keep the sarcasm out of his voice.

"But I will get my revenge. I will exact retribution. I will kill them and destroy everyone who they ever cared about. I must teach my people to fear me even as I love them.

"This one won't turn on me," he said petting the glass case again. "He was our favorite. We loved him. He wouldn't risk his family. He knows what would happen to them.

"I would disembowel all of the men and impale the women on spikes through their very womanhood."

"I'm sure he understands that, my prince."

"Then I say let's wait no longer. Prepare the door and I will release the Cybernetically Optimized Warrior."

The chamberlain elected to pick up a brand new, never fired Uzi, from a case of weapons beside the door. While out of practice, he pulled back the bolt to prepare it for use. He typed in the password for the door and waited by the handle.

The prince typed in another password on the glass case. The cyborg inside took its first breath in months. The prince smiled. "Come forth, Beant. We need you."

The warrior pushed open the unlocked glass and stepped forward, its footfalls making the floor shake. It extracted a large handgun from within its metallic forearm.

"Mission?"

"Bodyguard," the prince said, nodding to the chamberlain. The advisor opened the out door. "Clear us a path to safety."

Without missing a beat, the Cybernetically Optimized Warrior turned his gun on the prince, loosing a single large-caliber projectile. The bullet entered the stunned monarch's head and exploded out the other side.

"Safety achieved," the C.O.W. stated flatly. "Safety with you as leader can only be realized with you dead."

A dozen or more C.O.W.s poured through the now open door and saw the red abstract carnage on the wall and the prince's body slumped on the floor. "It is done," one of them said.

"No more pain," offered another.

The chamberlain, his shock now worn off, pointed his Uzi at Beant.

As one, all of the C.O.W.s dropped their weapons. Beant said, quoting another famous assassin, " 'I have done what I had to do. You do what you want to do.' "

The chamberlain lowered his weapon. "I would dispense justice, just as you have. Go with god."

THE MURDER OF DEREK VOLYNSKY

G.R. THERON

About the Author: Seattle based storyteller, photographer, and wanderer. He alternates between projects that sustain his living and projects that sustain his life. One day those will be the same.

The Murder of Derek Volynsky

G.R. Theron

"So, do we think this is a good idea?" Vitale asked.

"Well...it's your cow." I nodded at the husk. For two weeks, we'd been following reports of mutilated livestock. Two interminably long weeks. None of it made sense.

Not much passed for crime in Mineral County, and what did could often be settled with a few words, a stern glance, or (when all else failed) a night sobering up before I called the missus. But that was as far as it went.

These parts had good folk doing honest work. It's what drew me here. No sooner had I poured foreign sand from my boots and given my last salute before I headed for the mountains to make a life of it, away from things best left a decade in the past.

The Bitterroots had drawn Vitale, my deputy, too. Like generations before him, he'd headed west, looking for a fresh start. And Superior, Montana was about as different from New York as one could get.

At first, he worried I'd pause over his last name. Being from the Vocco family meant something in his borough. Meant something to the FBI, too. I didn't mind. One found a lot of things in the Bitterroot Range. If I was here for reincarnation, why not him?

"*My* cow?" Vitale quirked a brow. "You think you're funny, here?"

I grinned and took a sip of coffee. "I think I'm the sheriff."

He snorted. "How about you sheriff up some answers then, boss. This makes number three." Vitale knelt by the husk. "The eyes and reproductive organs are missing again. What would anyone want with those?"

The prior two had also been missing lymph nodes and brain tissue, or so I've been told. The vet would have answers, which would beget more questions of their own. Because no matter what he found, one thing was always missing: blood.

There was no blood anywhere, and there should've been plenty. That made mine run cold.

"Rancher see anything?" I asked.

Vitale stood and pointed north. "Some tracks in the mud, pair of headlights on the hill, and then the stampede. The other cattle ran that way." Vitale pointed south before shaking his head. "You think it's one of them in the hills? That kind ain't too shy what they kill and where."

"Not unless there's a border dispute I don't know about," I said.

"And they're keeping the blood for some reason..." Vitale said, shaking his head as his theory died.

I took a long breath and shrugged. "I keep trying to forget that part, too. Let's see these tracks."

I followed Vitale up the hill to where a forest road met the ranch. A cluster of Ponderosa pines framed the open gate; the chain meant to close it hung limp, the lock cut clean through. A set of tire tracks had carved a trench in the west soil, and splattered mud stuck to the trees and branches.

"More tracks here." Vitale stood about ten feet away from where the tire tracks began. "I can make out two sets. Then, right about here, only these large ones. Seems like the big guy was chasing the other. Then it disappears." He jerked a thumb towards the tire tracks. "Maybe he jumped into the truck?"

"One hell of a jump. That's eight feet if it's one. Short list of folk can make that kind of jump on damp soil at night." I walked over to look at where he pointed.

One set of boot prints disappeared abruptly, yet it was the *size* of the other feet that caught my attention. The imprint dwarfed my size eleven-and-a-half boots. Someone that tall would have weighed far more than the smaller of the two, but only the slight edges of the footprint were visible. They trailed away from the tracks and into the woods.

The radio from dispatch buzzed alive and Vitale stepped away to answer it. "This is Vocco. No, I'm with the Sherriff now."

Ignoring the conversation, I followed the tracks. They were spaced too far apart. As if the man had taken exaggerated leaps with each step. I tried to copy the spacing; every time, my boot sunk a half inch or more into the wet soil.

I didn't see the contorted remains of Derek Volynsky until I was almost standing on them. The twenty-year-old was curled into a fetal position with his head craned backwards, his now gaunt features drawn into an eternal, wordless scream. Vacant sockets stared into the forest as if searching for answers.

How I didn't empty my stomach right then and there, I'll never know. It'd been a while since I'd come across a dead body, and it hadn't prepared me for this. Even downrange, where the *why* of the killing became as blurry as lines in a sand, the *how* of it still made sense. I knew what the pressure on a trigger could do.

Here, the *how* muddled my brain almost as much as the *why*. What could drain a man dry, pull his eyes from his head, and discard him like a crushed can?

"Boss, folks from Fish and Wildlife are waiting at the station for us. Said they've got an idea on what's killing livestock," Vitale yelled up the trail from where I had left him. When I didn't answer he jogged up to meet me. "Hey boss, want me to tell them you'll call them back or—" He gagged and covered his mouth. "Is that what I think it is?"

"Yeah."

"What the hell is going on?"

I ignored his question. I didn't have an answer, or at least none that made any sense. "Call the coroner." I knelt by the body. Derek had been a troublemaker by local standards, which made him a bored young kid by mine. "Then track down whoever was with young Volynsky. Look for his truck. You know the one?"

"I do," Vitale nodded before pointing at his feet. "His boots are about right for the set we found in the mud."

"Sure are," I said. "I figure he and someone else came here last night. Stumbled into something they shouldn't."

He lowered his voice. "Boss, what do we have here? Cattle's

one thing, but this is something else. Everyone's capable of murdering when it comes down to it, but there's always a reason. I can't think of anything that would tie mutilating some cows with killing a young man."

"Someone drove that truck away. We start there."

Vitale was half right. The who and why of it prickled the hairs on the back of my neck but neither mattered more than how. The massive footprints had ended here as well. How had someone that big disappeared?

I needed that answer first.

It was late afternoon when I arrived back at the small, brick station that had become a second, occasionally first, home. Deputy Sarah Gailey met me at the door and asked for an update. Locally born and raised, she had proven herself as an unyielding and fair presence. I told her what I knew, trying to stay clear of speculations and provide a meaningful direction.

Which would have been great if I had one.

"That doesn't make bit of sense," she said when I finished. "Where did the tracks go after the body?"

I suppressed the urge to shrug. Vitale hadn't even thought about it, but I should have known I'd have no such luck with Sarah. "They didn't."

She quirked a brow, a thin smile turning at the corner of her lips. "You want me to take another look?"

I wasn't the best outdoorsman, generally competent with the broad strokes and confident enough to avoid embarrassing myself overmuch. Sarah, on the other hand, had forgotten more than I would ever know, and while she wouldn't come straight out and say it, she enjoyed finding things two city boys missed.

"I wouldn't want to waste your time but if you want..."

She smirked. "Oh, I think you'll need to be more concerned with time being wasted than me."

"I'm heading to my office."

She smirked and gestured towards the hallway that led to my office. "Yes, I know."

A moment later I knew what she meant. Two Fish and Wildlife wardens waited on the oak bench outside my office. They weren't what I had expected. Not by half.

The pair, a man and woman, could have passed for blond twins, or maybe the manifestation of a recruitment poster. Their pale skin and clean, pressed uniforms may as well have been a sign that read 'first time out of office' and the stiff way they stood to greet me did little to convince me otherwise.

A single, leather skinned warden would have made sense. This didn't, and I adjusted my tone and approach. I didn't have time for another mystery, and professional courtesy didn't extend to folks wasting my time.

"Caught me at a bad time," I said. "I've got to head back out-"

"Rangers West and Roberts," the woman interrupted me. The pair extended their hands to me in unison. She had a monotone way of speaking and, by the taciturn expression on his face, neither seemed to be the life of the party.

I shook their hands in turn. "Sheriff Alwin Danks. You both work for Fish and Wildlife?"

"Yes."

I walked passed them to unlock my door. I knew of a few differences between those in Fish and Wildlife and those who worked for the National Park Service, not the least of which was the former employed "wardens" and the latter "rangers." If these feds didn't have the courtesy of at least providing a decent cover it didn't bode well for the competence of the two they'd sent.

"Pleasure to meet you both and thank you for coming," I said, "but you wasted a trip. Not sure if you've heard but we're dealing with a fatality now."

"We have," Roberts said, in a somehow even more monotone voice than his partner. "We can provide answers."

"Alright." I gestured them inside. My curiosity about what

department (or possibly news agency) had *really* sent them got the better of me. "Hope neither of you are allergic to cats. Mittens is friendly, and not too particular about which lap she finds."

"We enjoy animals." West nodded twice.

No sooner had we entered than Mittens hissed and darted beneath my desk. I blinked. "Well, seems animals don't care for you."

They ignored the jest entirely, instead moving quickly to sit straight-backed in the two chairs at my desk. Any hope banter would loosen them up faded quickly.

"Vampire bats," Roberts said as soon as I sat down.

"Pardon?"

"That is the source of your cattle deaths."

"Bats?" I asked again, unsure if he was trying to make a joke or not.

"They're larger than average and work together."

I kept my composure, a feat particularly impressive given their ridiculous, if not outright absurd, notion. I kept my skepticism to myself, trying instead to determine what question to even ask at that point. "How can you be sure?"

"We've been researching incidents of rhabdoviridae aberrations present with wuchereria bancrofti infections in *desmondus rotundus*," Roberts said.

West nodded as if any of it made a lick of sense. "We are sure."

I scratched my tightly trimmed beard to hide a smile before saying, "You'll need to run that by me one more time."

"Run what where?" West asked.

I wasn't sure if he was joking or not so I spread my hands. "I've a passing familiarity with wucheria bancrofti. Anyone stationed where I've been would, I assure you, but bats? How does this impact bats?"

They looked to each other, puzzled, before nodding.

"Rabid vampire bats suffering from elephantiasis from a parasitic infection," West answered. "This explains the size and aggressive nature."

"Oh, of course." I leaned back in my chair and navigated the feelings of amusement and anger that churned in my gut. "Let me get this straight. Enlarged, rabid bats are working together to consume and mutilate cattle. Then, upon being seen, they turn on a human?"

"Yes," Roberts nodded twice.

West smiled. "We are quite certain."

"I'll take that into consideration." I stood and motioned them towards the door. "Thank you for your time. I'll keep an eye out for what you've described."

Neither stood. Instead, Roberts said, "We would like to be sure of our findings, however. May we see the body?"

I kept standing with my arm pointing to the door. "The victim and the cow are both being autopsied right now. As soon as I know something, I'll pass it on."

"They are doing the autopsy right now?" West asked quickly.

They both stood and Roberts gave a wooden smile. "We have taken up too much of your time."

West reached into his case, withdrew a thick file, and set it on my desk. "A copy of the research."

"Fish and Wildlife has spent money researching this? I asked.

"We have substantial resources at our disposal."

HOURS LATER, I STILL HADN'T MADE SENSE OF THE FILE OR THE pair of badly-disguised agents from some bowl of alphabet soup or another. But it was the duality of their guise that stuck in my mind like a bad song. Why provide a detailed file of research but not take enough time to know the difference between wardens and rangers?

I rubbed my weary eyes and took another drink of coffee long since gone cold. Time to start at the beginning.

Vocco's voice buzzed over the radio. "Vocco to Danks."

"Danks here."

"Found where Baumgardner went."

"Where?"

"Parent's cabin, apparently. No idea where that is."

Sarah's voice chimed in. "I know where it is."

"Good. I don't want to spend the night wandering the hills." Vitale said.

I held down the transmitter. "Send me the address, Sarah, and then meet Vitale. I want you both to go together."

"Something wrong?" she asked.

"Did you find any more tracks?" I asked.

The radio went silent for a long pause before she answered, "No. I think we're going to need a canine unit."

"What's this about footprints disappearing?" asked Vitale, his voice cautious even over the static of the radio.

"Sarah will fill you in," I said. "Stay together, bring Baumgardner here, and watch yourself out there."

"What did Fish and Wildlife say?" she asked.

I ran a hand over the pages of research that might as well have been atomic theory for all I knew. A picture of the largest bat I've ever heard of didn't hurt their case, but it didn't explain the footprints. "Nothing useful."

Vitale and Sarah decided to meet at an overpass and then he'd follow her to the cabin. My phone buzzed with Sarah's text and I checked the address. About a half hour away, if they didn't take a detour. I closed the absurd file and leaned back, shut my eyes.

I WOKE UP TO MY PHONE RINGING. RUBBING THE SLEEP FROM MY eyes, I slapped my face to wake up and answered. "This is Sheriff Danks."

The line went dead.

I glanced at my phone, and noticed the time; an hour and half had passed. I picked up the radio. "Vitale, what's your sitrep?"

No answer.

"Gailey, sitrep?"

No answer.

"Vocco or Gailey, copy?"

No answer.

"Dispatch, what's the location of deputy Vocco or Gailey?"

"Vocco and Gailey were en route to 456 Mountain View Road at 7:45pm." The dispatcher reported.

"Have they arrived?"

"Not yet, Sherriff."

"I'm en route," I said, checking my Glock. "Keep trying them. If they don't answer, send backup."

A QUARTER-HOUR LATER, I ARRIVED AT THE CABIN UNDER THE fading red sky of a late summer dusk. It was little more than a glorified shed overlooking a bluff that took in the Selway-Bitterroot Wilderness. A mud-covered, red pickup truck sat parked at the end of skid marks in the gravel driveway. Vocco's SUV and Gailey's cruiser were parked beside it.

A single light shone out from one of the back window, casting a dancing shadow against the trees. Someone inside moved.

"Dispatch, I'm 10-20 at 456 Mountain View Road, both vehicles are here."

Silence.

I tried the radio again. "Dispatch, come in." Only the sound of my own beating heart answered. Perhaps they simply couldn't respond? It was a comforting thought even if misplaced. There wasn't a reason they'd still be here if that was the case, at least none I could see.

I made my way towards the cabin and knocked on the door. Inside the low whining of dogs and a young woman's voice murmured over and over answered but no one came to the door. I knocked again, this time raising my voice, "Deputies, Ms. Baumgardner, it's Sherriff Danks. I'm coming in."

The acrid sent of dog urine tugged at my nose as I pushed the door open. Two german shepherds cowered in the corner. The furniture was overturned and pressed against the windows as if trying to block them. Light crept out from beneath the kitchen door. "Ms. Baumgardner? Deputies?"

A voice muttered over and over from the kitchen. Crossing the room, I drew my Glock and pushed the door open.

Eva rocked back and forth in the middle of the kitchen holding a red stained butcher's knife in her right hand. Blood covered her, dripping like morning dew from her gore matted hair. She turned her wide, unblinking eyes on me. "See you. They will see you when it comes. It won't take me. It won't."

"Eva, put the knife down."

She shook her head. "It comes for me."

"Eva, where are my deputies? Gailey and Vocco?"

"They came for me. Yes. They came. But it took them."

I flipped my safety off but kept my pistol pointed down. "Eva, are you hurt? Are they hurt?"

"You saw them. Didn't you?" she asked.

"Saw who?"

"The hunters. They hunt the beast, but it got away. Fires in the sky. They came but the beast disappeared. It killed him. It took his soul."

"Vitale! Sarah!" I called out, but no one answered. "Eva, where are they?"

She pointed the bloody knife towards the backdoor. For the first time, I noticed it sat slightly off its hinges. I stepped past her and pushed the door open with my foot. The scent of blood cursed the air and Eva muttered nonsensically.

It was Sarah's engagement ring, glinting in the fading sunlight, that drew my gaze to a severed hand that still clung to a blood-covered radio. Beside it, the tattered remains of what were once two people lay strewn like an elk on the side of the freeway.

"It tried to take me." Eva rocked back and forth faster, shaking her head.

"Did you do this?" Dread crept into me, and I raised my gun. "Drop the knife, now!"

Out of my peripheral, the bushes moved in the distance and something massive, larger than a bear, rushed towards the cabin. Eva screamed and I turned. It was as if the shadows themselves moved with it, shrouding it like a cloak, absorbing the light and giving only darkness in return. It crossed the meters between the bushes and the back of the house in the time it took Eva to scream.

I spun and pulled the trigger. The shock that traced up my arm paled in comparison to my surprise when the creature didn't slow. Unaffected, it crossed the last few meters to me. I grabbed the doorknob and pulled the ruined door between us.

Then it struck me. The impact lifted my body off the ground, my breath whooshing out in a single, painful gush. It carried me across the room with ease. The door splintered against my body, and a sharp pain stung my arm as a piece speared my forearm, tearing my gun from my hand.

Had it not been for the front window, I would have been crushed between the door and the wall. Instead, I sailed through the window and across the front lawn like a chew toy being flung by a playful dog.

I couldn't move; instead, I lay gasping, my lungs futilely trying to draw breath as my body spasmed. I knew things were broken. I was broken. And the image of Derek's contorted body came far too easily to mind.

The dogs howled inside, but that was drowned out by Eva. She screamed and screamed. The terror in her voice cut through me more painfully than anything else. I tried to call out to her, to rise, to do my job but I couldn't even utter a sound. With a final, desperate yelp the dogs cried out. Then nothing; a silence broken only by my wheezing attempts to draw breath.

The front door creaked open. In the dark of the house, three pairs of green eyes fixated on me. To what creature they belonged,

I couldn't guess, and what lurked in the darkness remained hidden by the shadows.

I looked up at the night sky. My last moment on this world to be of something beautiful if I had any say in it. A shooting star crossed the horizon, but it was a bit late to make a wish. The panting of the creature reached my ears and I knew it was near.

This was the end.

Then, unexplainably, the shooting star turned, moving towards me in an instant. Night became day; a burning, white light flooded the sky overhead. The shadowed creature seemed to cry out in pain and leap away towards the forest. I struggled to sit up, or at the very least cover my eyes from the light overhead, but my body wouldn't respond.

The best I could do was squint, and I did. For a moment, the shape of two people appeared between the creature and the tree line. The beast howled, and for a moment it almost sounded like words of a language I couldn't make out, or a voice recording playing an hour's worth of conversation in seconds.

The light blared anew, blinding me even with my eyes shut tight. An instant later, only the lingering spot in my eyes remained. I lay my head back on grass that had turned ash, allowing the sound of sirens to lull me into the afterlife.

IT WAS THE MORNING CHIRPING OF BIRDS WOKE ME FROM MY dreamless sleep. The sleep of the dead. That was if woke was the right word. More like brought consciousness back into my befuddled mind. I tried to look around but my eyesight was still washed out and blurry, good enough to make out shapes and little else.

"He's awake," a man said.

Suddenly I was surrounded by what looked like doctors and nurses. They asked me questions about my health and how I was feeling. Said they were glad I was alive, which was more concerning than it was encouraging.

My eyesight slowly turned from a white haze to even better shapes as one day turned to a couple. Deputies guarded my door. Why?

It was the fourth day, or maybe fifth, when two men in Brooks Brothers suits entered. They showed me their FBI credentials, but I knew who they were by the look of them.

"I am agent Rouche and this is agent Bendich. We need to ask you a few questions." Rouche sat in a chair beside my bed. "Has anyone explained what's happened to you?"

I waved their greetings aside. "Has anyone notified the families of my deputies?"

"That's being handled."

"It should be me."

"We understand you've been through a traumatic experience and so do they."

"Traumatic experience?" I spread my hands. "Guys, I don't know what I've been through but that doesn't even come close."

"We understand," said Bendich. His voice sounded like gravel being sifted for size over an iron grate.

"And Eva?"

"That's being handled as well."

Rouche pulled up a chair. "Why don't you tell us what happened?"

"It doesn't make sense," I warned them before I went over what I happened. What I knew. Not that there was a lot to say. More questions in the end than answers. And the more I explained what I had seen, the more I began to doubt my own sanity. None of it made any sense; in fact, it sounded downright insane.

"Tell us about the rangers again," Bendich said. "West and... Roberts I think you called them?"

I shrugged. "I'm guessing they work for you. Their cover story was absurd though. I expected better."

"What did they look like?"

I paused. "Why would that matter? Don't you know your own people?"

"They don't work for us" Rouche said, gesturing to Bendich and himself. "Though the names are familiar."

"How so?" I asked.

The two looked at each other, as if weighting a decision between them. In the end, it was Rouche that answered. "Sheriff, the two rangers you named went missing in the 70's. And this isn't the first time we've heard their name."

I stared mutely at him for longer than was comfortable for either of us. Unsure what to think or feel, I tried to work words to my dry lips but nothing came. My mind raced with ideas, all of them even more insane than the next. As was the case with any investigation, it was best to start at the beginning. "Where did they go missing?"

"In Wyoming. Apparently, there were reports of missing cattle and tracks the locals couldn't identify."

'TILL THE COWS COME HOME

KAYE THORNBRUGH

About the Author: Kaye Thornbrugh is an award-winning reporter, apprentice dungeon master and urban fantasy author. She lives in the beautiful Inland Northwest, and though she hasn't seen any faeries in the woods just yet, she remains optimistic. Visit her online at www.kayethornbrugh.com.

'Till the Cows Come Home

Kaye Thornbrugh

"So, do we think this is a good idea?" The look on Henry's face suggested that it wasn't a real question—he felt this was the best idea he'd had all day.

"Well... it's your cow," Filo said with a shrug.

Filo's shirt was sticking to his back; it was only midmorning, but the August heat was already oppressive. He would rather hoof it back to town and see about getting the car repaired than play cowhand—but he was traveling with his boyfriend, who took a picture of every missing-pet poster he saw, just in case. There would be no arguing with him.

They had been ten miles out of Donnelly, a speck of a town somewhere in southern Idaho, when the engine had started smoking. While the two of them stood squinting at the incomprehensible machinery under the hood, the cow had appeared in the middle of the road: a black-eyed, round-eared, reddish creature. Filo knew right away, just by the feel of her, that she didn't come from this side of the veil.

"Pretty sure it's *our* cow for the time being." Henry smiled and patted the cow's back, fondly, like it was a big red dog and not otherworldly livestock. "I've always wanted to see a crodh mara."

"Of course you have," Filo said, shaking his head a little. He couldn't say the same for himself. Where faerie livestock went, so did their owners, and it was too early in the morning to deal with the fey.

Crodh mara wandered out of rivers and lakes, sometimes, or out from under faerie hills, to be absorbed into human-tended herds. If a human treated it well, the crodh mara might remain for generations, bringing good luck to the whole farm. Filo had never heard of one this far west, but Henry tended to bring odd creatures out of the woodwork.

Henry had a way with animals—they understood one another's

intentions. It was a gift: a little light that he couldn't turn off. If he stayed in one place long enough, he attracted animals of all kinds. Rabbits and birds. Stray cats and racoons. A sea serpent, once. And now, possibly for the first time, cattle.

"Think she wandered out of her knowe?" Filo asked. The cow made him a little uneasy, staring with those big black expressionless eyes. "I haven't seen a hill in miles."

"Nah, she lives around here. There's a farm nearby."

Filo didn't ask how he could be sure of that. By now, he knew to trust Henry's instincts. They'd never steered him wrong.

Henry's power over beasts made him valuable within the magical community—a loose collection of humans, faeries and others being scattered across the world, mostly keeping to themselves, hidden from ordinary eyes. There was always another monster that needed to be tamed, or a rare animal that needed protection. In fact, that was why they were on this road to begin with: He'd been asked to help capture an escaped griffin in Boise.

When Henry had agreed to provide his particular services, he'd stipulated that Filo must accompany him—ostensibly because of Filo's extensive monster-wrangling experience, but really so that they could spend a few nights together in a hotel on someone else's dime. By the time Filo had heard about this trip, it was already a *fait accompli*.

This was the second day of their drive from Seattle to Boise. They could've made the trip in one day, but Henry wanted to take the scenic, and deeply convoluted, route. "If we're going all the way to Idaho, we might as well *see* it," he'd said, and because Filo had gone soft since they met three years ago, he agreed.

There wasn't much to Idaho so far, Filo thought: mountains up north, faded scrubland to the south, with a certain odor that seemed to grow stronger by the mile. But if Henry was happy to be here, Filo could be, too. Making him smile still felt good: like a victory.

Even Filo had his limits, however.

"Well, we can have a look around here. But I'm not walking for miles with a faerie cow," he said, resolutely.

THEY WALKED MILES WITH THE FAERIE COW, ALONG THE SIDE OF the road, with the sun beating down like they had personally offended it. For reasons Filo did not fully understand, they were letting the cow lead. It would've gone quicker, maybe, if the cow weren't so slow and plodding, pausing occasionally to gaze around with big black eyes.

No cars passed them on the road, which was lined with green pastures, rolling out endlessly. Filo only saw the fields to his right side, unless he turned his head; his left eye had been removed after an injury years ago. As they walked side by side, he trusted Henry to cover his blind spot.

There were a few houses in the distance, scattered, inaccessible from the main road. None of them appeared likely to have cattle—but then, Filo didn't know much about these things.

Breaking curses and building spells, on the other hand, Filo knew all about. Magic and monsters had been his life as far back as he could remember. It was the *ordinary* things that eluded him.

Things like taking a road trip with his boyfriend.

"What happens when we get to Boise?" Filo asked after a while.

"We show up at the Guildhall. They'll know where to send us—they're tracking the griffin," Henry said, passing Filo the water bottle they'd brought from the car.

"No, I mean—" Filo gestured vaguely, water bottle in hand. These two days on the road had felt like entering a world the size of their car, one that contained just the two of them. It was new to him, and strange. He wasn't sure how to navigate. "What happens *after* we get to Boise?"

"After?" Henry seemed confused by the question. Then he smiled. "Whatever we want. Once we deal with the griffin, it's just us."

"Oh," Filo said. "That sounds—"

"Good?"

"Great."

Another mile, and Filo saw why they had let the cow lead: a farmhouse, surrounded by pastures fenced in wood and wire. The slow-moving black and brown specks in a distant field must be cattle. They had to pick their way along a gravel road to reach the house, eight feet crunching along.

"They're not going to shoot us through the door as soon as we knock, right?" Filo asked, as they approached the house.

"Probably not," Henry said brightly, and bounded up the porch steps.

A woman came to the screen door a minute after he knocked, middle-aged and olive-skinned. She looked curious, but cautious; Filo guessed she didn't get many unexpected visitors.

"Good morning," she said slowly, without moving to open the door.

"Hey. So, ah—we found something that might belong to you," Henry said, jerking his thumb toward the red cow, which was bumping Filo with her nose.

The woman, who turned out to be named Carol, thanked them profusely while she returned the red cow to the pasture. While the animal seemed reluctant to part with Henry—normal, for him—he nudged her along.

Carol smiled politely at Henry as they spoke, but whenever she turned to Filo, there was a heartbeat when she wasn't sure where to look. Eventually she always settled on his eyes, but it seemed to be an effort for her to keep her focus there.

These days, Filo found that people fell into two categories: those who stared, and those who asked what happened. He wasn't sure which he preferred.

People who ran in Seattle's magical circles usually just stared, watching him out of the corner of their eyes, like they were attempting to see through a glamour. Meanwhile, normal humans were more likely to ask why he looked like he'd been mauled.

He usually just said it was a car accident. It didn't really match the visual, but by that point, most people felt too uncomfortable to probe deeper.

His face really wasn't as bad as it used to be, Filo thought—or maybe he was just used to it after three years. The thick, ropy scar tissue was more pink than red now, not quite so itchy and uncomfortable. The prosthetic eye looked the same as the real one, except for the fixed pupil; most people probably didn't realize he was blind on the left side.

The person he saw in the mirror each morning was no longer a stranger. In fact, Filo was starting to forget what his face had looked like before. But to other people, like Carol, his appearance was often startling.

Carol brushed her dark hair back with one hand, and Filo noticed that her ear came to a tapered point. Not half-faerie, he thought, studying her. The blood came from farther back than that. Perhaps she had a faerie ancestor who'd brought a crodh mara with them when they married a human.

Filo said nothing about; there was no need. It was possible this woman didn't even know; family stories became distorted over time.

"That cow's pretty old, I'm guessing," he said instead, with a glance at Henry. He knew nothing about the lifespans of cattle, but his knowledge of faeries gave him his suspicions. "Seems healthy, though."

Henry nodded wisely. "She'll be around for a long time, yet. But there are conditions—certain things you have to do each day, certain food you have to provide," he said, giving Carol a slow, knowing look. "Somebody explained that to you once. A grandparent, maybe?"

For a few heartbeats, Carol just stared at him. "I'm not sure what you mean," she said, her shoulders tense. "Now, I appreciate you bringing her back here, but—"

"It's okay," Filo offered, quietly. "We know she's... special."

"I've seen animals like her before," Henry said.

Carol hesitated a moment longer. "This was my grandparents' land," she said at last, glancing back at the old white farmhouse. "When I was a little girl, I found a coyote around the back. It was stumbling, foaming at the mouth. I didn't know what that meant. I froze when it came at me. But before it reached me—there was my grandmother's favorite cow."

She looked out to the pasture, where the red cow was peacefully grazing with the other cattle. A warm wind stirred the grass.

"I don't know how she got out of the pasture," she said. "All I know for sure is that she stomped on that coyote until it was dead. Never saw anything like it, before or since." Carol shook her head at the memory. "My grandmother said that cow would bring me luck, if I did right by her. And she'd outlive me, too."

That made Henry huff a laugh. "And she will," he said. "She'll outlive all of us, probably. But only if you keep up your end of the deal." He paused. "You missed something today, didn't you?"

Carol nodded. "I'll remember tomorrow," she promised. Then she looked from Henry to Filo again, somewhat hesitant. "In the meantime—"

"You know, it's usually easier just to look once and get it over with," Filo told her. There was no point in pretending he didn't notice. "I don't mind."

Carol's smile was half grimace, a little embarrassed. Still, she looked at him more directly. "So, ah—what happened to the other guy?"

"Dead," Filo replied, partly to watch her expression twitch, partly because it was true. The memory was hard to live with, but the word got easier to say.

The creature who had done this to him was dead, and he was alive, and that meant something. At least, he hoped so.

"Speaking of my end of the deal," Carol said. "There's got to be something I can do to pay you back."

"Actually," Filo said, lifting a hand, before Henry could politely refuse, "we could really use a ride into town..."

In the grand scheme of things, the car was only a small problem. They were back on the road by sunset, and green and brown landscape drenched in golden tones as Henry steered them along the highway. For the first time, Filo caught himself admiring the view.

"Well, I'd say that worked out," Henry said after a while—a little smug, Filo thought, but not undeservedly.

Filo hummed. "You surprised?"

"Not at all. You've got to believe in the inherent goodness of people, babe," Henry said, with a perfect sincerity that made Filo laugh. "I mean it—they'll surprise you."

"Sometimes," Filo said, no longer looking out the window, but at Henry, who was edged in light as the sun dipped lower.

Tonight, they would arrive in Boise, and tomorrow, they would round up a griffin. After that—well, maybe they'd take a few more days to themselves, before driving back to Seattle. Or maybe they would just take the scenic route again.

Filo felt the scars on his face pull as he smiled, imagining that. But it didn't hurt.

DEMON WITH THE GOLDEN HORNS

VOSS FOSTER

About the Author: Voss Foster lives in the middle of the Eastern Washington desert, where he writes science fiction and fantasy from inside a single-wide trailer. He is the author of the Evenstad Media Presents series, The King Jester Trilogy, The Mountains of Good Fortune, and the Immortal Whispers Series. His short work has been featured by various publications, including Vox.com, Flame Tree Publishing's Gothic Fantasy series, and the Alternative Truths series. When he can be pried away from his keyboard, he can be found singing, practicing photography, cooking, and belly dancing, though rarely all at the same time. More information can be found at vossfoster.blogspot.com.

Demon with the Golden Horns

Voss Foster

"So, do we think this is a good idea?" Karen's voice was tight and high and muffled by the full face mask.

"Well...it's your cow," said Wallace.

She nodded. It was her stupid, last-ditch effort to get out of this. Presented with the reality of the situation, it wasn't nearly as easy as it had been all the times she'd done it in her head. The steer stood in the tiny pen there in the field, silent as a sinner in the confessional. Karen had bred him and raised him for this, and he was sweet. Loving. Tending to him so directly for so long...well, she hadn't counted on this level of emotional attachment when the time came.

"This *is* the best thing that can be done, now." Wallace took off his mask, revealing a cragged, stubbled face. He was older than her by about ten years, but still attractive in a daddy-issues kind of way. He clapped her on the back, rubbed a gruff hand up and down her spine. "It's your decision, of course, but that's what he's for. All the work we've done has been leading to this sacrifice. Who knows if we'll even get another steer like Ricky...ever?"

He was right. Of course, he was right. Ricky was the right age. He had the correct markings, had been castrated at the right time with a gold-plated crusher, fed on only fruit and dark beer. And the stars were finally, *finally* right.

Karen drew in a deep breath, the air tainted by the flavor and scent of the carved wooden mask. "Okay. Okay, let's do it."

Wallace nodded, winked a dark eye at her, then slipped his mask back on. He grabbed the hammer from where it leaned against the tree and carried it over.

Karen sighed. "Bye, baby boy."

She watched Wallace swing the hammer high, but closed her eyes before she saw the head fall down. It didn't protect her from the noise. Cracking, squelching, and a cut-off, yowling moo. Karen bit down on the inside of her lip to keep from crying. *This is what Ricky was bred and raised for. This is important. We need this.*

"Come on, Karen."

Wallace's voice forced her eyes open. It was time to *really* get started. They'd made their sacrifice at the peak of the full moon. They had Kalivash's attention. The Demon with the Golden Horns. Now it was time for her to make an appearance.

Wallace laid the hammer aside. Ricky's corpse lay in the field, red leaking out across the green grass. A portable LED lantern cast a small, too-bright glow in the darkness. The blue-white of it reflected off Ricky's dead, dark eyes. The smell of iron filled the air around his body.

"You're up for this?" Wallace had already unpacked his supplies, laid everything out there on the ground. Knives and rods and crystals and little jars full of various ingredients. "We have just long enough for you to take a breather if you need to."

"No." She didn't want to take the time for it to sink in. Taking the life of a poor innocent cow—one of her own, nonetheless—had always been her least favorite part of this whole plan. *But now it's over.* "Let's just get this going." They needed to do it before first light of sun. Kalivash's eyes were too sensitive for daylight. She wouldn't appear if the sun was out.

Wallace took out the dagger, carved the ancient geometric patterns in Ricky's body. A small kindness for Karen, letting her prepare the rest of the ritual. She measured out ash and metal filings, powdered poisons and brimstone harvested from the outskirts of Hell... bought in the incorporated areas of Hell, Michigan, but they had to work with what they could get. A healthy dose of sherry, washed through her mouth then out into the bowl, finished it off. She took a swig from the bottle just to try and calm her nerves. It was happening. It was real. *Kalivash.*

"Is it ready?"

Karen nodded and handed the bowl to Wallace. He dumped it across the body, washing out blood from the headwound and filling the arcane symbols and sigils with gritty amber liquid.

Wallace grabbed an unmarked bottle from the ground and drenched Ricky's body in it. The sharp stink of raw alcohol seared Karen's nose.

"Stand back." Wallace slipped a book of matches from his pocket and struck one alight. He tossed it and the body went up in flames. It cast the gore in stark, flickering brightness. Darkness wouldn't hide the truth any longer.

Wallace moved back and started the prayers, muttering under his breath. Karen nodded. *Here we go*. She kneeled next to him. "Kalivash. Make yourself known. The feast is prepared. We urge you to eat and drink your fill. Kalivash. Make yourself known..." On and on she went, quiet, just under her breath. It could have been minutes, could have been hours. Her body ceased to exist. The world ceased to exist, and everything fell into the deep trench between her needs and the mantra.

Until the cracking clamor racketed through her ears. Her eyes burst open and she saw the crag in the earth. Ricky was gone, and the last remnants of flame sputtered out. But Kalivash was *not* there.

Wallace stood up next to her. "That... that's it?"

Years of preparation and studying, tracking down the handful of people who knew about Kalivash in the first place, breeding generation after generation of cattle until Ricky showed up. *Killing* him. Paying gobs of money for his food. Karen's stomach dropped straight into that hole after the burning carcass.

"Jesus!" Wallace tore off his mask and tossed it into the crack as well. "I... this isn't right! Everything... we must have gotten something wrong! Bad information!" He kicked a tree, as though that would actually do anything.

Karen forced herself to move, take off her mask. She walked to Wallace and put a hand on his shoulder. "We'll try again." The words tasted of bitter venom on her tongue, but she forced herself through them all the same. "I still have the cows. I can repeat the breeding until we get another steer."

"It's not going to do any good!" Wallace shook under her hands.

"We don't have any way to contact Kalivash, and without her, there's nothing."

"We did *something*, though." She gestured to the jagged opening where the pen had been. "Kalivash took notice. This is more than anyone else has done in decades. Centuries." The last time Kalivash had appeared in the corporeal was the 1700s. In China. And nobody knew exactly what they'd done. The ritual they used that night was pieced together from rumors and third-or-fourth-hand accounts. "We're close, Wallace."

Which was bullshit. It was years of work down the drain. She could die before another cow showed up with the same markings, and then it was still fifty-fifty if it would even be male. They both knew it... but freaking out would do nothing for either of them, and it certainly wouldn't make Kalivash suddenly appear.

Wallace grumbled under his breath. "This whole thing... I'm sorry about Ricky. I know you got attached to him. I assumed we'd have something to show for giving him up."

Me too. "Like you said. This is what he was for." The weight of it all tried and tried to press Karen into the dirt. But she held herself strong. "Come on. Let's... let's just go home."

Wallace sighed, but he nodded and gathered up his things. Karen headed for the car.

She had a solid thirty seconds to break down, bashing her hand over and over into the dashboard, widening the already present cracks in the plastic facing. Kalivash didn't come. She was supposed to appear. *Everything* was right. They even hunted down that god damn bottle of *palo cortado* for her... nothing. Just a crack in the ground.

She sucked in a few calming breaths. Wallace's lantern bobbed closer and closer to her. She turned the engine over and brushed the busted bits of plastic from the seat. There was no point getting angry. Anger was poison, and poisoning herself *also* wouldn't make Kalivash appear.

She would just have to... try again. And again. And again.

Summoning Kalivash was their only chance for justice. And she'd be damned if she'd let go of that chance for one failed attempt.

KAREN PORED OVER BOOKS AND ARTICLES AND SCANS OF OLD texts too expensive and delicate for her to actually ever touch. She'd spent every night since the botched ritual looking for *something*. An ambiguous translation. A missed page. A god damn ancient scribble that suggested something too outlandish to have been tried under normal circumstances.

Finally, a week in, she had to just look up at the ceiling. "Kalivash. Why? What the hell did we get wrong?"

And, of course, there was no response. The Demon with the Golden Horns couldn't hear them, couldn't see them. Not unless she was corporeal. The ritual was supposed to draw her into physical form and put her before her disciples. Where she could see their devotion and hear their pleas. Where they could *touch* her.

Karen slammed the books closed and pushed back from the table. "Well screw you, then." She shook her head as she marched away. She could go to bed, turn on the TV, and maybe take her mind off this week-long session of self-flagellation. It wasn't her fault. It wasn't Wallace's fault. It wasn't Ricky's fault.

It all came down to Kalivash. There was no reason she had to make it so hard to manifest herself in the first place. What was so important about staying separate? What if someone needed her? They were supposed to keep a sacred steer and a hundred-dollar bottle of sherry lying around just in case?

Into the bedroom. Karen turned on some mindless sitcom, then flopped herself into the little double bed. She was asleep before the end of the episode. Rage was exhausting.

When morning sun broke golden through the window, Karen's eyes creaked open. She turned over and the bed squelched. A few seconds for recognition. It was wet and it was warm and... the stink of iron. Her heart jumped to life, thrashing against her ribcage, and she sat up.

The sheets, the pillows, her bra and panties – all dyed crimson. An inch of red liquid sat on the floor, and a cow skull hung from the corner of the TV, obscuring the face of the cute little weather girl from Channel Seven.

Karen swallowed back her vomit. This was a nightmare. It was blood... but this couldn't be real. Except that she never woke up in her dreams. Ever. She was never asleep. Except in reality. Her skin raised in a million tiny bumps as bile wormed its way back into her mouth.

Screw me? A haughty, high-pitched voice filled her skull, pounding on the bone with each syllable. *Fuck you. It is not my duty to come at your beck and call.*

"Kalivash."

Yes, yes. How intelligent of you. Do you want a gold star?

It worked. It actually worked. They got more than her attention. In some small way, she'd come down. "Are you... are you corporeal?"

I am always corporeal. But no, I'm not on the mortal coil. It's so dull, and far too bright for that. The blood on the floor eddied and rippled, then slowly spun, spiraling toward some point under her bed. It drained out, sucked its way off the bed and out of Karen's underwear. *If you really want to see me, then fine. Bring the sherry and bring the boy. And cook the beef this time, for God's sake. I'm not an animal.*

"I don't have another cow. Not like Ricky."

Kalivash's laugh was sonorous and painful, vibrating Karen's skull and blurring her vision. *The first one was just seasoned properly. Or did you think that was some part of the ritual?* Another agonizing laugh, longer this time. *I like good food. Hence the beer and the wheat and the sherry. It's not magic. It's good taste. So make another roast from your precious supermarket and bring it back to the woods. If you underseason it, I'm leaving.*

Underseasoning the roast was the biggest worry, now? "Fine. When?"

When it's not so damned bright out. And I expect a little kinder tone when we meet in person.

Not so bright. Very specific. But Karen nodded. With no blood on the floor, and something *actually* happening, she couldn't keep the slight smile from her lips. "I will see you tonight, great Kalivash."

Much better.

Karen waited thirty seconds, just to make sure their conversation was finished, then bolted up and ran for the phone. She dialed up Wallace without even looking at the time. He'd be okay with it.

A creaky, muffled voice answered. "Hello?"

"Kalivash noticed us. We need to go out there tonight."

"What? What?" His voice cleared and sharpened on the second word. "Wait... what happened?"

"She filled my bedroom with blood, then told me to come back out to the woods tonight. With sherry and a beef roast."

"Are you serious?"

"I am serious."

"Oh my god... this might happen."

Karen nodded, though he couldn't see. "I know. You need to get another mask."

A slight beat of silence. "Crap. All right, yeah. Pick me up at 6:30?"

"Fine. See you then." She hung up, then slumped into an armchair. She had... she had to go to the store. And find a good roast recipe. Not in that order.

THEY WERE BACK TO WHERE THE PEN HAD STOOD, WALLACE'S

lantern making the path clear. It was a solemn, somber walk, though a palpable, electric energy skittered between them. The crack remained in the earth, but no other sign that they'd been there, performed any sort of ritual. It could have just been a natural oddity, a seismic screw-up. But it wasn't. *Any* chance of that flew right out the window when Karen's room turned into the Red Sea.

She set the roasting pan down, then slid on the mask. "I don't know when she's planning on making her appearance. Just sometime after dark."

Wallace nodded, then put on his own mask. "I suppose I shouldn't have gotten so angry before."

"Like I wasn't just as pissed?"

"Well, you were punching the car an awful lot, but I figure that's your business."

"You saw that..." Heat crept up her cheeks. "None of it matters now, anyway." Kalivash would appear. That night. And they could finally have their moment.

Night slithered on, further and further. The last glimmering rays of sunshine disappeared behind the trees. In the forest, dark was truly, truly black. No stars could twinkle through the thick canopy, no moonlight to seep between leaves.

You showed up. That voice again, overly loud and overly present. *With the roast, and the sherry. Thank you.*

The crack widened before Karen could even say anything. She stood and dragged Wallace to his feet. The darkness only seemed to grow, spreading like ink across the world. It snuffed out the LED lantern, and for a few silent moments, there was only black in the world. Karen clung to Wallace's hand, squeezed so tightly it even hurt *her* knuckles. And he never complained.

"The roast, please." A tiny glint of light. It took Karen a moment to realize that high, haughty voice was no longer in her head. It came from in front of her. From that gleaming point in the black. And the point grew and grew until pale gold illuminated the whole of the woods around them.

As wide as a car and nearly two stories high. Her fangs curved and snarled and spiraled into themselves. Bushy fur covered her legs down to char-black hooves. Her body was red as blood, eyes a pale, rheumy color. And the horns. Brilliant, unmarred gold. They cast all the light, like two tiny suns crowning the head of the great demon.

Kalivash hunched before them.

"Well? I didn't appear before you to not be fed."

"Of course, great demon." Karen opened the roaster and held it up for Kalivash.

She ate it, pan and all, in a single bite. "And the sherry?"

Wallace extended that. She took the glass bottle along with the wine.

Karen cleared her throat. "Kalivash, Demon with the Golden Horns, we praise you."

"So do a lot of people, though not as many as used to. But I'm here for you, so what is it you want?"

"Wealth." Wallace took over. Karen sucked in a few deep breaths. She had the dagger, this time. It was on her to get her hands dirty. She snuck around as Wallace continued his speech. "Both of us, we've gone into great debt in order to behold your golden glory."

"Is that all?"

"No. We want... revenge."

Karen had come closer. She feigned true, absolute fealty, running her fingers through so much fur, tangling it in her grip, pressing her face to it. Every inch of her smelled of fine wine and spices and hot metal. Karen gripped the dagger just as hard as she had Wallace's hand.

"Revenge on who?"

"Our families both died. It was senseless. Please, make this right. We seek revenge on the killer!"

"The killer?" Her voice went even higher. "One killer took out both of your families? You didn't need me for this."

Karen searched for the right spot as Wallace kept her

attention. "Please. We don't want their justice to be swift... it should drag out."

There. Karen found the soft area. Once before, Kalivash was wounded. And demons didn't heal the way anything else would.

Or at least Karen hadn't seen one do it in twenty years on the hunt.

She dug the dagger into that wound with a single driving push. Kalivash's head tilted back, mouth agape in silence. The trees all around her fell to the forest floor.

Wallace rushed up, slid a canteen out from under his coat. He opened it and tossed the contents across Kalivash's body. "*You* were the killer, Demon with the Golden Horns. They were sacrificed in an attempt to force you into the corporeal." Where the anointing oil touched her skin, it blistered and burned and seared to all different shades of red and black. And the spots grew. "We've put an end to the fool cultists who attempted to summon you... and now we put an end to you."

Karen's whole body jittered with electricity as she pulled out the second dagger. Demons weren't fragile. They weren't easy to wound. A thousand arrows and a thousand more could bounce clean from their bodies. But once that armor had been cracked... child's play. She knew of Kalivash's wound from so many years of research. She'd been pierced once by the Spear of Longinus. A glancing blow, but enough.

The silver knife was in. Now Karen dug in the golden blade, riding it along the silver. The power between them pushed back, but she broke through it and buried the knife to its guard. "What happens when a demon dies?"

Karen always asked, but none of them seemed to know.

Kalivash's hideous, malformed body literally cracked like pottery. That light from her horns raced through the openings, breaking her open. The ground cracked as though a meteor had struck. Karen and Wallace both toppled, their masks falling to the wayside. Karen glanced at his face — terror and bliss, swirling across his features.

Kalivash crashed to the ground. An arm fell off, shattered to dust. Then a bit of shoulder. Her face, her eye, part of her leg, the spines on her back. Karen crawled to Wallace's side and held him. Kalivash was all but dead. Her final moments after so, so long.

The air rushed away, and Karen struggled for breath... but the light remained. She peered over and saw... just the golden horns. Still glowing.

In another rush, the space filled back in. Karen collapsed against Wallace, and they stayed that way a few minutes.

Then, Wallace laughed. It shook his whole body. "We did it. We got the bitch." His laughs quickly gave way into sobs.

And still, Karen remained. She held him, and she cried. For the memories. For the time. For the relief. For the lost.

She was also the first to pull herself together. She moved back and wiped her eyes on her sleeve. "Are you okay?"

"Okay? Kalivash is dead." He blew out a ragged breath. "And we are rich."

"Rich?"

He pointed to the golden horns. "Sell them to a hunter. If no one else wants them as a trophy, smelt them down and make tools. Or just gold ingots. Either way... I suppose both of our wishes were answered by her."

"True." They had wealth and their families' killer was now dead. "Do you think she suffered enough?"

"No."

"Me either." She stood on shaky knees. A crater had formed around them and the horns. "But I guess I shouldn't expect a perfect deal from a demon."

Karen touched the horns, smooth and still warm. And at that contact... she saw the crater fill with blood.

What happens when a demon dies? The high, haughty voice. *We wait for those who wronged us. And the afterlife is eternal. I hope it was worth your one blow against me.*

Everything righted. Wallace came up to her, rested a hand on her shoulder. He had the lantern in his other hand. "You ready?"

"Yeah." No blood. No voice. But she couldn't ignore it. "I think we should camp in the car, tonight. We can call Irving tomorrow, have him haul these horns out for us." What good would telling Wallace do, anyway? They couldn't change their fate now... better to let him live out the rest of his life in peace.

Because death would not be so restful.

AUDUMLA'S APPLE

BETHANY LOY

About the Author: Bethany (Benny) Loy is a budding author working to explore the human experience. In her free time she enjoys video games and learning how to cook. She hopes to publish thought-provoking pieces in the future.

Audumla's Apple
By Bethany Loy

"So, do we think this is a good idea?" Anthony's voice wavered.

"Well...it's your cow." Brooks replied as he kicked some manure off his shoes.

Anthony grimaced. "But what if it hurts her?"

Beside them stood the cow known as Auddy, with her dark brown fur and pink nose, languidly chewing her cud. Brooks sauntered closer, wrapping his arm around her neck and hugging her.

"Look at her, dude. She's more than tough enough for a little mushroom." He looked into Auddy's left eye and spoke in a high pitched baby voice. "Isn't that right Auds? Yeah, that's right. It ain't nothing." Brooks continued making kissing noises at the apathetic bovine, his long, black, disheveled hair and straggly beard nuzzled beside her ear.

"Ok, so maybe it won't hurt her physically, but what about the ethics here? I mean, does she even have the level of consciousness necessary to enjoy a psychedelic trip?" Anthony gripped his right arm nervously and looked at the sandwich bag of mushrooms in Brook's hand. "What if she gets like... bovine PTSD?"

Brooks removed his arm from around Auddy's neck and glared at Anthony. "We either test them on the cow, or we test them on ourselves." He tossed the shrooms to Anthony.

Caught off guard, Anthony nearly dropped the bag, played hot potato with it between his hands, and finally managed to catch it.

He scowled at Brooks and stepped forward, closing the distance between them. Anthony's short, red hair stood on end as he angrily shoved the mushrooms into Brook's chest. "Or we could, you know, not use mind-altering substances and risk our health...or my cow!" Two mushrooms fell from the pack to the ground.

"Hey!" Brooks yelled back, his whole body rigid with anger. "I went to the trouble of finding these for you!"

"Ohhhh!" Anthony shouted, waving his hands. "Thank you so much for going to the trouble of collecting unknown, potentially dangerous fungi for my sake!"

Teeth gritting, Brooks said "At least I try! Sure, I don't know if I got the right mushrooms. But at least I make an effort!"

Anthony threw his hands out to his sides sarcastically. "Wow, thank you so much for trying to get me out of my shell by potentially killing me!"

"Get out of your zone, man!" Brooks said, leaning forward and staring daggers at his friend. "You always freeze up and miss out! Break through the surface!"

Anthony sighed, pushing his glasses up and pinching the bridge of his nose in frustration. "You're really going to bring that up?"

"Don't you want to work through your nightmares? Remember what you said?" prodded Brooks. "You're playing by the frozen lake, your friends are there and...?" he trailed off, gesturing for Anthony to fill in.

"I know, I know." Anthony relented, recalling the memory dejectedly. "They want to go play on the lake. I'm too afraid to join them. They ditch me. Then suddenly I'm trapped under the sheet of ice, watching them play." His posture deflated. "They never help me. They never even notice that I'm gone. They never see me pounding on the ice."

Brooks brought up his hand and flicked Anthony's nose, startling him out of his gloom. "Exactly, and as your *official* dream interpreter, I'm prescribing you three grams of—" He stopped short as the bell around Auddy's neck rang.

The two young men turned to look at the cow, who had finished her cud and leaned down to find something new lying on top of her grazing spot. The old girl sniffed loudly at the dropped mushrooms.

"Auddy, wait!" Anthony shouted, but too late. She was chowing down on the psychedelic fungi.

Brooks laughed and slapped Anthony on the back. "She has your interests at heart. Go Auds!"

"What do we do now?" Anthony said, anxiously approaching the bovine. Hesitantly, he stroked her side.

"We wait," Brooks said, leaning against the nearest fence post. He brought his arms up to rest behind his head.

TIME PASSED SLOWLY WHILE THE TWO WAITED FOR THE SHROOMS to take effect on the ponderous cow. Brooks drew in the mud with a stick, and Anthony distracted himself with his phone.

"How long does it take?" mumbled Anthony, his pale green eyes shining with the light from the phone screen.

"It shouldn't be much longer... hmmmm..." Brooks closed his eyes for a second, then dropped the stick and popped a pair of shrooms in his mouth.

"You didn't?" Anthony stammered, his mouth agape.

"It's been long enough, and she didn't get sick or anything, so I'm sure it's fine." Brooks shrugged.

"We aren't sure if it's affected her yet. How do we know if—" Before Anthony could finish, Brooks walked up and offered him a dose.

"Eat and be well." Brooks said. Imitating a servant, he put one arm behind his back, bowed slightly and brought up the hand holding the mushrooms in front of Anthony's face.

Jaw clenched and hand shaking, Anthony took the fungi from his friend's palm. He watched the cow for a moment, saw that she had calmly continued being a cow, and began to chew.

"This...tastes like crap." His face contorted into a disgusted frown.

Brooks laughed "Well that's a given, these grew in manure." He stroked Auddy's fur, continuing to chuckle.

Anthony halted his chewing "You're kidding! Brooks? That's a joke, right?" Anthony's eyes went wide with panic.

Brooks smirked. "Uh, Sure. Just a joke."

Anthony sighed with relief.

"IS IT SUPPOSED TO MAKE ME FEEL NAUSEOUS?" ANTHONY ASKED, rubbing his stomach.

Brooks turned his head down from looking at the clouds to Anthony. Brooks slowly stood up from where he'd been sitting on a rock, and walked over, placing his hands on his friend's shoulders.

"The adventure has commenced!" Brooks shouted, grinning.

Anthony frowned, "Seriously man, when is this supposed to—" and then a wall slammed into him at sixty miles per hour, then phased right through him and left him somewhere else entirely. Anthony was transported.

"We are not in Kansas anymore, kiddo," Brooks whispered, staring wide-eyed into the distance.

Anthony surveyed the landscape. The rolling hills danced with greens, which shifted into swirling blues, warmth welled up in his lungs, and his breath filled with peace. Brooks took his hand and led him to Auddy, placing both their hands on her snout. The soft velvet coalesced with his hand; Anthony was Auddy, and Auddy was Anthony.

Motion drew his gaze to her head, where a pair of bulls' horns emerged above her ears. He pulled his hand out of the cow, and the horns receded. Experimentally, he pressed his hand back onto her side, which rippled like a disturbed pond, and the horns grew back.

"How are you doing that?" Brooks asked, his mouth gaping.

"You see it too?" stammered Anthony. "The horns?" He continued removing and reapplying his hand, but now the horns ceased to sink back in.

Auddy reared her head back and looked at Brooks. She grew in height, towering over the men as the scenery turned a shade of deep red.

"I am Audumla! What must the primordial provider bestow unto you?" the bovine bellowed down at the two.

"Jesus," gasped Brooks as he fell back, grasping at Anthony's pant leg.

Anthony, taken aback, blanched pale as a ghost. He froze completely before this being.

Audumla stepped closer to Anthony, huffing at his scent. "Let your wishes be known!" she commanded.

Brooks slowly pushed himself further from Audumla, his eyes fixed on her grand horns. "...T-t-tell her!"

Anthony clenched his fists, shaking as the wind danced around him. Closing his eyes, Anthony concentrated on slowing down his breathing.

He stepped forward, and with a stern determination called out, "We require a guide out of the frozen lake." The ground trembled below him as he spoke.

The red haze that surrounded them shifted to deep blue. Ice cascaded across the ground and covered the dirt as far as the eye could see.

"Commence the journey!" boomed Audumla. She turned towards the distant snow gathering on the hills, her bell clanging in low, eldritch tones as she strode.

Anthony and Brooks followed the great bovine into the blizzard.

Trudging through the building snow, Anthony looked at the surrounding trees; the branches formed from icicles. He leaned close looking through the trunks of ice, and observed his surroundings through the tall, leaf-covered looking-glass.

Walking around one tree, he viewed Brooks through the trunk of ice. Brooks was clasping his hands together near his mouth, warming them with his breath. From this vantage point, Brooks was more lanky, tall, and a strange shade of yellow. Anthony leaned out from behind the tree to look to Brooks again, but he shifted back to normal.

Brooks gave Anthony an inquisitive look. "What?"

"Nothing. You're just bright, is all," said Anthony.

With a laugh Brooks replied "What do you mean by that?"

Anthony could only shrug in reply. He understood, but found it impossible to articulate his understanding. Then, noticing that they were lagging, Anthony wove his hand forward at Brooks, urging him to quicken their pace and catch up with Audumla, waiting ahead.

Audumla stopped in the snow. With another clang of her bell, she turned to them. "Unearned knowledge is a dangerous thing. Climb that tree and obtain an apple for me."

As she spoke, a tree sprung from the ice. Tearing through the dirt and ice, the tree trunk raced towards the sky. Finally, reaching the end of its height, many branches fanned out. The majestic tree wasn't frozen like the others; it appeared normal except for its immense size.

Brooks gaped at the tree "Climb that? Are you sure this is a good idea?"

The tree branches looked to parlay with the clouds, swaying in the wind. Leaves periodically detached from above and floated down.

He looked at Brooks, then the tree, and finally to Audumla. "Well... It's my cow, and she needs an apple," Anthony answered, now approaching the great tree.

Brooks scratched his head, grinned and then laughed. "Careful what you wish for. We called for adventure and now we got it," he said.

Brooks sauntered up to Anthony, then placed his hand on his forehead. Shading his eyes, he looked up into the branches. "How do you suppose we get up there? I don't see any apples either," Brooks questioned.

Anthony walked along the base of the tree looking for a way up. "There! If you lift me a little I could reach that branch." He pointed upwards.

As Anthony had instructed, Brooks allowed him to stand on his back giving him extra height to reach up.

"Watch where you step! Your heel is grinding into a nerve cluster, dude." Brooks grunted below.

Anthony's fingertips grazed the branch, "Sorry, I just need a little more...almost," he sighed.

Brooks panted. "It won't work. Come down."

Anthony jumped down from Brooks' back and stared at the lowest branch, racking his brain for a plan.

With Anthony's weight off his shoulders, Brooks straightened out his back. "What a pain," he complained as he stretched.

Putting his hands on his hips, Anthony surveyed the tree once again. The contrast between the orange sky and the green leaves captivated him. Another gust of wind blew, and the tree danced along. The surrounding landscape of ice and snow left little in the way of life; the giant tree buzzed with it. Countless birds and beetles restlessly moved about the branches.

"Yo! Do any of you know how to get up there?" Brooks yelled to the creatures above.

Laughing Anthony turned to Brooks. "Will that do anything?"

"Worth a try." Brooks shrugged.

As if in response, a black mass of buzzing beetles began to collect above. They swirled down the trunk, weaving their paths down into the bark. The grooves they left behind glowed with tree sap. Finally grouping all together at the base, they formed into one mass and stopped. Then they gnawed into the oak, chewing away at excess wood until an ornate doorway appeared.

Anthony, eyes wide in amazement, said "Well then...Good call, Brooks." With that, the two entered past the doors.

They ran their hands along the wood walls as they walked forward. As they stepped, Anthony's feet would catch on the roots that sprawled across the ground. Fortunately, the two managed not to trip in the darkness.

Once further into the tree, a curve up ahead became visible. Light stretched around the corner. Both quickened their pace, glad to see an end to this tunnel.

Together, they exited out of the darkness and into the bright light.

Anthony had to shield his eyes from the sudden change in brightness. Once their pupils adjusted, they found themselves in a forest. Thick with flowering foliage and fog, the expansive environment seemed to go on forever. They heard sounds of flowing water in the distance and saw monolithic piles of stone towering above the trees.

The two continued onward into the forest, searching for Audumla's apple.

Brooks reached out to run his fingertips along some flowers that hung from the trees."It's all beautiful. I imagined more of a hellscape, maybe some monsters." He sighed.

Pushing past bushes trying to get a further look into the depths of the forest, Anthony replied, "Are there any apple trees? I see raspberry bushes, peach trees, and the like, but no apples."

Anthony jumped on a large rock jutting from the ground to get a better view. Squinting his eyes, he still couldn't see through the foliage. In the distance, they heard a cowbell softly chiming ahead. "That way!" Anthony pushed on, heading for the sound.

Just as they were passing a juniper tree branch, a large parrot dropped down, startling the two. They flinched back as the bright yellow-and-green avian stared with one unblinking eye. Where the other eye should have been, a large scar was all that remained.

"No wisdom given free. It comes with a price, it comes with a fee," squawked the feathered being.

Anthony repositioned his glasses on his nose and asked, "Would it be safe to assume that you know where to find an apple?"

The bird bounced its head up and down excitedly. "The apple of your eye. The apple of your eye." In a sweeping motion, the bird turned around and flew off.

Blowing his hair out of his eyes, Brooks mumbled, "Real helpful."

"Let's go." Anthony motioned to move on, looking for a moment towards where the bird headed.

Trudging once again, they made their way towards the sound of the cowbell. They came upon a small crystal-like pond. On the left stood a rock altar facing the water. On top of the altar was some viscous substance a shade darker than the carved rock. Dark stains ran down the sides of the stone, dried and faded to different hues over time, but all matching the substance on top.

Anthony approached the altar; the color intrigued him. Placing his hand down, he felt the partially-dried substance.

Brooks peered over Anthony's shoulder "Maybe someone would prepare fruits or something here?"

Examining his hand, Anthony didn't think it was fruit. He brought his hand to his nose and smelled a coppery tang, then froze. "I think it's blood," he said.

A quiet, brushing noise startled Anthony. He looked down to see a yellow serpent climbing up the altar. Pulling his hand away, Anthony watched the snake coil atop the stone. Slinking his head around, the snake stared into his eyes.

"Wissshing to obtain anssswers, I sssee." The reptilian hissed, bringing its tail under its chin in a pondering manner.

Catching his stilted breath, Anthony said, "Y-yes. Where may we find an apple?"

The snake chuckled as he rose up to get a better look at the men. "Thisss pond hasss the wisssdom you need, but I won't give it freely. For wisssdom, there isss alwaysss a priccce." It swayed side to side in cadence with its speech.

Anthony unconsciously rubbed his blood covered fingers together again. He had a clear idea of what this price entailed.

Smirking at the recognition on Anthony's face, the serpent continued, "Hmm... It ssseems to me that you have eyesss to ssspare. Give me one of them, and you can drink."

Brooks clenched his fists. "He will do no such thing!" he said, gritting his teeth.

Paying no mind to Brooks the snake drew in even closer to Anthony, it's tongue flicking out periodically. "Unearned knowledge is a far more dangerousss option, my friend..."

Horrified and pale, Anthony slowly lifted his hand to his face. Quickly catching his wrist, Brooks stopped him.

"We don't need that murky pond scum. Let's go," Brooks said, pulling on Anthony's arm worriedly.

Anthony's voice shook "It... It will be okay." He stepped away from his anxiety-stricken friend.

His hands shook and trembled as he brought them to his face. The snake was watching with gleeful anticipation, wagging his tail slowly, a broad, malevolent smile on its face. Brooks looked away, clasping his hands over his ears.

Anthony removed his spectacles. Folding the sides of the frame, closing his eyes and breathing in deep, he attempted to calm himself. Grabbing the edge of the altar, then placing his eyewear on the platform, he got ready to gouge out his left eye.

Just before his fingers grazed his eyelid, the hissing voice interrupted him.

"The deal isss complete," the snake said. Wrapping around Anthony's glasses, the serpent began to slither away. "The pond isss all yoursss. I thought it was ssselfisssh enough that you had limbsss, but four eyesss as well. Sssuch greedy creaturessss!" The serpent escaped into the nearby foliage.

Shocked, Anthony stood there, the snake's intent slowly dawning on him. He began to laugh maniacally out of relief. Folding over, wrapping his arms around his waist, he laughed maniacally at the sheer, marvelous absurdity of it.

Brooks turned back around, cautiously still covering his ears; he peeked at Anthony.

"You... alright?" his voice croaked.

Wiping a tear from his eyes, Anthony chuckled. "It took my glasses."

"Eyes to spare..." Brooks said.

Anthony nearly skipped to the pond, then crouched to drink. The pond water traveled down his throat, refreshing, soothing, and ice cold. He stood up again, water dripping from his chin.

Looking expectantly at him, Brooks crossed his arms over his chest and asked "Any wisdom?"

Savoring the liquid, some iota of understanding wisped around Anthony's brain like a half-forgotten dream. He couldn't grasp the knowledge, but he could follow it.

Using the wisdom from the pond, Anthony led the way.

As they walked, Brooks looked at Anthony "You cool without your glasses?"

"I should be fine. Things are blurry up close," Anthony replied, moving a branch out of the way.

ANTHONY AND BROOKS PUSHED ONWARD INTO YET ANOTHER new world. It was getting darker, and the thought of a night in here frightened the two. Pushing his fears aside, Anthony opted to instead focus on forging the path ahead.

After sliding his form between two large rocks Anthony stopped. Brooks made his way between the stones, catching his foot once in the small crevice of the boulders.

Looking upwards, Anthony pointed. "Up this mountain," he said. Beginning again, he started grasping at the steep incline.

Jutting upwards stood a mountain, its form imposing. The mountain consisted of dark black stone, with jagged edges. The air pulsed like a heartbeat around it, no life encroached at its base or on its slopes. It was barren, yet strangely felt alive.

Brooks inhaled audibly as they viewed the elevation, but followed Anthony onto a black rock face. Upward they climbed, knocking small rocks down as they stepped. They stopped only to test the strength of the next handhold, hoping not to make an error.

As the summit came into view, their fingers and palms were scratched and sweaty. The wind buffeted their bodies, and they clung for dear life. Anthony slowly brought his hand up the edge, desperately pulling himself up. Nearly losing his grip, he shimmied his torso over the side, his feet dangling in the air. He had made it.

Anthony reached down to Brooks and helped lift him up. Brooks laid on his back, panting "If there is a God, never again," he grunted.

Sitting on the edge, Anthony surveyed the gorgeous landscape. The trees swayed in the wind and birds fluttered from branch to branch. To his right, he saw a clearing with a herd of large elk grazing, their antlers reaching up to the heavens. Looking to the far left he saw a green river rushing through a long canyon.

After the short breather, they stood up turning towards their goal. An opening in the rock beneath their feet formed a beckoning cave, leading back down into the mountain.

Much as when they had entered the tree, they ran their hands along the walls to guide their steps. The cave sloped into a downward incline, moving deeper into the mountain. The cave floor progressed from stone to moist sand, and water dripped from the ceiling.

Mid-step, Anthony's foot clipped a rock and he began to fall. He felt Brooks reach to grab for his arm but succumb to gravity as well.

Painfully, they rolled down the decline. Even after they stopped rolling, they still slipped further into the throat of the mountain. Anthony tried to dig his feet into the ground to stop, but it proved futile. All he could do was scream until the reserves of breath in his lungs depleted.

They splashed into water. A torrent washed them down the dark tunnel. The force of the water flow was too high to fight. All Anthony could do was hold onto both his breath and his friend. His eyes clamped closed as they swirled through the tunnels. With one final thrashing, they were cast into a large body of water. Desperately clawing towards the surface, Anthony's hands smashed into a sheet of ice blocking his way.

Anthony's lungs burned; he needed oxygen. The two beat at the ice with their hands, it wouldn't budge.

Anthony felt like he was about to pop but continued to pound the ice. The skin on his knuckles split open and his blood began to taint the water around him, but he could feel the ice begin to crack. The word '*break*' repeated over and over in his mind. He knew he and his friend were fading, and put all he could muster into one, final strike.

His bleeding hand burst through the ice. Clawing madly around, he widened the hole large enough for first his head, then Brooks'.

Coughing up water, Brooks pulled himself out next to Anthony, then collapsed face down on the ice.

With difficulty, Anthony lifted himself onto the ice as well. Succumbing to his exhaustion, consciousness left him.

Much time passed in the darkness; the only change Anthony could sense was warmth. No longer wet, no longer cold. Heat reached out and caressed his body. Once and again, a rush of hot air hit him; he could also hear the wind periodically blowing. It passed again, blowing his hair back. He found himself thinking, still half-asleep, '*Strange winds... breathe life into the dead.*'

Something prodded his leg, then shook it. Sleepily, he protested, "Hold on, let the dead have peace." He stretched his legs out, then brought them back to his chest.

A stronger gust tore at his clothing. Startled, he opened his eyes. His blurred vision focused on the green mass before him. Slowly lifting his head to scan the thing, his gaze met with an enormous yellow eye.

Quickly sitting up, Anthony looked to his left to see a horrified Brooks. The two were no longer cold, but shook, all the same, in fright. Anthony scanned the beast before them. Scales layered over scales covered its hide, and its long neck extended into a broad horned head.

Anthony realized he was in the presence of a dragon.

The great drake raised itself to look down upon the men, then opened its treacherous maw, its many teeth glistening ominously. With a booming voice, the monster began to speak, "I know not why you have come, but I am sure you realize the great danger you are in." The enormous creature's eyes widened threateningly.

Anthony nervously gulped. After this entire journey, it would end here. He looked down defeatedly, observing the gashes he had inflicted upon his hands for nothing. Some obstacles were simply impossible to overcome.

Once more, the monstrosity's breath raced between them, tearing at their hair. The dragon looked past them, to the shattered ice behind the two, then spoke once more. "Clearly you have no wishes to die today. I respect that, and honor your perseverance. However, I do not give mercy freely." He lowered his head, peering closer at the mortals.

"Much like the wounds on your hands, I too am in pain. My scales have stopped many blows from all manner of weaponry, but in my haste to swallow a foe I also consumed his spear. It has unfortunately lodged itself in my throat, and it pains me greatly." His breath gushed from his nostrils.

Stuttering Brooks asked, "H-h-how do we know you won't j-just eat us..."

Before he could finish the dragon's eyes widened angrily and he spread out his enormous wings, "You dare accuse me of deceit!" he screamed as his claws dug into the ground. "Human, if I wished to devour you I would simply *do so.* Do you believe me so weak as to need to rely on *treachery?*"

"No!" Anthony yelled against the howling wind around him. "Our apologies. We—uh, that is—this is a new situation for us."

The dragon brought his eye to Anthony's face. The abyss-like pupil, dilating, stared him down. Brooks was violently shaking as Anthony's eyes locked with the dragon's.

"Remove the spear and your lives will be spared," the monster calmly stated.

Anthony stood up with quaking knees as the dragon laid his head on the ground and opened his mouth. Taking a firm hold of one of the protruding fangs, he lifted himself into the opening. Large globs of saliva dripped and rolled off the beast's teeth. The dragon's steaming breath poured out and his feet sunk into the giant tongue.

He was far too afraid to be disgusted. Anthony moved deeper, holding one hand to the roof of the dragon's mouth. Covered in slippery saliva, it would be all too easy for him to be gulped whole. Gritting his teeth, he approached the uvula, hoping to find the spear soon.

He was at the entrance to the throat. "I don't see the spear," Anthony called out.

"It is further inside, you coward. I will not swallow you," the dragon murmured, his tone annoyed.

Anthony leaned to look further into the depths. Shifting his weight caused his feet to slip from under him, and he grabbed the uvula. From outside the dragon's eyes widened as it attempted to hold back his gag response, digging his claws into the stone below him in further anger. The walls of the throat convulsed as he held to the uvula, desperately trying regain his footing.

As the esophagus writhed, Anthony caught a glimpse of the shaft of the spear stuck in the flesh. Lowering himself by the uvula, he reached out for the spear. The dancing walls were bringing it closer, then further from his hand. He felt his hand begin to slip in the dragon's saliva.

Stretching as far as he could, Anthony's fingers grazed the weapon. After another convulsion, he felt the rough wood in his hand. The thing was firmly stuck, and he fought against the waving walls as they tried to wrest it from his grasp. Even pulling with all his waning might, the spear would not come loose.

More saliva poured down, and his grip on the uvula slid further. Panicking, he dug his nails into the dragon's flesh. He heard the dragon make a retching sound, then watched a massive convulsion of the throat approach him.

As it came, he dropped his grip on the uvula and grasped the haft of the spear with both hands. It loosened, and with a wet pop, the impaled object let loose as the force of the esophagus and throat pushed him up and out.

The beast continued to retch even after Anthony tumbled out of its mouth. It raised itself on its haunches and angled its head down, gagging.

"By the gods..." the dragon said as his breathing began to calm.

Panting, Anthony muttered, "That will teach you to chew first." With that, he threw away the spear.

Brooks limped to Anthony's side. "You alright?" he asked.

Anthony grinned and brought up his slimy hand, giving a thumbs up.

Regaining his composure, the dragon looked to the two, "You have earned your lives." Spreading his wings, he readied himself to fly.

Brooks jumped up. "Wait! Can you take us to the apple?" He asked, waving his arms pleadingly.

The dragon froze. "I am no servant to mortals!" he said furiously.

Narrowing his eyes, Anthony glared daggers at the creature, "I helped you, and I don't even get a thanks!"

Grimacing menacingly, the dragon huffed. "You got your life, insolent ape! Why do you need the apple?"

"Because Audumla has requested it," Anthony said.

The large eyes of the dragon dilated in recognition. "What sorry champions she has chosen. Even so...come along," he said, shaking his head.

The two climbed up the beast and held onto his scales. The Dragon spread out his wings, reared back and jumped up. Flying up and out of the opening at the top of the mountain, they soared.

The wind blew furiously as Brooks and Anthony held on for life. The grand wings of the dragon flapped and waved with tremendous power. One moment they passed the forest, the next they glided over an expansive sea. Miles passed in the blink of the eye. It wasn't long until he landed on the crest of a hill. On the top was a lone tree with one fruit hanging from its lowest branch.

The men dropped down, and the dragon carried on his way

without a word, only glancing back once as he flew. The two approached the tree, staring at the fruit before them.

The fruit was shaped like an apple except that its glistened white instead of red or green. "Strange..." Anthony brought up a finger to touch it.

When he removed his finger, some of the fruit stuck to his skin. Licking his finger, he grimaced.

Brooks worriedly asked, "What?"

"It's salty." Anthony shivered, the taste not leaving his mouth.

Even so, he reached out, the object of their mission literally at hand. He wrapped his fingers around the apple and, with one motion, plucked it from the branch. Everything went dark.

Anthony felt the chill as he laid on frozen ground. Strangely, it felt as though a hand was rubbing sandpaper against his face. As he awoke and opened his eyes, the stroking hand turned into a tongue. Auddy, now lacking both her horns and her sense of majesty, calmly licked his head.

Straining to sit upright, he looked at the cow; she was back to being ordinary Auddy. He heard a grunt and saw Brooks getting up, stretching out his arms and yawning.

"The trip is over," Brooks said, stretching his back and popping a few joints. He smiled at Anthony.

Leaning back, he cooed to Anthony, "Left the lake?"

EVER AFTER

MANNY FRISHBERG

About the Author: Manny Frishberg has been making up stories since he first stared out a window. He spent the first half of his life learning how to write them and the second half learning what to write about. He is now spending the third half of his life making up stories, just like when he was eight years old.

When he is not doing that, he writes about things he hasn't made up for several magazines, and provides freelance editing and writing coach services. Visit his website: mannyfrishberg.com and like him on Facebook (MannyJFrishberg).

Ever After
Manny Frishberg

"So, do we think this is a good idea?"

"Well, it's your cow." Jill sounded skeptical, but there was a dare shining in her eyes. Neither one of them had ever come within even breathing distance of magic.

Jack looked at the impossibly old woman standing in the road, and then to the brown and white cow, her dusty hide stretched over extended shoulder blades. She was half-starved and well past her prime.

"I don't know. Half a dozen beans — that's hardly even a mouthful," he said, starting to walk around the frail woman dressed in ragged black clothes.

"*Magic* beans!" Jill and the old woman said at once.

Something about the way their voices melded stopped Jack in his tracks. He didn't think he'd changed his mind, but he could not shake the feeling that, if he passed up this opportunity, his life would return to an endless series of days spent scrabbling for a half-full belly and a roof that didn't let the rain in, as gray and ordinary as every one before.

"What's Mamma gonna say?" It was a half-hearted objection. His hand was already reaching the hemp reins to hand the old cow over to the ... was she *really* a witch?

If they truly are just beans, then we'll starve a few days sooner. For, if they had anything left, he would not be taking his cow to market in the first place. He handed over the rope and let the beans fall from the old lady's wrinkled hand into his outstretched palm. Magic, they were. Or, at least, they looked the part, iridescent colors swirled on the shiny black surface of the beans — they were mesmerizing.

Sun shined through the branches, lighting up the edges of the leaves, a glowing, brilliant green, greener than the leaves had been on the way here, the sky through the leaves a deeper, crystal blue. Even the freckles sprayed across Jill's cheeks and her fiery hair were brighter than before he held the beans. The hollow rumble in his belly reminded Jack that not much had changed, yet.

What happened when Jack got home has been told before – how their mother, distraught over having sold off her last possession and dearest friend for nothing in return, threw the beans into the tall grass through the kitchen window. How, in the morning, the beans had grown into a vine he climbed to another world in the clouds, and how Jack became the most celebrated house thief in the history of fairy tales. But stories end — lives go on.

After his experiences with the giants in the cloud castle, Jack tried to settle down but, as the song says: How ya gonna keep them down on the farm after they've seen Paree? Jill did not know what a paree was, but Jack had to have seen one up there when he was fleecing the giants, hadn't he? Because nothing on their little farm suited him.

With all the gold and the money they claimed from selling off the magical harp, and alike, Jack had bought up the neighboring farms and filled the meadows with sheep and even a few cows. For his mother and sister, he built up the house, as they had no wish to move out, so he hired carpenters and thatchers to add rooms and balconies, and a separate kitchen so the house would not heat up from the ovens in the summer. Still, it never seemed enough to fill the yearning in his chest. Now that he had exalted in the feel of the magic, he needed its touch again; he could not drive it from his mind.

So, Jack took to wandering the woods surrounding his properties, first covering the length and breadth of his hunting grounds, his holdings kept in their pristine state to supply fresh meat, then ever wider afield, a knapsack with cheese and bread, and whatever fruit was available – enough to share, and a fine rapier because there were bandits and highwaymen to contend with. He left the management of the lands to his sister and the work in the fields to the farmers he had dispossessed, cultivating what used to be their fields for him.

One day, at last, he came upon what he had been searching for. An aged hag, gnarled teeth and a long, warted nose, a mole sprouting stout hairs capping her chin, sat idly beneath a towering willow, half-hidden behind its cascading branches.

"Ah, a kind young man, I can tell by your eyes," she said before he had even spotted her behind the leafy curtains. Jack almost cackled with delight. He could do kind if it suited him.

"How do you do, madam?" he bowed deeply, hiding his smile. "How can I be of service?" He hoped she would ask him for food, as witches in the stories often did, rewarding the generous youngest brother with fortunes and magic wishes. He had plenty.

"A foolish old woman, I dropped my tinderbox down yonder tree," she said, pointing to a large oak, split down the middle by lightning. "A fine, strong young man like you could easily climb down and get it for me." Jack looked skeptically at the tree. "Tie this rope around your waist," she said, "and I'll help you back up. Of course, there is something in it for you, as well."

At that, the light in Jack's eyes brightened, and his stomach churned with stored anticipation. He allowed the smile to spread across his face before he bowed again. The old woman stood up and untied her apron, handing it to Jack.

"When you get to the bottom of the tree," the witch said, her own smile spreading wide, letting a breath of rotten fish spread with it, "you will find yourself at the entrance of a large hall, lit with fifty candles, with a strongbox in the center of the room. Your reward is in the box, more gold and fineries than your knapsack can hold or you can carry when you climb. But do not forget my tinderbox." It all sounded too easy. And Jack had experience with magic before; he knew that there were always complications. He waited for the trap to snap shut.

"My box is in the far corner of the room. Go and retrieve it first, because you will need it to claim your prize. For, lying on the box—laying guard, if you will," she said and cackled at her little joke, "is a great hound with eyes as big as saucers, and he is a fierce guardian. But lay my apron on the floor and put the tinderbox in the middle and the dog will go and sniff it. Then, while he is distracted, you'll have your chance to grab as much as you can carry. When you pick my box back up, he will go back to his post atop the strongbox, and you can make your escape."

When he arrived at the surface, Jack held the worn tinderbox with its cracked leather hinges tacked to the lid out to the witch. But, then she reached for it, he pulled it back, feeing the magic emanating from its essence.

"Why don't you want at least a share of the treasures I have retrieved?"

"Baubles and gold are fickle friends and only disappear with time. A useful thing is a constant servant." The old woman moved faster than she seemed capable an instant before but Jack dodged nimbly and knocked her behind her head as she sailed by, sending her sprawling.

"What's so special about that box? Tell me now," he bellowed, "or I'll cut off your head!" The witch just cackled again, and Jack did as he had threatened.

For the second time in his life, Jack had bested and dispatched a magical creature and walked away, as they say, healthy, wealthy and, in his own estimation, wise. Unastoundingly, all this swelled his head.

Jack moved to the capital and proceeded to set himself up as a dandy. He purchased a carriage from a bankrupt viscount in a distant duchy and with it purchased the herald emblazoned on its door, so he became viscount, in name if not in deed. He had himself dressed in the richest brocades, embroidered with silver and gold threads, stockings of rare Chinese silk and shoes of the softest calf hide. He moved into a grand apartment and hired musicians and composers to play symphonies for his supper and hosted grand balls on every occasion.

In that way, he came to the attention of the king, whose daughter, his only child, had reached the age to marry. The king was delighted at Jack's sudden appearance and invited him to court, anxious to avoid his mage's premonition that the princess would wed a commoner.

Jack was delighted, as well. He redoubled his efforts — throwing even more lavish parties, catered with platters of hummingbird tongues coated in gold leaf and oranges brought all the way from Serendib. He gave the princess an emerald necklace, the biggest bauble in his collection, as a Saint's day present. And so, his fortune disappeared over time.

Nearing the bottom of what had once seemed his bottomless coffers, Jack panicked. He thought of scouring the forests for yet another elf or sorceress to take advantage of, but he remembered how many fruitless days had turned to years before he had found the witch. At once, he remembered the tinderbox — "a constant servant," the old woman had called it. He took it out of its hiding place and took out the flint. He made a small pile of twigs and dry leaves from the box and struck the flint from inside it. He heard a scratching on his door and, rather than send for a servant, he opened it himself. In ran the dog from down under the tree, the one with eyes as big as anything.

"What," said the dog, "is my lord's command?" What else was Jack to do?

"Fetch me more gold, more gems and jewelry, enough to fill my knapsack," he said and hung the old bag around the great hound's neck. In less than a flash, the dog was gone and returned, the knapsack fairly bursting at its seams with more riches that Jack had brought up from the hollow tree himself.

His fortune replenished and the dog at his hearth, Jack imagined his fortunes replenished, as well. He threw himself wholly into his new goal, to woo and marry the princess, and thereby, to one day become king, himself. And that is just how it all unfolded.

Until the day it did not. Or, the night.

It happened the night the happy couple's engagement was to be announced. Naturally, the king had thrown a gala ball, the biggest that had been held since anyone could remember, so glad was he to have skirted the premonition so smoothly. Invitations had been dispatched far and wide, to every noble house in the kingdom, and several of the neighboring principalities and duchies. It was inevitable, in retrospect at least, that some near or distant relatives of the real viscount would appear. When an aged aunt arrived, she shocked the room, demanding to know, who was this, posing as her disgraced nephew?

Jack was summarily arrested and tossed into a dank cell in the subcellar, still in his fine brocade jacket. The princess arrived soon after, on the other side of the cell door, of course, tearful and confused. Who was he, if not the fine young noble he had presented himself to be? What was he?

Jack confessed everything. He told her of their destitute condition when he was growing up, how he had taken their last cow to market, in hopes of simply having food to last the winter, and how he had, foolishly everyone thought, traded for a handful of magic beans.

He told her of the beanstalk growing to the castle in the air overnight and how he had climbed it to find his first fortune, glossing over the gory details to not offend her fine sensitivities. He explained that he, thereby, had secured a comfortable life for his mother and sister, but how he had also had been driven from that comfortable home by the fires of his ambition.

Then, Jack recounted finding the hollowed oak with a great hall at the base of its roots, and the magical dog, who had been the guardian of the treasure, and now slept at his hearth, a faithful servant. As he told his truth, Jack watched the princess's face through the bars window cut in his door and felt sure he had her sympathies.

Emboldened, he told her: "If anything, I should think this makes me, even more, your perfect mate and Lord, for I have not come to my nobility by accident of birth but by my own ingenuity and the gifts of the Graces." Immediately, he saw his mistake reflected on her face. The princess's tears dried up, and her gaze grew steely instead.

"If anything, your ambition blinds you," she said coldly, "and in that, you are common, indeed." With that, she turned and marched away without a backward glance.

Bereft, Jack thought he had lost everything, and expected to lose the one thing left to him — his life — when the sun arrived. It cheered him slightly to think that he had no windows to show when that would be, such was the depth of his depression. Sitting down on a bed of moldy straw, he remembered the magic box in his apartments.

He bribed one of the guards to go there and get the box for him, promising he would tell the guard the secret location of a golden chalice. What seemed like days later, the guard returned and, true to his word, Jack told him where the chalice was stashed. Left to himself again, Jack took out the flint and struck it, expecting to see the dog with giant eyes or to hear it, at least, outside the thick cell door.

Instead, he heard a familiar voice.

"Whatever am I doing here? What's happened to me?" Jill sounded terrified, speaking to no one.

"You're here to help me," Jack called through the window. "It's me, your brother, Jack."

"Like I have another. Where have you been all this time? Our mother has sent messengers in all directions, looking for word that you yet survived. She'll be relieved to know you have."

"I won't for much longer if you don't help me out."

Jill nodded. She moved out of Jack's line of sight, and he heard her grunt. Then a large bolt snapped back with a dull metallic ring, and the door swung open.

On their way out, he gave away the hiding places of more and more of his possessions, bribing the guards to let Jack and Jill slip past. By the time they had reached the road outside the capital city's gates, Jack's latest fortune was spent. Still, he counted himself lucky to have escaped with his hide intact. He would rebuild his fortunes, one way or another, he was sure.

The family farm was more than a hundred leagues from the capital, and the way Jill had arrived was not available for their return trip, nor did they have a carriage or a cart, or even a dog to pull one. So, they walked.

On the first day, they came upon a small country village holding a market day. Jack traded his fine brocade jacket for three ewes but no ram. On the second day, they came to a crossroads where several tradesmen had set up canvas stalls. Jack traded ewes for a leather harness. Jill berated him gently for trading his livestock for a harness, leaving him nothing to lead. But, on the third day, they came upon a large market fair where Jack traded again, the harness for one of a farmer's daughter's pet calves.

As they headed away from the fairgrounds, back to the road home, they passed in front of an elderly woman in black weeds, a small velvet bag in her outstretched hand. Jack had to stop and look. Jill turned around and stared incredulously. She clacked her tongue and shook her head slowly.

"Seriously?" she asked. "I'd think by now you'd have cured your thirst for magic, seeing what it almost brought you to." Jack shrugged sheepishly.

"So, I take it you don't think this is a good idea."

"Well, it *is* your cow."

The End

REMNANT DAWN

RYAN RIDDELL

About the Author: Ryan Riddell is a native of the Pacific Northwest and lifelong follower of fantasy and science-fiction. As an author, he searches for ways to blend the genres together in his novels and short stories. In his free time, he enjoys a friendly game of darts, online gaming, and spending hours discussing genre fiction and film.

Remnant Dawn

Ryan Riddell

"So, do we think this is a good idea?"

"Well... it's your cow. You saw what it did to the rest."

"It's the only option we have."

Hudson stared at the red-lettered transcript as it flashed beneath the thin layer of ash covering the monitor. There was no date on the monitor to tell him when the incident took place. As was so often the case on an Info-Recon mission, he'd entered a slice of the past with only his thirty-year-old memories of the world before the Blast from which to guess what this particular place was.

"Hud, scroll back up," Leslie ordered with her usual, indifferent tone. "It didn't collect."

She held her tablet closer to the monitor. The green, neon LED light flickered in the darkness. Hudson did as she asked. The keyboard's button depressed with slightly less resistance than before, and just as it had a few moments ago, the dull, green monitor flickered on and the same red message flashed across the screen.

"There we go, caught it that time," Leslie said. He couldn't see her face through the radiation mask, but he could tell she was smiling. "Is that it?"

"Seems to be," Hudson said.

"Pity. Go ahead and let go; I got the scan running," Leslie said. "So, why a cow?"

"Who knows?" Hudson said.

"Well, you should. That's why you're here, isn't it?"

Hudson ignored the accusation. "Towards the end, people got desperate. They tried all sorts of cures. Maybe they tried one on this cow before taking it themselves."

"The cure wouldn't have worked on a cow."

"Like I said. Desperate."

"You ever see one? A cow?" Leslie asked.

"Years and years ago. I was on a field trip to a farm."

"Damn. Bad luck there's not more." Leslie shoved the tablet back into her satchel.

"Not quite what Captain Miller wants, right?"

She shook her head. "Let's keep moving. There's three more signals near us. Let's hope that they give us more than a few idiots debating whether or not to poke a cow with a needle. Hurry, I want to find it before the Miller or Jenkins."

Without anything further, Leslie led the way out of the lab and down the littered hallway. Sometimes, Hudson pitied her. Leslie was born after the Blast. She never knew the fear people had in those moments leading up to it. To her, the Blast and the Rot that followed were simply dates in a history book.

But she also never knew the world as it was, either. As Hudson followed her, he remembered. Leslie would never feel the warmth of a summer day on the beach. She'd never have rain fall on her face or be refreshingly shocked by a dive into a clear pool of fresh water.

For Hudson, he still thought of life as it had been. Three decades underground, and he still woke up thinking he was back in his old apartment sometimes. The past was his world. This...this present was a crooked nightmare; the result of a warning nobody'd ever thought would come to pass.

Hudson watched Leslie stride ahead, paying little attention to his laggard, middle-aged pace. Somewhere, out in the ruins, a lovely set of high-school track trophies with his name etched on them rested. He wondered if anyone would ever find them, and if they did, what type of man they would imagine James Hudson to have been.

He hoped they thought the best. Not that it mattered. Nothing mattered but the signals, or at least that what he had been told when he was selected as a guide. The signals held the answer for the future.

Finally, Leslie turned around and held her arms out wide.

"When I read your report, it said you were more than capable of keeping pace."

"I am. You don't see many sixty-four-year olds now-a-days who can walk more than five hundred yards with a mask on."

Leslie dropped her arms to side. "Well, hurry up, gramps."

Hudson quickened his pace, but only a bit. Truth be told, he *was* one of those old men who had a hard time running with his mask on. It was heavy, awkward, and obviously repurposed. He fought the urge to rip it from his face and take a deep breath.

Of course, if he did, he would be dead within a couple minutes. Resurfacing missions in the face of the Rot had only been possible for two years.

Hudson had reached his shelter before he saw the biological weapon ravage his home-town. Being young, healthy, and single, he was a perfect candidate for the continuation of the human-race. But he had seen the live reports.

It came shortly after the Blast. First people thought it was the flu. Then they thought it was radiation poisoning. It wasn't until it started changing people and animals from the inside that they realized it was something different. Something man-made.

"Now, the second signal's coming from that building over there," Leslie said once he reached her. She pointed to the remnants of a storage shed.

"That?" Hudson said.

"Yeah, why?"

"Check the signal again," he said.

"I did before we got out of the rover. It was positive. Why, what is it?"

"Nothing," Hudson said.

"No, if you got something to say, say it. That's the only reason you're here. You remember all this shit. If we are going to find the Remnant Dawn, you're our best bet. Maybe not you in particular, but your generation. You're here to guide us. So, out with it, what does '*that*' mean?"

Hudson pointed his finger at the shed, mimicking the way

Leslie did, and said, "*That* is a storage shed. You won't find anything in there but tractors and tools or, more than likely, old mop buckets. The computer you'll find in there won't have anything more valuable in it than the janitor's schedule. And I really doubt that that's going to be the bit of info that lets us come back up."

"Well, you said people were desperate back then, right?" Leslie said.

"Yes, I did. They were."

"Then maybe we'll find what we need there."

"I highly doubt that the cure would be stored in —."

"I'm not asking," Leslie said.

"I thought you wanted me to tell you what I was thinking?"

"I do," Leslie said. "But it's my mission. Understand? We aren't to leave any leaf unturned. Your job is to give me the information. My job is to do something with it."

Hudson laughed and gave up. What did it matter anyway? The likelihood of the Info-Recon teams finding the mythical cure was about as good as the odds that he'd be alive long enough for the shelter's scientists to figure out how to use it. These Info-Recon missions were no more effective than poking a cow with a needle. Humanity needed one, last, desperate resistance to the Blast and the Rot before just accepting and moving on.

The shed was exactly as Hudson said it would be. A rusted Ford truck with deflated tires and a broken windshield lay parked halfway in the shed. One of the shed's walls was blown out, leaving scattered pieces of wood and brick strewn across the floor. Whatever tools had been in here were long gone. More than likely, they had been used as weapons after the shelters closed. What few reports came through after the last person was allowed to enter had been grim at best.

He found the shed's computer nestled behind an overturned desk. Like all the computers that were connected to the compound's nuclear power supply, this one was also built into the wall. Hudson tapped the monitor. It was scratched and stained from some fluid Hudson couldn't identify.

It looked like it was as useful as a one of the bricks. *When was the last time anyone turned this on?* he thought. Thirty years was a long time for any computer, much less one that had been exposed to the elements for three decades.

Leslie pulled out her tablet. "Turn it on," she said.

Hudson plugged in his portable battery and wiped away the layer of ash from the keyboard. Most the keys were still in place. Luckily, the power button was still there. He pushed it in, then winced as it ground and crunched into life.

A green menu screen loaded on the decrepit monitor. Its lettering flickered through the stains as the old piece of hardware struggled.

"Can you make a connection?" Hudson asked.

"It's faint. Starting the scan," Leslie said as her radio crackled with Miller's voice.

"Leslie, do you copy?" Captain Miller said.

"Copy," Leslie said.

"What's your location?"

"In a storage shed, of some sort," Leslie said. "Signal two. Where are you? Find anything yet?"

"Not yet. I'm en route to meet Jenkins. I want you to rendezvous at our location when you're done."

"Jenkins find something?"

"Maybe. How long 'til you're done?"

Leslie tilted her head up at Hudson.

"There's nothing on this menu but a few recordings. Rest is what I thought — inventory lists and the like," Hudson said.

"How long are the recordings, Hudson?"

"Not long," Hudson said. "Less than a minute each."

"I'm sending you Jenkins' location, Leslie. Come meet us when you're done there. Don't bother going to your third signal quite yet. Jenkins sounded pretty confident he found something good. Understood?"

"Understood," Leslie said.

"See you soon. Miller out."

"Can you play the recordings?" Leslie asked.

"Just about," Hudson said. The menu wasn't the easiest to navigate. Well, none of the remaining computers were, but the missing buttons made this one a slight more difficult.

"Well, hurry. I don't want the Captain and Jenkins waiting for me."

"You mean you don't want to miss them finding Remnant Dawn without you?" Hudson said, mockingly emphasizing the words *Remnant Dawn*. He always thought it was silly naming the hypothetical cure before it was found.

"Don't you want your name in the history books, Hudson?" Leslie asked.

"Not particularly."

"Really? Why not?"

"It's been a long time since wanting anything meant much at all. We *need*. That's it. *Wanting* is for when you don't need anything. I haven't wanted something since I wanted Sally Tennett's number the week before my name was called."

Leslie laughed. It was the first time he ever heard her laugh. He wasn't totally sure she was capable of it. "Did you get it? Her number?"

"Well, I got *a* number," Hudson said. "For a Pizza Hut, though."

"A what?"

"I'll tell you later. Okay, got it." Hudson stepped away from the computer as the message played.

"...Barton here...it's the twenty-first of June, 2032. I'm not sure how long I have...Newell should be joining me soon. We're going to take his F-150 and go get the others. Our attempts have failed. We've abandoned the main campus. Buildings A, D, and L are closed off. Building T has been overrun by ...Dr. Mcdowell has closed off T's server room. Jesus, I'm not sure what to say. Newell will be bringing our samples. Our lab was compromised. I'm not sure if the others are going to join us. I'm leaving this message should anyone find...go to..."

The rest of the message faded into indecipherable static.

"What's an F-150?" Leslie asked.

"That," Hudson said, pointing to rusted truck.

"Play the other message," Leslie said.

Hudson hit play and stepped back again. He had expected to hear Newell, or both Newell and Barton. But instead, there was only the white noise of someone holding the record button down and the indistinct sounds of something moving around the room with loud thuds that stood out from the static and dead noise.

"That's it?" Leslie asked.

"Appears so," Hudson said.

"What do you make of it?"

"What *can* you make of it," Hudson said. "He was scared, whoever this Barton guy was. And they obviously left their truck. They probably died here. Maybe they were eaten. Who knows?"

"Dear god," Leslie whispered.

"One things for certain, these messages aren't your cure. Do you have them downloaded?"

"Yes."

"Good, now let's get the hell out of here. Don't want to miss having your name in the history books."

Leslie nodded and showed him her tablet. Miller had marked the location on the map. It was a thousand yards away from their third signal. There was no telling what the building had been. Just like every map the Info-Recon teams had, it had been constructed solely from drones flying overhead, which only gave the general outlines of the structures. The nature of the buildings themselves had remained largely a mystery until boots hit the ground.

So much had been lost in the hurry for safety, Hudson thought. He remembered movies that would never again be seen, songs never to be heard. On his first recon out, he'd found a piano in the middle of a mall. The uneven keys had reminded him of a cobblestone road that had been undermined by a nearby tree's roots. He wondered if there was anyone still alive who knew how to play a piano...

"You're doing it again," Leslie said once they were outside.

"What?"

"You're slowing down for no reason."

"Sorry, I was thinking."

"Can't you think *and* walk?" Leslie said, waving him on with an irritated gesture. Then, once he was keeping pace with her, she asked, "What were you thinking about?"

"Music," he said.

"Are you losing it on me?" Leslie asked.

Before he could answer, her radio crackled again. *"Leslie, copy, copy? This is Ca...iller"* Miller's voice cut in and out of static.

"Leslie here, I barely copy. Captain Miller? Do you copy?" she said.

"If you can hear me...quick....get here quick. We found some..." Miller voice then died out completely.

"Come on!" Leslie said.

Hudson followed her as quickly as he could. For the first time since they arrived, she didn't seem to care if he kept her pace. And for the first time, he wanted to. They darted through the scattered remains of what looked like a communications building toppled by a fallen radio tower, but at a sprint, Hudson had little time to focus on the details.

Finally, after a few moments, Leslie paused, but only to look at her tablet. Hudson took the opportunity to clutch his knees and try not to pass out. More than ever, the warm, damp feel of his breath made him want to throw up.

"Les..." the radio crackled.

"Miller!" another voice came through. Jenkins. Hudson had only met Carly Jenkins on the deployment rover here, but he could pick out her scratchy voice anywhere.

"They must have found it," Leslie said.

"Stop." Hudson pulled on her arm.

"Let go!" Leslie screamed. "Can't you hear them?"

"Yes, I can," Hudson said. "We need to think."

"Think? About what?"

"Just try to reach them again," Hudson said. Suddenly, he felt open in the emptiness. Nothing living remained above ground. At least, nothing that the drones could detect. Yet, he had the same gut reaction he remembered when he entered a dark alley or a lone place in the woods where anything felt like a threat.

"If you need a breath, I can go ahead," Leslie said.

Hudson shook his head. "Give it a try."

Leslie stutter-stepped away for a brief moment before giving in. "Miller. Jenkins. Do you copy?"

Nothing but radio silence answered back.

"Once more," Hudson commanded. She tried twice more. Each time, nothing but silence came across the channel.

"We're wasting time," Leslie said.

"Pull their beacons up on the map," Hudson said.

The other two teams' beacons flashed on the screen. Each one moved around whatever room they were in.

"Satisfied?" Leslie said.

"It doesn't make any sense that their radios were cutting out," Hudson said.

"You used them underground, right?"

"Several times."

"And did you ever cut out?"

"No."

"Exactly, and that was *underground* with miles of pipe and stone between you and them. But now they're no more than two hundred yards away and we can barely make out a single word?"

He knew what she was thinking. People who survived the Blast and Rot were paranoid. Kids he grew up with never got over the nightmares. He wished he could see her face. It would give him some indication of what she was thinking. Did she think he was paranoid? He passed all the mental tests to come aboard. Surely, she saw that?

"I'm going ahead, Hudson," she said at last. "Look at the map. They're moving around. Digging things up. It's there. I know it is. And I'm out here arguing about...about...God knows what we are talking about. The Remnant Dawn is in there. They found it! Who knows why the radios don't work? I don't care. Everything we have is built from some old blueprint of thirty-year-old technology. Perhaps their batteries died, or there's a solar flare. I don't give a shit right now. You coming?"

What choice do I have? Hudson thought. He couldn't stay here. Standing in one place wouldn't make him feel any better, or help him get back to the shelter safely. Nodding, he said, "Yes, but we get clear ASAP."

"Think I wanna stay here forever?" she said.

When this was all said and done, he wanted to sit her down and have a drink and a long conversation. If they were going to be a team, then he needed to detect her sarcasm when he couldn't see her face.

They ran the rest of the way in silence. Their target structure was much larger than any other building on the compound, and the least decayed. Several broken antennae dangled over the roof, along with detached cables that looked more like jungle vines.

"What do you think it was?" Leslie asked.

There were no signs. Four out of the five floors were obviously offices. Surprisingly, a few of the windows were still somewhat intact. "Admin building, I imagine," Hudson said. "Are they still moving?"

"Yes," Leslie said. "Come, let's go."

Together, they slid open the steel door. Once, it had opened automatically. The main foray was probably built as a sleek entryway into a high-tech compound. The reception area had been shaped like a giant half-moon and contained five separate workstations. Idly, he checked one of the computer monitors at the desk. Splintered glass framed a small flower growing inside the monitor.

"How much farther?" he asked, turning on a flashlight. The scattered midday sunlight only reached as far as the desk. Squinting, he saw a rotunda staircase leading to the second floor.

"Not far," she said, checking her display for Jenkins' and Miller's team beacons. "Just up the stairs."

He flashed the light up the stairs, illuminating a list of names etched in the marble walls. Hudson's eyebrows rose as he realized that each name began with the initials "Dr."

"There must be a second way in," Hudson said.

"Maybe that's what he was trying to tell us," Leslie said.

Hudson hoped she was right. They reached the top of the stairs and peered down the dark hallways. Each end looked as endless as the other. Whatever sense of urgency Leslie had was now gone as she checked the tablet again. The beacons flickered nearby.

"Jenkins?" she called out. Her voice rang down the empty corridor. "Miller?"

Then, the beacons on the tablet stopped moving.

Hudson wanted to turn. He wanted to grab her shoulder and spin her around and tell her to go. Fear had died a long time ago, but Hudson's instincts had grown around the concept of caution — the knee-jerk reaction of someone who had outlived ninety-nine percent of the human population.

Something wasn't right.

Trying to keep his hands from shaking, he scanned the hallway, looking for any clue or indication that the rest of the team was there. Then, another thought crossed his mind.

"Leslie," he whispered. "They would have only called us if they found a computer signal, right?"

She nodded, slowly inching herself to the room where their beacons had stopped. Her hand slipped down the gun holstered at her side. Hudson wondered if she had ever fired it.

"Then why didn't it show up before?"

"What?"

"When the drone did the initial scan, it found nine signals. This wasn't one of them."

"No," Leslie's voice shook. "It wasn't."

"I know where we are," Hudson said, flashing the flashlight on a wall of circuitry that had been shut off. "We're in Building T. That's a server. Any information the building has would be stored in there."

"That's excellent!" Leslie said. "Why do you sound like someone punched you in the face."

"Remember the recording? Barton said they secured the server room. Does this look secure? It's not even turned on."

"That was thirty years ago. That's probably where Jenkins' and Miller's teams went, to turn the power on. Here look —" she pointed at the tablet. Jenkins' beacon flashed behind them.

Hudson spun around. The beam from the flashlight briefly illuminated a bovine face with red eyes glaring at them from darkened hallway. Bloody strips of clothing hung from its mouth, caught on an unnatural fang that protruded from the beast's mouth. He recognized the clothes from the rover over. They belonged to Jenkins.

Leslie's voice quivered behind him, "Hud, don't move."

The beast continued to stare at them as it gradually moved forward. More of its misshapen body inched into the shaky glow of the flashlight. Three horns protruded from its skull, one of which had been snapped in half. Grunting, it scraped its hoof against the floor.

The clicking sound of Leslie's gun almost echoed in the silence and then, with a flash, she fired. Hudson jumped to the side with the sound of the shot, and the beast charged forward. Hudson hit the ground; his flashlight popped out from his hand and skidded across the floor, but he rolled into a semi-crouch. Leslie fired three more times, each one quicker than the other and then, with a scream, the bovine monster slammed into her, carrying her off into the darkened room.

Two more pairs of red eyes flashed in the corner of the room. Frantically, Hudson jumped to his feet and looked for Leslie in the darkness. *She's gone*, he realized.

Without thinking, he ran. Thirty years had passed since he'd felt any sense of urgency, but as he sprinted down the dark hallways, rapidly thinking of where to turn, the adrenaline pumping through him convinced him he was a young again.

He sprinted down the stairs, nearly falling down the marble steps as he focused on the fading daylight retreating from the threshold. Then, as he reached the bottom of the stairs, his footing slipped. He had a split-second to understand what had happened before he heard a loud "pop" followed by a pain he could only describe as a shotgun firing into one of his ankles. Screaming, he grabbed his rolled ankle.

Keep running, he thought as the first pair of red eyes looked down at him from the darkened top of the stairs. *Get up*!

His ankle felt like it was connected by only a thread, but the former high-school track star reached the doorway before he collapsed. With his remaining energy he slid the steel door shut just as the beast crashed against it with a resounding thud.

Again and again, the beasts slammed against the massive steel door. It wasn't just one of them now. All three beasts beat against it, denting it more and rattling the hinges slowly towards their breaking point.

"If anyone can hear this," he said into his radio, "do not come here. Miller, Jenkins, and Leslie are dead. I believe they were killed by an experiment gone wrong. We encountered three malformed cows that were, from what I can gather, a mutated result from some test. Or maybe the Rot? I'm not a scientist. My name is James Hudson. All I know is this: don't come here."

Everywhere he looked, he saw nothing but open ground. The rover was still parked a quarter mile away, on the other side of buildings and ruins. Even with the head start the failing hinges could buy him...

He shook his head. Then, with a sigh, he removed his mask.

To his surprise, the air didn't feel any different than it did before the blast. He closed his eyes and took a deep breath. For one last time, he was back again in the clean air and open streets of a city bustling with life.

CPSIA information can be obtained
at www.ICGtesting.com
Printed in the USA
BVHW071747270922
647885BV00002B/13

9 781732 247710